DENIM WARS

a novel

BARBARA A. DAVIS

the three
tomatoes
Book Publishing

Published: Febuary 2026
Paperback ISBN: 979-8-9947313-2-1
Hardcover ISBN: 979-8-9947313-3-8
Library of Congress Number: 2026902887

For information address:
The Three Tomatoes Book Publishing
6 Soundview Rd.
Glen Cove, NY 11542

Cover Art: Erin Discordia Davis
Interior Design: Susan Herbst

DEDICATION

To you, Dad. I finally wrote the book.

And to those thinking of giving up because life feels too hard and too much… please don't.

This story takes place in a time that no longer exists, except in my memory. Like all things in life, everything is temporary. We borrow what we need for a while and then let it go, by choice or by circumstance. I much prefer the first.

I'm grateful this story is finally being told, because it deserves to be. It was a magical time when Seventh Avenue was alive with creativity and chaos, when garment titans reinvented denim from utilitarian farm wear into high fashion.

Through the rise of brands that turned blue jeans into symbols of independence and freedom, a new culture was born, one that celebrated rebellion. The young models, the glossy ads, the showroom wars, Studio 54, they all collided in a moment that changed everything.

Denim Wars, a work of fiction based on a true story, captures that electrifying moment in the late 1970s and early 1980s when New York fashion was changing by the minute. Three powerhouse denim companies were locked in a fierce battle to be first, redefining style. Behind the glitz and glamour stands Julie Glass, caught in her own crossroads of career dreams and personal loss.

It was an incredible time, one that will never come again. But for those of us who lived it and those who can only imagine it, *Denim Wars* is a reminder of what it felt like to dream in blue or bleed in blue, depending on how you landed. It is a reminder of what happens when you give everything you have, against all odds, and how, sometimes, the fiercest battles are the ones we fight within ourselves.

If you recognize yourself in this body of work, it's because I love you, and because my respect and admiration for what you endured and accomplished is endless.

To you, dear readers, if these pages touch your heart, mind, or soul, then I have lived the dream that carried me through every chapter.

"You're never ready for what you have to do.
You just do it. That makes you ready."

~ Flora Rheta Schreiber, author *Sybil*

— 1 —

She wasn't ready to leave Seton Hall, to walk away from the chapel with its glistening steeple that had marked so many of her days. She wasn't ready to kiss her mother goodbye, or to let go of Wayne, New Jersey, the town that still felt like it was part of her. She wasn't ready when she packed her car with boxes and drove east toward Manhattan. She wasn't ready when she stood beneath the skyline, the Twin Towers glittering like a promise. And she certainly wasn't ready for the whirlwind world of Seventh Avenue.

Julie had repeated Schreiber's words about never being ready, to herself more than once, though she couldn't remember where she had first read them. Maybe in an old, tattered paperback on her nightstand, maybe in a magazine someone left behind on the train. It didn't matter; the truth of it clung to her.

But she went anyway. And that was enough.

— 2 —

Back in fourth grade, Mrs. Moody had told her she was a born leader, the kind of girl you would want by your side if you were stranded on a desert island. Julie believed her, too. She even ran for class president under the nickname Cool McCool, sure that a name like that would give her instant recognition. Her opponent and biggest rival had his own strategy and decided to go with a name almost identical to hers, hoping to confuse everyone and steal a few of her votes in the chaos. It worked. Cool McCrunch won by a very close margin.

That was the day that Julie learned a hard truth— good intentions don't always win, and some people just don't play by the same rules. There was one more thing Julie Glass learned that day— she was a very sore loser.

Mrs. Moody glanced her way just as the school principal's voice came over the loudspeaker announcing the winner, and she quickly rushed to her side.

"I don't feel very well," Julie said softly, staring down at her desk.

Her throat ached, and she was fighting back the tears with everything she had.

Mrs. Moody gently rested a hand on her shoulder. "It's really all about trying in life, young lady, not about winning." But her words fell flat. Maybe for most people, Julie thought, but not for me.

Mrs. Moody walked her down the hallway to the nurse's office, past the school posters hanging on the wall, each one a reminder of a goal that had not been met. She had lost, and the sight of those posters staring down at her, mocking her, wasn't helping. She sat on one of the cots in the nurse's office. The room smelled of antiseptic and Band-Aids. Ten minutes later, her mother appeared in the doorway, wearing her beautiful, warm smile and open arms, ready to scoop her daughter up and make everything right in her world.

As they pulled out of the school parking lot, Julie's mom glanced over at her very depressed daughter and said, "Hey, you, how about we skip going home and grab a pizza instead? And, maybe, just maybe, then head over to Dairy Queen for a double-dipped chocolate vanilla cone? Sounds pretty good, right?"

She didn't wait for an answer.

By the time they sat across from each other in the booth, a slice of gooey cheese pizza between them, Julie felt a little better. Her mother took a sip of Coke, leaned in, and said gently, "You know, Julie, you should be very proud of yourself. You gave it your all, and that's what matters most." She paused, then sighed. "I hate to tell you this, sweet pea, but most of the things you try for in life you won't get, at least not right away, and sometimes not at all. But it's the trying that makes all the difference. That's how you grow as a person."

Julie looked up from her pizza and managed a small smile. "That's what Mrs. Moody told me, Mom, but it sounds much better coming from you." Her mom laughed, gently brushing a crumb from Julie's cheek. She smiled again, touching Julie's hand. "Your posters were amazing, and that

   — — — B A R B A R A A. D A V I S

speech you wrote? Fantastic. I couldn't be prouder of you."

Julie smiled back. Between the pizza, her mother's words, her heart, and stomach felt full again. It was the kind of full that made everything, even losing, somehow okay.

That day stayed with Julie longer than she expected. Losing had stung, but it hadn't silenced her. If anything, it sharpened something inside her, an instinct to step forward instead of shrinking back. It happened back in fifth grade. She raised her hand before she even thought about it. "I'll wear the red tights! I'll play Puck!" Julie blurted out, her hand shooting into the air just as Martin Abrahamson's went up, for the exact opposite reason.

"There is no way I'm wearing red tights, Mr. Greene. No way!"

And that was that. Martin became the gravedigger, and Julie got the lead role of Puck in *A Midsummer Night's Dream*.

She caught the look of hesitation in Mr. Greene's eyes as he handed her the script. "You really want to do this, Julie? It's a big role," he said, clearly second-guessing himself but too kind to change his mind.

Nothing made her prouder than winning the MacDonald Middle School Award for Best Actor in a Play. Mr. Greene's grin as he handed her the trophy was something she never forgot. She also never forgot her last line of the play— "Lord, what fools these mortals be!" While she stood there, the spotlight aimed only at her, looking out at the audience while delivering those lines as the final curtain closed around her.

As she walked back to the car with her family, holding that small gold statue, Julie made a quiet promise to herself— she would never let anyone else define her role in life. From that day on, she would ask for what she wanted, even if it cost her.

High school only seemed to prove her right. Everything she went after seemed to fall right into place. She was voted cheerleading captain, won prom queen, made the honor roll, and was voted most popular. She had the best boyfriend any girl could ask for, one who surprised her after school one day with the cutest little tabby cat they named Shakespeare. She wore every title proudly, collecting them as if they were charms on a bracelet. Her grandfather Ed was especially pleased that Julie had won the same award he had in high school, the "I Dare You Award for Leadership." It made her so happy to see how proud he was. It felt as if the universe itself were cheering her on with two giant blue pom-poms. Life was as perfect as she had imagined it to be.

Almost too perfect, as if God knew what was coming and wanted her to soak up every bit of joy and happiness before the floodgates opened.

— 3 —

It had been what felt like an eternity since Julie's mother, Mimi, had come for a visit. She loved surprising her daughter, sitting on the edge of Julie's bed in her dorm room at Seton Hall, waiting for the doorknob to turn so she could see the look of surprise on her face. It always made her smile just as much as it did Julie.

Mimi tried to be brave as she spoke the words that shattered Julie's world. "I have cancer," she said quietly, "and it has spread." She promised she would do everything in her power to fight it. She promised she would be ok, but their bond was so close, Julie saw right through the lie.

"You'll be ok, Mom. I know you will," Julie whispered, going along with the charade her mother was trying so hard to create for her.

The moment her mother's car pulled out of the school parking lot, Julie took off running across campus until she reached the chapel. She pulled open the heavy doors and fell to her knees in prayer.

The chapel had always been her special place, the place she went to ask for direction and guidance, even to pray for a passing grade when she knew an exam would be hard. But not today. She gripped the back of the pew in front of her, tears streaming down her face, and begged God, Jesus, Mother Mary, anyone in heaven who was listening, to help her mother get better. Her voice broke on the words, the sound swallowed by the stillness of the chapel. When the tears finally stopped, a bone-chilling numbness settled in, something she had never felt before. Her thoughts drifted back to the center of the stage. For a brief moment, she was Puck again, her voice ringing out the lines—

> *If we shadows have offended,*
> *Think but this, and all is mended:*
> *That you have but slumber'd here*
> *While these visions did appear.*

Back then, she hadn't really understood what those words meant. Mr. Greene had explained that it was about endings and beginnings, that as one life fades away, another begins, a kind of passage from one world to the next. But Julie didn't want a new life. She didn't want to be handed a new script. She loved the old one, the one she already knew by heart. Still, deep down, she understood, it wasn't her decision. Life decides for you sometimes.

She sat in silence, watching the white wax drip from the candle, each drop splashing against the gold candlestick like tears of its own, as if the church itself were crying with her.

Julie left Seton Hall in the middle of her sophomore year. Her father had lost his job, and there was no insurance to cover the enormous medical bills that arrived each month. It was too much for him. He struggled to care for the love of his life while trying to hold on to what little stability he had left. Decisions had to be made, and sacrifices, too. Seton Hall tuition was one of them.

She hugged her perfect roommate, Linda, goodbye, packed up the yellow floral bedspread she had bought at Bamberger's with her mother, and with it folded away the dream of becoming the next Barbara Walters. She said goodbye to her childhood, too, stuffing it between duffel bags and cardboard boxes until her car was crammed full of everything from her dorm room.

When she closed the trunk, the rearview mirror caught the bronze statue of Mother Seton holding a Bible, her cape looking as if it were blowing in the wind. "I'll miss you," Julie whispered into the mirror.

She turned the key in the ignition and felt the finality of it all, the campus fading in her rearview mirror, the chapel steeple shrinking against the blue sky. Every mile on the Garden State Parkway pulled her further from the girl she had been and closer to the unknown. The passage from one world to the next had begun.

— 4 —

Phillipe **Leon was the number** one dress manufacturer on Seventh Avenue, or at least that's what the Help Wanted ad claimed in the back pages of *Women's Wear Daily (WWD)*. Fashion had always been Julie's second love, and since the Barbara Walters dream was no longer within her reach, this felt like the next best thing. They were looking for a fit model. Measurements required—36-24-36, height 5'7". Contact Mr. Morris Schaffer.

It was 1977, and the Garment District was alive with incredible energy, a heartbeat of New York itself. Delivery trucks clogged the curbs, steam hissed from grates, and cutters and seamstresses hurried along sidewalks with muslin draped over their arms. Julie stood in the middle of it all, overwhelmed by everything she saw. The air smelled of roasted chestnuts from the corner cart mixed with a nervous tension that seemed to vibrate through the streets.

Horns blared from impatient taxis, the roar of delivery trucks echoed between the tall buildings, and somewhere someone was singing along to a radio playing from an open window.

Every doorway she passed seemed to open into another world, pattern rooms crowded with sketches, elevators jammed with garment bags, showrooms bursting with racks of silk, satin, and polyester prints. And then there were the leggy, beautiful runway models. They walked down the sidewalk like it was their own personal stage, like the whole city was built just for them. Julie found herself staring, thinking she'd never seen anyone move with that kind of confidence. She couldn't take her eyes off them.

She clutched the ad in her hand, cleared her throat, and pushed through the revolving doors of 1372 Broadway, the towering skyscraper that housed Philippe Leon and several of the city's top fashion designers.

The lobby was jammed with people, everyone talking at once as if the whole building was in on the same conversation. Elevators rattled open and shut, spilling out a stream of people so colorful they seemed plucked from every corner of the world—buyers with bulging garment bags, models gliding past in impossibly high heels, businessmen in a hurry to get to their next appointment, and messengers weaving through the crowd with manila envelopes tucked under their arms. Everyone looked busy, important, as if they were all running the same invisible race. The walls were lined with framed magazine covers, glossy reminders of the industry's icons.

Julie felt her stomach twisting in knots, the nervous excitement rising inside her. This was no school play, no prom queen crown. This was Seventh Avenue, and she was about to step into it.

As Julie stood by the elevator, she heard a ripple of whispers and turned to see what the commotion was about. A shiny, copper-colored Rolls-Royce Corniche had stopped abruptly in front of the building. A chauffeur, dressed in a uniform straight out of London's finest, stepped smartly to the curb and opened the door.

A man appeared, skin bronzed by the sun, as if he had been dipped

    - - - B A R B A R A A. D A V I S

in it. Impeccably dressed, his silver hair worn like a crown, a folded newspaper in one hand. But it was his eyes that stopped her cold— crystal-clear
blue, the kind you don't forget. He carried the air of wealth and success so
effortlessly that Julie stared, almost intimidated, as if she were seeing the
type of person she had only ever read about.

He moved across the lobby without hesitation, his private elevator
waiting. Just before the doors closed, his eyes swept quickly over her,
from the top of her head to the tips of her shoes. In that split second, she
felt a vulnerability she had never felt before. It was as if he were wearing
glasses that could see right through her. It left her cold and uncomfortable.
Whoever he was, she decided right then that she did not like him.

"Who in the world is that?" Julie whispered to the woman standing
beside her.

"Oh, that's Mr. David Rosere," the woman said, almost reverently.

"He owns Philippe Leon." Julie stood stunned. The noise of the city
faded into silence. For a moment, it felt like everything around her just
stopped. She took a breath and reminded herself why she was there. The
whispers died down, the elevator doors closed, and her brief encounter
with Mr. Rosere became a moment she couldn't quite shake.

Clutching the ad in her hand, she walked toward the reception desk.
"I'm here to see Mr. Morris Schaffer," she said, her voice steadier than she
felt. Within minutes, she was being ushered past mannequins draped in
muslin and sketches pinned to cork boards, into a small office where her
fashion career was about to begin. She waited for what felt like an eternity.

The chair beside her was piled with fabric swatches and rolls of
trim, smelling faintly of starch and dye. A fast-moving man in a vest and
ascot suddenly stopped short in front of her, his arms full of muslin.

"Bonjour, madame," he said with a flourish, balancing the fabric
with practiced ease. "I'm Frenchie. Are you the new fitting model?"

Julie laughed, caught off guard, but playing along. "I hope so," she
said, extending her hand. Instead of shaking it, he bent and brushed the top

of her hand with a kiss.

"Well, then, I certainly hope so too. With that, he was off again, muttering curses under his breath about not having enough time to finish samples for a major department store.

The whole place pulsed with an urgency Julie had never experienced before. Everyone who walked by seemed dressed in the latest fashions, sleek wrap dresses, wide-lapel jackets, platform heels, racing across the dusty, uneven floor. Julie glanced down at her own outfit. *What was I thinking?* Suddenly, her skirt felt a little too plain, her blouse not fitting quite right. A wave of insecurity washed over her, like she had accidentally gotten on the wrong bus and landed in a world where everyone else knew the rules but her. She pushed down the panic rising in her chest and convinced herself this was exactly where she belonged.

At last, Mr. Morris Schaffer appeared. He was older, slightly balding, with a slouched back that suggested a lifetime bent over cutting tables and showrooms. He gave Julie a quick once-over, sighed, and said flatly, with a thick Jewish New York accent, "Go back to school, kid. You don't want to be in this meshugge rag business."

For a moment, her stomach dropped. The words stung more than she expected, like someone had slammed a door before she had even stepped inside. But then something in her straightened. Julie lifted her chin, forcing her voice not to shake.

"Mr. Schaffer," she said quietly, "I wouldn't be here if I didn't need the job. I need this job, and I promise you will not be sorry."

Schaffer's eyes narrowed. He leaned back, scratching his jaw as though the decision was more difficult than it was. "Okay, kid," he muttered at last.

"Lemme think about it."

Julie blinked. "How long do you need to think about it?"

He looked at her, expressionless. "Not sure." And with that, he pushed himself out of the chair and disappeared through the door.

  — — — B A R B A R A A . D A V I S

– – – – –

Julie stayed put. Minutes crawled into hours. She didn't move, not even when the ache in her bladder begged her to find the bathroom. Three hours later, Schaffer finally returned. He glanced at her, still sitting there, and gave a short laugh through his nose. Finally, he exhaled and shook his head.

"You've got nerve, kid, I'll give you that. Nerve might get you through a day in this business. Might."

He gestured vaguely toward the pile of fabric swatches beside her. "Alright, Julie. Let's see if you've got more than just nerve."

Her heart pounded so hard she swore it might burst right through her blouse. She fought to steady herself, biting back the grin tugging at her lips as she leaned forward. Whatever test was waiting next, she felt ready for it, just as soon as she found the ladies' room.

— 5 —

It was the saddest of days. In a quiet hospital room at St. Joseph's Wayne Medical Center, Julie whispered her final goodbye and her last thank you to the person who had been her everything. Mother Seton had tried to save her, but sometimes prayers simply cannot be granted. Nothing could soften the reality of sitting there, holding the hand of the woman who was her best friend, her rock. She was her entire world.

Julie's sister Malerie, her brother Richard, and her father all circled her, a family joined in grief, standing together to say goodbye to the person who had shaped their entire existence. Who would carry their memories forward now?

With tears that felt endless, Julie leaned close, her voice breaking as she let her gratitude spill into the silence of the cold hospital room, a thank you that carried the weight of a lifetime of love.

After the funeral, returning to the life she once knew felt impossible. The familiar patterns of her everyday life no longer fit. The world at home didn't feel like hers anymore. Julie knew what she had to do. She loved her father deeply and hated the thought of leaving him, knowing how much he depended on her and how hard letting go would be for both of them. Her sister and brother were still there, he wouldn't be alone, but she still felt guilty.

He had made his famous meatloaf and baby potatoes to cheer everyone up. And after dinner, they settled onto the old burgundy plaid couch in the den, Jeopardy playing softly in the background.

Before saying anything, Julie's eyes drifted to the brown leather chair across the room, the one where her mother had spent her last days hoping for a miracle. She stared at it for a moment, as if silently asking her mother for permission. Then her gaze fell to her father's hand resting beside her. When he was younger, a talent agent once spotted him and asked if he had ever thought about being a hand model. He always laughed when he told that story, wiggling his fingers with a grin. Now those same strong hands appeared wrinkled and old. He had never taken off the black onyx ring her mother had given him when they were engaged, and Julie knew deep down he never would.

She took a breath, steadying herself. "Dad, she said quietly, "I want to move to New York City. I can't stay here. It's too hard."

He didn't answer right away. His thumb brushed slowly over the back of her hand. "I know," he said at last.

"I feel like if I stay," her voice catching, "I'll never...every room...everything reminds me of Mom."

He nodded, his eyes fixed on the television, though neither of them was watching. "This house has been your home for a very long time, Julie. That doesn't mean you're meant to live here forever."

"I don't want to leave you, it feels like I'm running away" Julie said.

"You're not leaving me," he replied gently. "You're going where your life is now." He turned then, meeting her eyes. "It isn't running he said. "It's what comes next. Your mother would have said the same thing."

"You're really ok with this, Dad?" she asked.

"Your mother and I raised you to go after the life you want," he said. "I would be more worried if you didn't want to go."

A small smile tugged at his mouth. "Just don't forget to call your old man once in a while."

"I won't," Julie said, managing a faint smile of her own.

"And remember, he winked, meatloaf tastes better at home than it does in the city."

Before she packed up to move to New York, Julie helped her father go through her mother's things. She couldn't bear the thought of him facing that heartbreak alone. They made three piles. Keep. Donate. Throw away.

Together they opened drawers and closets, each piece of clothing a reminder of how beautiful her mother had been. Her turquoise jewelry box spilled over with treasures she had carefully put away, her father's fraternity pin from college, charms from a bracelet she loved, tiny baby teeth wrapped in tissue, faded ribbons from first baby hair bows, and love letters her children had written to her over the years. At the very bottom lay Julie's high school graduation program. She picked it up and stared at the list of names, remembering a time when her life had felt simple, and full of promise. Her mother used to say that the people with the best coping skills in life were the real winners.

Only now did Julie understand how true that was and how impossibly sad life could be. There were a few pieces of clothing she couldn't part with. She pressed one sweater to her face, breathing in the faint trace of her mother's perfume. Wrapping her arm around it almost felt like a hug.

The hardest part came when she reached for the wig mannequins lined up along the top of the dresser. Her mother had despised them, hated what they symbolized, the life of illness they tried to disguise. If she had her way, she would have walked proudly with her bare head showing.

But for Malerie's sake, her baby girl, too little then to understand, she wore them, even gave them names that made everyone laugh despite the sadness— Itchy Irene, Frizzy Franny, Helga the Helmet, and her favorite, Flatty Patty. Julie lifted the first one carefully. "Okay, Itchy Irene," she murmured. "Time to go." She placed it in the box, then reached for the next. "You too, Frizzy Franny. You were never my favorite." A small, unexpected smile flickered and disappeared. She hesitated with Helga the Helmet, smoothing the stiff strands as if Helga might feel it. "You tried your best, "she whispered. Last came Flatty Patty. Julie held her for a moment longer, pressing her forehead lightly against the plastic band. "You were always Mom's favorite," she said softly. "Mine too."

It took the whole day to clear away the last physical reminders of her mother. Priscilla, her mother's Persian cat, kept curling up on the scarves Julie had piled at the foot of the bed, her green eyes blinking slowly as if she, too, refused to let go. Prissy began walking slowly toward her, her mother's scarf tangled around one paw, and Julie completely lost it.

That was the breaking point. Julie sank at the end of her parents' bed, her body folding in on itself as the floodgates finally gave way. She sobbed until she could hardly breathe, Priscilla pressing against her side, trying to purr her tears away. Her father was in the kitchen making them something to eat, leaving Julie and Prissy alone in their grief, swept under by the unbearable weight of losing the most important person in their lives.

Julie turned her thoughts toward New York City. She had the job. She packed her car again with boxes, clothes, a few framed photos she couldn't leave behind, and drove east on Route 3 toward the skyline that shimmered in the distance like a promise. The closer she got, the taller the buildings rose, steel and glass catching the afternoon sun. The World Trade Center's Twin Towers stood like sentinels over the city, glinting in the light, daring her to begin again.

To Julie, they weren't just buildings; they were symbols of possibility, of promise, of a world where she could carve out a place for herself. She felt so small, she felt so alone.

Apartment hunting in Manhattan was nothing like paging through the real estate section of the *Star-Ledger*. Landlords barely looked up from their desks, brokers hustled her from one shoebox-sized room to another, quoting rents that made her head spin. She climbed endless flights of narrow stairs, saw kitchens smaller than closets, bathrooms with pipes that rattled like subway cars, windows that looked out onto brick walls and the rats. Big, ugly, hairy rats that seemed to scurry around every street corner.

But Julie was determined. Somewhere amid the chaos of the Village stoops, the Upper East Side brownstones, and the midtown walk-ups with rattling pipes, there had to be a place with her name on it. Each rejection, each disappointment, only sharpened her resolve. Somewhere in this sprawling, unforgiving city, there had to be a place that was hers, however small, where she could call home. And until she found it, she wasn't going to stop looking.

She sat alone at Harry's Coffee Shop in the heart of the Garment District and ordered their famous strawberry cheesecake. The "find an apartment clock" was ticking; she had only one week left. Her high school friend Mary Trotter had been kind enough to let her crash for a few weeks, but with Mary's boyfriend returning soon, Julie knew three would be a crowd.

Julie had tacked a "roommate needed" notice on the New York Public Library bulletin board, hoping someone would answer her prayers. Then came the call she had been praying for; her name was Kerry Turnberry.

Kerry was stunning, with a movie-star quality that drew eyes the moment she walked into a room. She had once been married to a very wealthy, much older man who had inherited a trust fund designed to last for generations. For the first five years of their marriage, Kerry lived a life most girls only dreamed of— maids, butlers, yachts, European vacations, and a clothing allowance that would make any fashion editor jealous. That was until one summer afternoon on their yacht, when Kerry picked up the receiver of the ship-to-shore phone and heard her husband's unmistakable deep voice telling a stranger that he loved her. Six months later, Kerry was out. No maids, no yachts, no allowance. She had not read the fine print in the prenup.

She found herself living in a tiny, dark studio on the Upper East Side, just around the corner from Bloomingdale's, with nothing but her looks, what was left of her pride, her modest alimony check, and a little black poodle named Pepper.

Kerry had not been on her own for long when she met Frank Sisto at a friend's dinner party. After that night, he called her every day for two weeks before she finally agreed to meet him for dinner, making it clear over the phone that she had no intention of ever dating again. But Frank was persistent, and patient, and in just three months he had won her over. Frank asked Kerry to move in with him. There was only one problem—no dogs allowed. He was allergic, or so he said.

The phone call to Julie was brief, almost businesslike. "The apartment is yours," Kerry said, "if you agree to take care of Pepper. She's my baby. I'll cover the rent difference, and I'll have visiting rights."

Julie pushed her plate aside, the last bite of strawberry cheesecake untouched, as her mind drifted back to her conversation with Kerry. A roof over her head and a poodle named Pepper, it wasn't much, but it was a start.

— 6 —

It didn't take Julie long to learn what was expected of her at Phillipe Leon. Arrive at 8:45 a.m. sharp. Head straight to Frenchie, her favorite part of the day. He had come to the company from Paris ten years earlier and quickly earned a reputation as the best pattern maker in the house, a title he wore as confidently as the silk ascot around his neck. The ascot was his badge of honor, and the ever-present cigarette in his hand served as both a prop and a pointer as he spoke. And without fail, there was always a warm, buttery croissant waiting for Julie, slathered with the homemade jelly his wife Patricia made.

"Only one, Julieee," Frenchie would tease, wagging a finger. "We need those measurements to stay exactly where they are."

"Yes, Frenchie, yes," Julie would fire back with a grin, pretending to surrender. It was Frenchie's small ritual of kindness, a reminder that even in the frantic chaos of fittings and deadlines, there was room for a little sweetness.

Frenchie was a funny little man, and always on edge, a bundle of nerves wrapped in charm. The days were never long enough for him, and he moved through each one with the restless energy of a man racing an invisible clock. He would line up each dress in a neat row, waiting for Julie to step out of the dressing room, only to swoop in with pins and quick fingers, fussing and adjusting until the garment molded to her body as if it had been born there.

"Juleee," he would say in his charming French accent, tugging at a hem, "can you move? Can you sit in it?" Julie would oblige, twisting and bending, trying not to laugh as Frenchie fluttered around her, muttering to himself and stabbing pins back into the fabric.

Next came the walk to the vice president's office. Justin Weiss not only carried the title of vice president at Phillipe Leon, but more importantly, he was Mr. Rosere's son-in-law, married to his daughter, Karen. He was polite enough, but certainly not warm. Julie learned early on not to engage beyond what was required. She would knock softly before stepping into his office, which was at least twice the size of her apartment and said to have been designed by Lauren Minkoff, one of the city's top interior designers, whose waiting list stretched for months.

Justin always asked the same three questions: "How do you feel in it?" he said barely looking up.

"Fine," Julie answered, smoothing the fabric.

"Are you comfortable?"

"Sure."

"Would you personally buy this for yourself?"

"Absolutely," Julie said.

She turned away from the mirror so Justin wouldn't see her face. This one was especially bad. In the three months she had worked there, there had only been one dress she would have bought for herself. It wasn't the flashiest piece in the collection, or the most daring. It was simple, a slip of silk in the palest shade of blue, cut on the bias so it skimmed her body without clinging. The neckline was soft, the straps delicate, the hem

     --- BARBARA A. DAVIS

brushing just below the knee. When she caught her reflection in the mirror, she hardly recognized herself. The dress didn't try too hard; it didn't need to. It was elegance in its purest form.

Frenchie had stood back that day, cigarette dangling, a rare smile tugging at his mouth. "Juleee," he said, "that one… it is made for you."

Julie had believed him. For a moment, she felt not like a fitting model, not like a stand-in for someone else's vision, but like herself, exactly as she wanted to be.

The afternoons moved in a blur of fittings, notes, and last-minute changes. By the time the clock neared 5:30 p.m., Julie had settled into the same routine of closing the day, slipping out of the last dress, handing the garments back to Frenchie's frantic assistants, and grabbing her things to go home.

On her way out, she had to pass Mr. Rosere's office. He sat behind his desk, broad-shouldered and imposing, talking to his son Alan, who had inherited the title of president. He never looked up, and for that, Julie was thankful. She never lingered in front of his office for too long, but today her eyes caught a glimpse of the walls. They were lined with oil paintings, each one a portrait of his pride and joy, not his children, but his thorough-bred racehorses. Names she had only read about in the papers stared back at her from expensive, gilded frames, sleek bodies captured mid-stride, nostrils flared, black manes flying.

Above his desk hung the largest painting of all—the Rosere family gathered proudly around their prize horse, Lancelot, immortalized in oils after his Kentucky Derby win. David stood tall in the center, his wife Barbara at his side. Around them, his children, all so young, standing proudly by their parents' side. They seemed like a happy family dressed in the finest clothes money could buy. Julie noticed at once how different Mr. Rosere looked in the portrait, so much younger, his face less hardened, his posture lighter. It had to have been painted years ago, before time and business etched themselves into his features.

The canvas radiated power, a portrait of wealth and legacy meant to last forever, the kind of triumph that could not be earned in a single lifetime. For some reason, she always avoided eye contact with the man who paid her salary. Something about him made her uneasy. Maybe it was the unspoken truth that their worlds were too far apart, her in her tiny studio apartment with its squeaky pipes, borrowed furniture, and a dog that wasn't even hers, and him presiding over Seventh Avenue as if he owned it outright. What could possibly connect them? It seemed impossible, like the distance between their lives was measured in more than just dollars and square footage. It was an entire universe.

And yet, as she made her way home, Julie couldn't help but wonder, did the universe have its own way of closing distances she could never imagine crossing? As she walked toward the elevators, the vision of that family portrait followed her out into the evening rush of Seventh Avenue.

Julie first met **Toni Rubin** in the employees' ladies room, a chance encounter that turned into something so much more. Toni, confident and quick with a smile, introduced herself right away. She worked as a designer for Philippe Leon and carried herself with the kind of poise that made her seem wise beyond her years. Within minutes, she had Julie laughing, the awkwardness of a first meeting gone.

One afternoon, she invited Julie to The Bird Cage, a charming tea house and restaurant inside Lord & Taylor's flagship store on Fifth Avenue. They were famous for their tea sandwiches, and Julie's favorites soon became the crustless triangles filled with egg salad and tuna. For dessert, she and Toni would share the layered sponge cakes that melted in your mouth. They were served on the kind of pretty little plates that reminded Julie of when she was a little girl, dressing up in her mother's heels and pearls, pouring imaginary tea for her dolls. Only this time, it wasn't pretend; the tea party was real.

Over lunch, Toni was stunned to discover Julie had never been to a gynecologist. "That's crazy," Toni gasped. "How old are you?"

"I'm twenty," Julie whispered, fumbling for an answer. "Have you had sex with anyone? Are you on birth control? How can that be?" Toni shook her head, amazed at just how naïve Julie was. Right then, she took it upon herself to teach the Catholic girl from Wayne, New Jersey, a thing or two.

She had a lot to catch up on. Toni quickly became more than just a coworker; she was Julie's tour guide to New York, introducing her to a world she had never imagined. She took her to Elizabeth Arden's Red Door salon for her first facial and made her an appointment at Vidal Sassoon for a hip new hairstyle, declaring that the "Jersey girl" look had to go. At Bloomingdale's, Toni showed her how to work the sales racks like a pro, mixing one perfect designer piece with a handful of basics so she could look like she belonged on Seventh Avenue without spending a fortune.

Toni taught Julie how to hail a cab in the rain, "Elbow out, arm up, don't be shy," and where to find the best Harvey Wallbangers and Pink Squirrels at happy hour. She pulled her into SoHo galleries on Saturday afternoons, whispered the names of Wall Street men to avoid, and laughed as Julie tasted sushi for the first time, grimacing at the texture, not sure if she would ever order it again. It wasn't just life lessons; Toni taught Julie the little things, too.

The small pleasures that made the long days feel lighter. She introduced her to the best corned beef and Reuben sandwiches at Lou G. Siegel's on West 38th Street, a deli so legendary it seemed like every cutter, designer, and sales rep in the Garment District had a story that began there. Julie could hardly finish half a sandwich, but she loved the warmth of the place and the way it made her feel as soon as she stepped inside. The place was alive with the kind of energy Julie adored. Fun. Loud. Chaotic... Perfect!

Julie never said no when Toni invited her to dinner at La Grenouille, her favorite French restaurant on 52nd Street, where fashion elites and celebrities all met. Their Christmas parties were the stuff of legend, gorgeous floral arrangements, escargot and French delicacies laid out on linen-draped tables, champagne flowing, the Christmas spirit alive and well in the Jewish garment district. Julie had never tasted food like this before, had never seen a room full of people who carried themselves like they owned the place. It was overwhelming, almost dizzying, but it thrilled her too. For the first time, she felt herself edging closer to the life she had always dreamed of, one she had only ever seen from the outside, looking in.

— 8 —

The endless days of fittings and parading in front of out-of-town buyers were wearing Julie thin. For more than two years, she had been doing the same job, and the glamour that once thrilled her now felt like drudgery. Even Frenchie, her beloved Frenchie, was beginning to grate on her nerves, his relentless nervous chatter and the constant cloud of cigarette smoke clinging to him like a smelly shadow.

One afternoon, as Julie stood numbly in yet another ill-fitting muslin, Toni slid up beside her. With a glance to make sure no one was watching, she slipped a folded note into Julie's hand.

"Call him," Toni whispered, eyes sharp with insistence. "Go call him now. My husband's new company is hiring. You're too smart to be a human pincushion. Go."

Julie felt her pulse quicken as she closed her fingers around the note. It was the first spark of escape she had been handed, and she wasn't about to ignore it.

Julie ducked into the narrow hallway by the freight elevators, the note burning in the palm of her hand. She unfolded it with trembling fingers. A name. A number. Jérôme Gérard. Scrawled in Toni's impossible-to-read handwriting. Her throat went dry as she fed coins into the pay-phone, each clink echoing louder than it should. She pressed the numbers, her heart pounding with each push of a button.

"Hello?" a man's voice answered with an accent she wasn't familiar with. It was warm, sexy, touched by something foreign that set it apart from the loud, brusque New York voices she heard every day. Julie couldn't place it, not then, but that unfamiliar voice would linger in her mind, an echo of something that would matter later, far more than she could imagine. Julie cleared her throat. "Hi…my name is Julie Glass. Toni Rubin suggested I call. She said your company might be hiring."

There was a pause, the kind that stretched just long enough to make her wonder if she had made a mistake. Then the man's voice came back, warmer this time. "Ah, yes, Julie, I've been expecting your call. When can you come in for an interview?"

Julie closed her eyes, gripping the sticky receiver tighter. For the first time in months, maybe years, she felt something shift inside her. The possibility of a door opening.

She had only been gone for ten minutes, but when she returned to the office, it looked as if a bomb had gone off. Desks were abandoned, phones left ringing. The usual bustle of fittings and small talk had vanished. Julie caught a glimpse of Morris in the office foyer, waving her over with a face full of worry.

The entire back room and sales staff were gathered there, too, their voices hushed and nervous, their eyes fixed on the office directly across the hall…Mr. Rosere's.

Julie's curiosity was getting the best of her, and she couldn't shake the feeling that something bad was about to happen. David Rosere, President of Phillipe Leon, rarely called his employees together, and when he did, it never ended well. The nervous whispering fell silent as he stepped out of his office. He wore his gold-rimmed glasses, the ones reserved for the most serious conversations with department store vice presidents over markdown money and returns. The frames meant business. He looked perfectly composed, a man in full command, though the tension in the room was electric.

Julie had seen those glasses before, and she knew what they meant. She remembered the day Saul Kaplan, the CEO of Macy's San Francisco, sat across from Mr. Rosere and calmly announced his plan to launch a Wednesday "Sale Day" every week of the month.

"Are you fucking crazy?" David exploded, ripping the glasses from his face and hurling them across the office. "You'll ruin the business, Kaplan! Who's going to buy anything at regular price during the week? Everyone will wait for Wednesday!"

The silence after his outburst was deafening. David's face had turned bright red as he slammed his hand against the edge of his desk, his voice shaking the walls. "You'll destroy everything, Saul! You think you can just do whatever you want? Don't you dare fucking walk out on me, Kaplan. You think you're bigger than this company? Bigger than me?"

Julie could still picture Saul standing there, calm but cold, as he picked up his black leather briefcase with steady hands. He met David's rage with a blank stare that made it clear the meeting was over.

"I'm doing it, David. Like it or not," he replied with icy resolve. "And one day, you'll see it was the best decision I ever made."

Julie never forgot that moment. Never forgot the thud of his fists slamming the desk. It was never a good sign when the gold-rimmed glasses came out.

The head designer, Ozzie, held a copy of *WWD*, its front page folded open. She had torn out an article earlier that morning, the kind of news that spread through the building like wildfire. Whispers had already begun—Was it true? Had he really done what the article claimed?

Without missing a beat, Rosere confirmed it, his voice calm and precise, as though he were merely asking for the salt to be passed.

"I have sold Philippe Leon."

The words struck like a lightning bolt. Julie heard the gasps ripple through the room. David's voice remained firm, leaving no room for discussion. "The terms of the arrangement secure the license agreement to manufacture Gordon Gabriel Jeans. I'll be moving forward to launch Gordon's new denim business."

She watched in disbelief as his son Alan and son-in-law Justin closed in at his side, like Secret Service agents guarding their protectee. Code name: VULTURE. The name fit.

Before walking away, he glanced at the receptionist. "Black coffee and a tuna on rye," he announced calmly, clueless to the impact his words had left on the people still standing in the room. He simply turned and headed down the hall to his office, answering no questions and making no mention of what would happen to their jobs.

Something ignited deep inside Julie. She knew he had the right to do whatever he wanted; it was his company, his rules. But did that give him the right to leave years of loyalty standing in silence? What kind of a man does that to people who had worked tirelessly for him, who had helped him build his business stitch by stitch? She felt her face burn with anger. The silence was unbearable. Julie gave Frenchie a fierce hug, then straightened her shoulders.

For years, she had hurried past that office door, eyes down, afraid to even glance at the man who signed her paycheck. But not today. Her pulse raced as she marched across the floor and past the rows of stunned faces. *How dare he slip back into his office without so much as an explanation? These were people who had worked tirelessly for him, some for decades, and he couldn't even tell them what would become of their jobs?*

The rage inside her left no room for hesitation. She reached his office, threw his door open, and for the first time locked eyes with his steel-blue stare. The unannounced intrusion startled him. David stumbled backward, his heel catching the edge of the oriental rug. Julie stood rigid as he crashed into the massive portrait of Lancelot hanging on the wall. The gold frame wobbled, then crashed to the floor, the frame cracking open.

Julie's glare met his, steady and unflinching. She stood her ground, staring at the man sprawled on the floor like a spoiled child, his glasses knocked sideways and hanging crooked on his face. He pushed himself up from the floor, brushing off his hands as if to steady both his body and his pride. Slowly, he straightened and turned to face her, a woman whose last name he wasn't even sure he knew. His voice came low, edged with contempt.

"How can I help you, Julie? It's Julie, correct?" he asked.

"Yes, Mr. Rosere, it is. Julie. Julie Glass." She didn't move. At first, her words came steady, controlled. "Start by telling us the truth…" Then louder, "…what's going to happen to everyone out there?" And finally, her voice filled the room, fierce enough to rattle even him… "They deserve to know!"

The silence that followed was uncomfortable. Then, almost as if the moment itself conspired against her, the folded piece of paper that Toni handed her slipped from Julie's pocket and landed right at Mr. Rosere's feet.

He bent down, picked it up, and unfolded it with deliberate care. His face tightened as he read the words, and through gritted teeth, he repeated them. "Gérard Jeans…" His eyes lifted, hard and unblinking. "Why do you have a note in your pocket that says Gérard Jeans?"

Julie's glare met his, steady and unflinching. "So it seems," she said coolly, "we both have questions and no answers."

Every instinct told her to shrink back, to look at the floor the way she always did when she passed his office. But not this time. She ignored his question, lifted her head, and locked her eyes on his. "And so, I'll ask again," she continued, unwavering, "what happens to them?"

Neither of them moved. The slip of paper still hung between his fingers like a threat or a test. Julie didn't look at it. She wouldn't give him the satisfaction.

"Maybe the question isn't them or me," she added evenly. "Maybe the real question is, who are you without them?" The words landed, sharp and final. And for the first time, David Rosere had no answer. Julie stayed silent for only a few seconds before turning toward the door.

At the doorway, she paused, glanced back at him one last time, and said quietly, "Goodbye, Mr. Rosere. May God help you." Then she was gone.

David buzzed for Toni the moment Julie stormed out of his office. He shut the door behind her and slid a crumpled slip of paper across his desk.

"Look what fell from Julie's pocket," he said. He had recognized her unique scribble of handwriting right away. "Do you know where this came from?"

Toni met his stare without blinking. She knew better than to deny it.

"Yes," she said calmly. "It came from me. My husband, Barry, was just hired by Gérard Jeans at Carol Tanaka's request. And you know as well as I do, Mr. Rosere, no one says no to Carol Tanaka." She let that land before continuing.

"The moment I read the article this morning in *WWD* that you had sold Philippe Leon and were opening Gordon Gabriel Jeans, I joined as well. My resignation letter is already on Justin's desk." That was all. She rose slowly, shook his hand, and walked out of his office, carrying the uncomfortable feeling that ambition sometimes feels like betrayal.

Toni's mind was racing as she walked back to her desk. She packed quickly, hugging the people she had grown so close to over the years. They were more than colleagues; they were her work family, and the thought of leaving so suddenly was harder than she thought. She lingered over the small mementos she placed into the box, each one a reminder of something that at one time had meant so much to her.

David stood silent, watching Toni walk toward the elevator doors. For a moment, his mind flickered back to the first time he had met her, how confident she had been when his oldest son, Alan, first introduced them at a polo match in Palm Beach.

"She'll be great in design, Dad," Alan had insisted. "She's got the eye. She knows everyone. The buyers will love her, and they will listen to her." Alan wasn't wrong.

Toni Rubin began her career at Loehmann's Department Store as an assistant designer and took to the role like a natural. Her fashion director was stunned by how quickly she picked things up; nothing seemed too much for her. Within weeks, she was running circles around designers who had been there for years. Promotions followed in quick succession— first head designer, then VP of Design. Under her leadership, Loehmann's stores flourished.

It was at an all-store meeting that Alan Rosere truly noticed her. He had flown in all the designers, buyers, and Loehmann's management from both coasts to unveil Lucky Girl, a new private label dress line Phillipe Leon would design exclusively for Loehmann's. There were the usual presentations, a fashion show to preview the line, and then a luncheon followed by a stroll through the racks filled with all the new designs for the season.

Toni, halfway through Alan's pitch, had excused herself for the ladies' room, interrupting him mid-sentence, as if it were nothing. That small gesture alone caught his attention. But it was while she was weaving through the new racks of clothes, slipping between the metal bars and hangers, that she sealed her reputation. She stopped, turned, and met the President of Phillipe Leon head-on. Without a flicker of hesitation, she told him exactly what she thought. "You need a new designer." Alan blinked, caught off guard. He fumbled with his cufflinks, forcing a thin smile, all the while thinking, Who does this girl think she's talking to?

"This line won't sell. The colors are off; the shapes are dated and matronly. And just look at the stitching on this thing, it's awful! In six months, they'll be begging you for markdown money," she said, her tone firm and certain.

The words cut sharply and clean, carrying the weight of truth. Alan had heard whispers about Toni's instincts, her uncanny knack for spotting what would sell and what would flop. Now he was seeing it for himself, and as much as he hated to admit it, she was right.

"And who would you suggest I hire to design Lucky Girl, Miss Rubin?" he asked, his voice half-amused, half-curious.

"Well… me, of course, Mr. Rosere," she replied without missing a beat. Then, with the faintest edge of a smile, she added, "And it's Mrs."

Alan paused, taken aback for only a second before his expression shifted into something almost admiring. "Mrs., it is," he said smoothly. "When can you start?"

David felt the irritation rising as his mind slipped back to when Toni had first joined the company all those years ago. She had been a force from day one, sharp and unstoppable, reshaping everything around her. And now she was walking out. The sight of his beloved portrait of Lancelot, shattered at his feet, only added to the sting. He wasn't sure which upset him more, her leaving or the broken glass on the floor. But the thought didn't last long. He brushed it aside quickly. After all, he told himself, everyone was replaceable.

_ 9 _

G ordon Gabriel was already a household name in couture, a women's line that had graced every major department store window for over a decade. His sharp tailoring, his daring use of color, his unapologetic slogans, I don't care if people are talking about me, as long as they're talking about me, had cemented his place in fashion history. But this was different. This was denim. And the timing could not have been more volatile.

It was the mid-70s, and the denim wars had just begun. The rules of fashion were shifting for everyone. A famous socialite, Astrid Peyton, had stunned the fashion world by introducing a "dressy" pair of jeans, cut slim and fitted tight to the body, with her new iconic embroidered butterfly stitched onto the back pocket. The moment her jeans hit the floor, women scrambled to own not just one pair, but two or three. Department stores fought bitterly for distribution rights, each one desperate to be the first to splash full-page ads across the glossy spreads of *Cosmopolitan*, *Vogue*, and *Harper's Bazaar*.

At the same time, four brothers from Roubaix, France, Jérôme, Daniel, Bernard, and Sami, sold their family's one-hundred-year-old fabric mill and launched their own denim label, Gérard Jeans. The factory had been a working-class operation, producing sturdy bolts of wool, cotton, and eventually denim, the kind of fabrics destined for uniforms, workwear, and the everyday clothes of ordinary people. The brothers had grown up among the noise of looms and the smell of dye baths, learning firsthand the grit of the trade. But they weren't content to remain suppliers in the shadows. They wanted to move beyond fabric, to put their own name on the finished product, and so Gérard Jeans was born, sleek, sexy, and made for the dance floors of Studio 54. Their rise was meteoric.

And now, David Rosere was stepping into the mix. He had built Philippe Leon into an empire of cocktail dresses and evening gowns, but he wasn't about to watch from the sidelines while denim took over the fashion world. He wanted a piece of it, no, more than that, he intended to own it outright.

— 10 —

Carol Reynolds Tanaka was the granddaughter of Dr. Kenneth Reynolds, a name that regularly appeared in society pages from coast to coast. Carol had grown up in a world of privilege. Her childhood was shaped less by her parents, who spent their days jet-setting from one glittering location to another, and more by the nannies who raised her in their absence.

Her life had been a carefully curated itinerary—private schools, summers at elite camps, personal shoppers at Bonwit Teller, and a credit card with unlimited spending power. There were debutante balls and coming-out parties at The Plaza, lessons in manners, and finishing schools that prided themselves on turning out young women of perfect poise. Weekends brought trips to the museums, summers meant the family's Hamptons estate, and afternoons were filled with charity luncheons where she was introduced to the city's most eligible young men from families just as prominent as her own.

Through her father's connections, Carol stepped into the role of Associate Director of Design Relations for The Fashion Institute of Technology (FIT), introducing new designers into the market, those with promise and talent.

Her work required taste, discretion, and an understanding of the market. An ideal fit tailored made for her. She loved her job, loved the connections that came with it, but most of all, she loved surrounding herself with the young talent emerging daily, all of them hungry to claim their place in New York's fashion world. Everything Carol had been given came wrapped like an exquisite gift, tied with colorful ribbons. When she opened it, the contents were always the same: the proverbial silver spoon.

She was grateful for it, of course, but somewhere in the back of her mind lingered a question she could never quite silence: *could she do it without one?* So, when Jérôme Gérard reached out and asked her to head up his new company, she didn't hesitate. She went for it. It was the first thing she had ever taken without a bow on top.

And then by chance, Carol met the love of her life, Kenji Tanaka.

Nothing about it could be traced to her parents' careful orchestration of her future. They had dreamed of a Wall Street investment banker or a corporate lawyer from a white-shoe firm on Park Avenue, the kind of match that promised prestige and stability. Her mother had tried a hundred times over to arrange introductions. But life had a way of laughing at carefully drawn plans, and Carol's path turned out to be anything but the one her parents had imagined. Fate had rewritten the script.

Carol had just left Susan Bennis/Warren Edwards, the legendary flagship shoe boutique on West 57th Street, where New York's elites shopped for the latest designs. The store itself felt less like a shop and more like an art gallery, its mirrored shelves gleaming with bold, sculptural shoes that seemed to whisper of daring nights out and fancy Fifth Avenue parties.

Carol, of course, had overindulged. Her arms strained under the weight of eight shopping bags, half of them filled with Maud Frizon shoe boxes, the rest just as extravagant, when she collided head-on with a man hurrying down the sidewalk to meet his parents for dinner. Her bags spilled everywhere, shoes skidding across the pavement like runaway kittens.

"Oh my God, I'm so sorry!" Carol gasped, scrambling to gather her shoe boxes.

"I think your shoes are trying to escape," the man replied with a grin, already kneeling to help. His voice was warm, and his hands were quick but careful, as if even her chaos deserved respect.

When their eyes met, something stopped her, a feeling she couldn't name. Kenji handed her a wayward heel, their fingers brushing for only a second. "You might need a bigger closet," he teased.

She clutched the shoe box to her chest, still trying to steady herself, when he reached into his backpack and pulled out a pen. Without hesitation, he scribbled a number across the top of the box. "I would love to hear from you... does the shoe lady have a name?" he asked, half-teasing.

Carol smiled, finally setting the shoe down. "Carol," she said softly. "And yes, you will be hearing from me."

For the first time in a long while, she laughed, not the polite laugh she saved for society dinners, but the one that lived deep inside her, the one she hadn't heard in years. He wasn't from her world of Plaza debutante balls and Hamptons summers. No introductions, no pedigree, no planning. Just a chance collision on a Manhattan sidewalk.

It did not go well when she told her parents about Kenji. Nothing had prepared Pauline and Bob Reynolds for a nearly penniless, struggling artist whose family still lived in Japan and whose parents spoke very little English. Carol fought for him anyway. She invited Kenji to every holiday, every family vacation, determined to make them see what she saw. Slowly, Pauline began to soften, catching glimpses of the charm and quiet intensity that made her daughter so devoted.

Bob was another story. There were closed-door conversations, arguments that ended in ultimatums. At one point, he even threatened to cut her off, no trust fund, no allowance, no inheritance. But for the first time in her life, Carol refused to budge. She adored her parents, but if it came down to a choice, she would choose Kenji over them.

They married in the backyard of the Reynold's summer home in Bridgehampton, right on the water. White sailcloth tents lined the lawn, flags snapping in the ocean breeze. Peter Duchin and his orchestra played under the lights, the same band favored by presidents, movie stars, and the city's most powerful families. The food was flown in by Glorious Food, the caterer of choice for Manhattan's elite, and Moët & Chandon's prestige cuvée champagne flowed endlessly, refilled in crystal flutes before a single bubble had the chance to fade. Liza Jones, the "Grand Dame of New York," covered it as the wedding of the season. Everyone who was anyone was there. But none of that mattered to Carol. All she cared about was the moment she said, "I do," and became Carol Tanaka and said goodbye to Carol Reynolds.

A few months after the wedding, Kenji Tanaka was no longer just Carol's mysterious artist husband; he was becoming a name. Kenji knew, without question, that without Carol, he would never have come as far in the art world or received the recognition that was now beginning to surround his name. She had opened doors he had not even known existed, introducing him to collectors, curators, and society figures across New York. It was dizzying, almost impossible to keep track of them all.

His signature style emerged in modern, vibrant abstracts, including a series of bold shoe paintings, each one a playful nod to the moment he and Carol first collided outside Susan Bennis/Warren Edwards.

It had started as nothing more than fooling around in his art studio in their three-story brownstone on East 63rd Street. Kenji never imagined it would become anything serious, just sketches and experiments, bright splashes of color across canvas. But fate, once again, had other plans.

One evening, during a dinner party in their home, one of Carol's friends, a successful Upper East Side gallery owner named Simon Guez, asked for a tour. Carol, beaming with pride, led him straight into Kenji's studio

Simon stopped in his tracks. He scanned the walls, then turned sharply, gripping Kenji's arm. "I want twelve," he said, eyes gleaming. "Make me a dozen paintings. I'm opening a new gallery downtown in a few months, and I want the entire show to be yours. We'll call it The Sole Experience by Kenji Tanaka. A little play on words. Shoe sole. Get it?" Simon laughed, looking at Kenji. "How much fun is that!" Kenji was stunned. But he nodded.

Two months later, twelve paintings were finished. And when Simon opened his new gallery in the Village, a star was born. The opening night was electric. Critics and collectors packed the gallery, along with curious passersby, until the walls seemed to hum with energy. Carol stood proudly at Kenji's side, her hand resting lightly on his arm, her eyes fixed on him with quiet admiration. Both sets of parents had come, Carol's mother and father mingling politely, while Kenji's, who had flown in from Japan, did their best to bridge the language gap with broken English and warm smiles.

The Gérard brothers, Jérôme, Daniel, Bernard, and Sami, all arrived together, loud and full of life. Carol had invited them after meeting them the week before at an FIT luncheon. She was taken by their magnetic charm and how effortlessly they became the center of attention. Carol saw something in them, and it was only a matter of time before her intuition sparked a connection that would send the entire fashion world on tilt.

They commissioned a painting for their office lobby and promised it would hang where every visitor could see it. More than decoration, it was a statement, a bold reminder that Gérard Jeans wasn't just selling denim anymore; it was shaping culture.

Friends, colleagues, and New York society filled the rest of the room. Champagne bottles were popping, murmurs of "genius" whispered over the canvases, and the kind of night that every artist dreams of but few ever experience. By the end of the evening, Kenji's twelve paintings had sold out.

And just like that, Kenji Tanaka was no longer a struggling artist from nowhere; he was the name everyone was talking about in the New York City art world.

— 11 —

Jérôme Gérard had first heard Carol's name whispered by Paula Jennings, the veteran buyer at Bloomingdale's who had taken him under her wing. Paula had been a buyer for over twenty years and had the kind of eye that could spot greatness before the rest of the world caught on. She wanted Gérard Jeans for Bloomingdale's, not just wanted them, she wanted to own them. Exclusive styles, the first ad campaign, the first delivery, and anything else she could get her hands on. In exchange, she dangled an introduction that would change everything—Carol Tanaka.

Carol, Paula told him, wasn't just someone who could run his business; she could take charge of it. She was smart, relentless, and known across Seventh Avenue for running a tight ship. Fashion wasn't just her career; it was in her bloodstream, her baby.

Jérôme's brothers had been eager to see Studio 54, so he asked if Carol could meet him there. She was a little surprised at the invitation— after all, they could have discussed whatever it was he wanted to talk about at Kenji's art exhibit in SoHo instead of this place. Who discussed a business transaction in the middle of Manhattan's hottest nightclub? But then she reminded herself, as Dorothy did, that she wasn't in Kansas anymore. This new world of denim jeans was foreign territory; a universe far removed from the polite runways and quiet, exclusive showrooms she knew. What the hell, she thought as she agreed. What do I have to lose?

The music pounded, bass lines pulsing through the walls, while the lights strobed in dizzying bursts of color. Models, actors, and Wall Street traders mingled on the same dance floor, all pretending for a few hours that the world outside didn't exist. And then, as if choreographed by the gods of insanity, a nude woman rode slowly past on a white horse, her skin shimmering beneath the mirrored disco ball. People gasped, applauded, and leaned in for a better look. Jérôme barely noticed. His eyes were locked on the woman Paula had insisted he meet.

Carol carried herself with a composure Jérôme wasn't used to. He had grown up around noise and improvisation, where instinct and survival drove every decision. But Carol was different. She moved through the chaos of Studio 54 with the calm of someone who knew she was above it all. She spoke in a crisp, deliberate, hypnotic rhythm, each word weighed and measured, as though she had already mapped out the next ten moves in whatever game was being played.

Jérôme wasn't sure about her at first. She came from a world of polish and connections, so unlike his own raw, scrappy world. Yet something about that contrast intrigued him. Within an hour, he knew Paula had been right.

Carol wasn't just sharp; she was the kind of force who could steady the storm. She would help him run the company and make Gérard Jeans the number one denim line in the country. She had better, he thought, because he had just agreed to pay her one of the highest salaries on Seventh Avenue.

                                   - - - B A R B A R A A. D A V I S

— 12 —

Jérôme had asked Carol to interview Julie for him; his meeting with Macy's had run over, and he didn't want her left waiting. Carol leaned back in the corner office at Gérard Jeans, her leather swivel chair creaking softly as she crossed one leg over the other. The New York City skyline stretched behind her. She studied her with a cool, appraising smile, the kind that made it impossible to tell whether she was impressed or merely amused.

"So," she said at last, her voice smooth but edged with curiosity, "you must be the portrait crasher, Julie Glass."

Word had already spread up and down Seventh Avenue, through showrooms and buyers' offices. A young girl who had dared to speak her mind in front of David Rosere had earned herself a nickname and a reputation.

Julie sighed. "Guilty. But in my defense, it was the portrait that started it."

Carol let out a quick, sharp laugh, though her eyes softened with warmth. She leaned back in her chair, shuffling the papers on her desk as if to buy a moment. "Well, if you are going to crash something, I suppose making it memorable isn't the worst way to go."

Julie straightened her shoulders. "Memorable's fine, but I would rather be employed. I know this business, Carol, buyers, margins, deadlines, and I'm not afraid of hard work."

Carol tilted her head, studying her carefully, as though weighing not just Julie's words but the conviction behind them. "Not afraid of David Rosere, not afraid of the Seventh Avenue rumor mill… Tell me, Julie, what scares you?"

Julie hesitated for only a second before answering. "Standing still. Watching everyone else move ahead while I stay in the same place. That terrifies me."

"Good answer, Julie, I'm impressed."

Julie leaned forward. "You won't be sorry. When do I start?"

Carol shook her head at the audacity, but she admired it. "You are bold Julie Glass, I will give you that. Let's just say, you have already started. Welcome to Gérard Jeans."

Toni had stayed deliberately out of sight, giving Julie her space with Carol, but now she was right in front of her, arms wide open. It felt so good to hug her. After the upheaval of the past week, there was something grounding about standing across from the person who always had your back. Toni had called Julie the night they both walked out of David Rosere's office, telling her she had joined Gérard Jeans, and promising she wouldn't be far behind.

"I'm really glad we're doing this together," Toni said quietly. "It just feels right."

Julie nodded. She felt it too. In an industry that shifted without warning, having someone by your side was no small thing.

Before Julie could respond, a man stepped forward from the office doorway. Toni's husband, Barry, extended his hand, "So, finally we meet," he said to Julie. "Toni told me about the note. I'm so sorry that happened, "but I'm very happy you're joining the team."

Julie took him in quickly. He wasn't loud or showy like so many of the men she had met on Seventh Avenue. There was something measured about Barry, a quiet confidence that made her instantly alert. She had the sense he missed nothing, that even as he shook her hand, he was already calculating. He had a reputation to uphold, after all, known by everyone as the man who moved mountains. And now, standing before her, he was deciding whether Julie Glass would be an asset worth keeping in his world.

Barry had been one of the first hires at Gérard Jeans, handpicked by Jérôme, Daniel, Bernard, and Sami. The brothers had agreed without hesitation—he was the man. Soon, he earned the nickname the fifth brother, and he wore the title proudly.

He knew exactly what he was up against. He knew the players in the denim wars, and he had no intention of letting Astrid Peyton or David Rosere walk away with the prize. Where Toni was bold and outspoken, Barry was her opposite, quiet, reserved, measured, and sly as a fox. Julie could see it already. He understood what it would take, and he had no problem rolling up his sleeves and doing whatever was necessary to claw out the market share that would earn him the bonus he had been promised if he hit the target number.

Julie could hardly contain herself. Of all the twists Seventh Avenue had thrown her way, finding Toni already settled in at Gérard Jeans and meeting Barry felt like the best one yet.

— — — — —

To Julie, Carol Tanaka would forever be her greatest role model. The woman opened the door to the world of sales and showed her how to walk through it with confidence. But what impressed Julie most was not Carol's connections; it was how she used them. Carol introduced Julie to buyers who treated Seventh Avenue like their personal chessboard, teaching her how every handshake, every cocktail, and every whispered word at a runway show could tip the balance of a million-dollar order.

She taught Julie the art of walking a floor, moving through a department store to see what others missed—the way merchandise was displayed, the way customers picked up and put down a garment, the subtle signals from a sales staff that revealed whether a line was selling or failing. She introduced her to the charity circuit as well, where fashion wasn't just clothing but currency, traded at luncheons and gala dinners that filled the pages of *WWD*. Julie learned how to make small talk with men in tuxedos and women in ballgowns, how to hold her ground in conversations where everyone else seemed older, richer, and far more polished.

And then there were the lunches. Not the Bird Cage at Lord & Taylor anymore. Carol swept Julie into the power spots—The Four Seasons, The Pierre, Le Cirque at the Mayfair Hotel. Places where editors, buyers, and designers sat at the next table, and where Julie realized that the deals were often sealed over a glass of Sancerre rather than a boardroom table.

Through it all, Carol hammered one lesson home—sales were not about numbers; they were about relationships. And in her polished, worldly way, she passed that truth to Julie, who carried it like gospel. From human pin cushion to deal closer, her story flipped overnight. It reminded Julie of her favorite quote, the one about never really feeling ready, but doing it anyway. She couldn't wait to get started.

— 13 —

It was Thanksgiving, and the holidays were still unbearable since Mimi had passed. She was the holiday, the person who filled the house with light, warmth, and laughter. Without her, it all felt unfinished, like a puzzle missing its most important piece. With a heavy heart, Julie boarded the bus at Port Authority Bus Terminal with a box of everyone's favorites pastries from Zabar's and headed home to Packanack Lake in Wayne for the long weekend with her family.

Port Authority was a strange place. Busy travelers hurried toward home, stepping around homeless men and women wrapped in filthy blankets, holding torn paper coffee cups stained with old brown spills, begging for anything. It was depressing, especially when you were already stretched thin, when your own emotional well-being was being held together by a thread.

Buses always amused her, the way elevators did. Everyone climbed aboard, found a seat, and then sat perfectly still, eyes forward, each person sealed inside their own private thoughts, almost daring you to look away.

There was one seat left open in the back. Julie took it immediately. The bus was full, and the last thing she wanted was to stand for over an hour.

As the bus pulled away, her thoughts drifted, not far, just enough. She noticed a little girl sitting across from her, clutching a tiny black-and-white stuffed dog. The sight stirred something unexpectedly tender. Julie looked away, pressing her head lightly against the window, watching the city blur past.

She didn't need to unpack the memories now. She didn't have the room for them. Grief had a way of doing that, crowding everything else out. For the moment, it was enough to sit still, to let the bus carry her forward, even if she wasn't sure where forward really led yet.

As the bus neared Wayne, Julie looked out the steamy window, taking in the familiar scenery. She remembered how the lake used to shimmer on a windy day, kids riding their bikes barefoot, and the smell of barbecues drifting on summer evenings,

She thought of how much she had taken for granted, the way everyone waved to each other, the way crossing guards knew your name, how grocery runs turned into twenty-minute conversations with neighbors. Those invisible threads were what made a place home. In a world that spun too fast, those small-town moments had been her anchor. Back then, it wasn't just school schedules, cheerleading practice, and band concerts; it was connection, it was community.

The bus pulled into the Willowbrook Mall park-and-ride, and Julie spotted her father's car waiting. He always flashed his headlights on and off when he saw the bus arrive, as if to say, "Welcome home, Julie." The moment the doors hissed open, she ran toward the car, where her father was already leaning across to push open the front door for his girl.

"Zabar's… oh great," he teased, pretending to be more excited about the baked goods she carried than about her.

"How's my favorite girl?"

"I'm so happy to see you, Dad," Julie said, and she meant it.

On the ride home, she glanced over at him and wondered how he always managed to pretend to pull it together. His hands rested firmly on the steering wheel, steady and sure, even though she knew how sad he was. Grief had carved lines into his face that had not been there before, but his eyes still held that same twinkle, the same quiet strength that had anchored her all her life. Julie leaned her head back against the seat, comforted by the familiar streets passing by as the car made its way home, and for a moment, it felt like nothing had changed at all.

She loved her family deeply, but after her mother died, grief hung heavy over them all. Her father especially seemed so lost. Without Mimi, he had lost his identity, his anchor. It was as if he were drifting between the life he once knew and the uncertain one he was trying to navigate without her. Julie saw it every day; it was as if he were waiting for something, or someone, that would never come back.

And yet, if you asked him, he would be the first to say he still had many blessings in his life. He adored his parents, Edwin and Ethel, and his older sister Doris. They had lived a very comfortable life. His father, Edwin, had started in the mailroom at the Nestlé Chocolate Company at the young age of seventeen, after his own father died, leaving him to support his mother and siblings. Thirty-five years later, he retired as Vice President, a title that ensured the family never worried about money again. Edwin Glass was affectionately called the Mayor of Palisades Park, not for holding office, but because he was the first to raise his hand when someone needed help. During the Depression, neighbors often came knocking, sometimes for advice, sometimes for a handout, and Ed never turned them away.

When he was a little boy, Julie's father would hide on the third step of the family's long staircase, listening as neighbors stopped by to ask his father for advice or help. It was there he learned the lesson that would guide him for the rest of his life— if you were lucky enough to grab the brass ring, it became your duty to share it with those who had not been as fortunate.

At fifteen, Julie's father, full of patriotism, lied about his age and tried to enlist with the 50th Armored Division of the Army National Guard. Word traveled fast, and within hours, his mother, clutching her embroidered handkerchief, and his father, eyes caught between pride and disapproval, brought him back home. His father had other plans for his young son—Bucknell University, Nestlé, and eventually the passing of the chocolate baton.

But life had a way of redirecting dreams. When Ed's aptitude test results arrived, his father placed the envelope on the kitchen table, silent for the first time his son could remember. The smell of the homemade blueberry pie his mother had just baked couldn't sweeten the disappointment. Nothing on that test pointed Ed toward business… just the opposite. It suggested he was "best suited for a strong outdoor/ nature interest, enjoys working with living things and natural surroundings. Prefers open air environments to office or factory settings and shows potential for forestry and animal-related occupations."

His father read the results twice before folding the paper and tossing it into the fireplace, the flames curling around it, consuming the dreams of both father and son. Dutiful but conflicted, young Ed watched in silence, already sensing that his own life would be one of responsibility over passion.

After one difficult semester, he knew he was on the wrong path. He came home, walked into the kitchen, and declared he was done with Bucknell. Instead, he planned to marry his high school sweetheart, Mimi Florio, the girl with the prettiest eyes in their yearbook. His parents gave their blessing, and soon Ed and Mimi were married.

The young man who once longed to fight for his country, who loved trees, mountains, and wildlife, accepted a job through his father's connections, selling Birdseye frozen foods. The closest he came to working with nature was the company's logo itself, a bird swooping across the front

   - - - B A R B A R A A. D A V I S

cover of a cardboard box. Julie thought it sad, but almost comical, how her father's passion for the outdoors had been reduced to a frozen mascot.

How hard must it be, Julie wondered, to spend your life in a job that only paid the bills and, in her father's case, barely even that. Work that left the soul empty and dreams shelved. Yet she had never once heard him complain. He was so gracious and kind, a man who did his best, even if he never came close to grasping his own brass ring. But even without it, he was always there to lend a hand. Her grandfather, she hoped, would at least be proud of that.

Birdseye had transferred Julie's father to run the Midwest territory. Julie remembered her mother calling her and her brother, Richard, to the kitchen table, saying she had a surprise.

"I think it's a pool," Julie whispered excitedly to her brother as they slid into their seats at the chrome dinette set with its gleaming Formica top. She held her breath, certain her wish was about to come true.

"You're going to be a big brother, Richard, and you're going to be a big sister again, Julie."

Julie burst into tears, inconsolable. At nine years old, she only wanted three things in life—a horse, a canopy bed, and a pool. A baby was not on the list. Her mother knelt beside her, hugging her gently, rocking her as she whispered, "I hope it's a girl, Julie. You'll always have a best friend."

She was right. Malerie came into the world during one of the worst tornadoes East Lansing, Michigan, had ever experienced. She blew in at Sparrow Hospital, the prettiest little thing Julie had ever seen. They were complete opposites: Malerie with sparkling blue eyes, beautiful pale skin with cherry cheeks, and a mop of curly blond hair; Julie with dark bronze eyes, shiny straight brown hair, and a complexion brushed with gold and honey.

Richard, as usual, sat in silence. As long as his apple crate was parked in the driveway, he was content. He loved sports and was a superstar in almost everything he played. Stubborn but fair, Julie often wondered if he might have been happier being raised by Mickey Mantle. Sports were his life, and more than one Thanksgiving dinner ended in chaos when he stomped away from the table because his beloved Dallas Cowboys were losing. Julie and Malerie would exchange knowing looks, half-exasperated, half-amused; it was just Richard being Richard. Thankfully, he grew out of temper tantrums and running away from home every other week and became the kind of person Julie was proud to call her brother.

But her mother was right, Julie always had a best friend in Malerie. From the moment she first held her sister's hand, she never let it go. And she never would.

The first Thanksgiving without her mother was pretty much as impossible as it gets. Julie was quietly grateful that Dallas had pulled off a win; at least her brother's mood wouldn't ruin the day, something everyone could be thankful for. Her father had outdone himself in the kitchen, as if determined to hold the day together. The turkey was tender, the stuffing was delicious, and the giblet gravy, his pride and joy, was perfect.

Julie kept catching herself glancing at the chair her mom always sat in. Families, she thought, always seemed to fall into their own quietly assigned seats, unspoken, but constant. Now, the emptiness of that one chair felt heavier than words could ever describe. She swallowed the last bite of apple pie and whispered so softly no one could hear—"I miss you, Mom. Happy Thanksgiving."

— 14 —

Tuesday morning arrived in a blur, the scent of Thanksgiving stuffing still lingering in Julie's nostrils. At 9:00 a.m., the Gérard brothers gathered around a polished conference table, waiting for Debra Wilbers from J. Walter Thompson, the oldest and most prestigious advertising agency in New York City to arrive. Jérôme leaned back in his chair, his eyes moving slowly across his brothers. Pride swelled in his chest. It had been a whirlwind few months. It was hard to believe that not long ago, the four of them had stepped off a plane from France at JFK with nothing but ambition, a single denim prototype, and a very large check they received from selling the family business.

He thought back to the moment it all began. Paris was alive that afternoon, the hum of Boulevard Saint-Germain spilling into Les Deux Magots, thick with smoke and conversation, when Daniel spotted her. A tall, striking woman walked past, and though she turned heads with her beauty, it was her jeans that caught his eye. He crushed his cigarette into the ashtray and shot up from his chair, weaving through the tables to catch her.

"Excuse me, miss! Excusez-moi, Mademoiselle." His voice carried a rough urgency. "Your pants… what are they?"

She hesitated, not sure if she even wanted to answer, but Daniel pressed on.

"I'm Daniel Gérard. My brothers and I run a fabric mill in Roubaix—"

She wrinkled her nose. "Where?"

"Northern France," he clarified, "near the Belgian border." He leaned a little closer. "Are those denim? And what's that embroidered on the back pocket?"

The denim they manufactured back in Roubaix was nothing like this. Their bolts of fabric became stiff overalls and rugged work clothes, made for farmers and laborers who needed durability, not style. Fashion was the last thing anyone thought of. Yet here it was, shaped and fitting her like a glove. A pair of jeans that made heads turn. Daniel was amazed.

She tilted her head, amused by his persistence. "I bought them in New York, at Astrid Peyton's fashion show. Out of her Seventh Avenue studio. Everyone's trying to get a pair, but they are nearly impossible to find."

His eyes dropped again to the pocket, following the delicate stitch. "What is that? A flower?"

She shifted her hip just enough for him to see. "No. A butterfly, silly. That's Astrid's logo. Every pair has it. The moment you see it, you know they are hers."

He studied it closely, so small, yet impossible to miss. "It's simple," he murmured, "but powerful."

She smiled knowingly. "That's why people love them. It's more than fit. The butterfly makes them recognizable. It tells the world who you are wearing, and more importantly, she smiled slyly, everyone knows how much they cost."

The words struck him harder than he expected. It wasn't just denim,

   - - - BARBARA A. DAVIS

it was identity. A status symbol stitched in thread. In that instant, Daniel understood that if the Gérard brothers were going to make jeans, they couldn't just sell fabric. They needed a mark of their own, bold, unforgettable, a stamp the world would know at a glance. He imagined four G's, one for each brother. Jérôme, Bernard, Daniel, and Sami Gérard. Gérard Jeans was born.

"Please don't move," he begged, before sprinting back to grab his brothers. And right there, on that Paris street corner, in front of a girl they would never see again, the Gérard brothers made the decision that would change everything— they would go to New York, and they would rewrite the rules of women's fashion.

Now, sitting in his New York office, Jérôme smiled faintly at the memory. The girl was gone, but the spark she lit was still burning.

After they arrived, the brothers had only two months to pull off the impossible—secure a showroom, build a sample line, and find the buyers who would take a chance on their jeans.

Barry Rubin, Toni's husband, turned out to be the answer to their prayers. Within a week, he had a lease signed at 1411 Broadway. Three weeks later, they were moving onto the twelfth floor, fully painted, screened, mirrored, and carpeted. Barry built a powerful sales force almost overnight, and from there, they were on their way.

Two weeks before Market Week, Jérôme had a brilliant idea. He understood how quickly a single week could make or break a label. Market Week happened only four times a year. Spring. Summer. Fall. Winter. Buyers descended on a few crowded blocks in the fashion capital of the world to decide what designers would survive and which would quietly fall by the wayside. Jérôme walked into the lobby of every building on Seventh Avenue and Broadway, introducing himself to the young women at the front desks, the gatekeepers who directed buyer traffic to the showrooms upstairs. He charmed them all with his boyish good looks and sexy accent, learning their names and their stories, and most importantly, their pant sizes.

A few days before Market week arrived, he showed up dressed like Santa Claus, bearing gifts, a pair of Gérard Jeans in each girl's size, with one request: that they wear them during market week. In return, Santa promised to come back with another pair.

It worked like a charm. New York and out-of-town buyers couldn't miss it. Everywhere they turned, lobby receptionists were in the same jeans, each pair embroidered with four bold white G's stitched on the back pocket... two on top, two on the bottom, stacked like a code the fashion world was just beginning to understand. Curiosity spread fast. "Where did you get those?" people asked, certain they were seeing the next big thing. And right on cue, the girls, armed with Jérôme's freshly printed business cards, handed them out with a smile.

The orders arrived faster than they could process them. The brothers scrambled for more denim, more yarn, more trim, shipping by the thousands to meet the demand. Their first week of selling was beyond anything they could have imagined. But they had a secret source. The fabric mill they had sold to launch Gérard Jeans became their lifeline, and it was running hot.

And unlike most new labels, they had an edge—they knew the mills, the weavers, the suppliers. Years in their family's business had taught them the ins and outs of the supply chain, and that knowledge gave them speed when everyone else was still learning how to walk.

There are no secrets in fashion, and this was no exception. Word soon reached David Rosere at Gordon Gabriel Jeans and, of course, Astrid Peyton, who couldn't help but notice the uncanny coincidence—embroidered G's stitched onto the back pockets of the Gérard brothers' jeans. She wondered where in the world they had gotten that idea, as an annoying smirk spread across her lips.

                          — — — B A R B A R A A. D A V I S

— 15 —

He was not having it. David turned in his chair, his eyes locking on the oil painting of Lancelot that hung proudly above his desk. Refurbished after Julie's abrupt exit, the stallion's gaze seemed to follow him, its defiance mirroring his own. There was something in that horse's eyes that stirred David, an unspoken reminder that defeat was not an option. He would not and could not accept that four brothers, strangers to the industry he had devoted his life to, could possibly beat him at his own game. The door burst open, and his son, Alan, rushed in, breathless, clutching what he believed was the answer.

"Dad, she's going to do it," Alan said, his words tumbling over each other in excitement. "Riley Spencer's mother just signed the contract."

David straightened, his interest piqued.

Riley Spencer was the top teenage model in America, fresh-faced, innocent, yet carrying an undercurrent of seduction that had the fashion world at her feet. The perfect muse. The perfect weapon.

Alan pressed forward, "Her mother signed this morning. And James

Clive has agreed to photograph her, wearing nothing but a pair of Gordon Gabriel jeans."

It was exactly the kind of ad campaign they needed to steal the spotlight back from Gérard Jeans. David and Alan knew they were sitting on something big, something that could put Gordon Gabriel back on top. David could already picture the buyers' reactions once it launched.

James Clive's photo shoot landed in the April issue of *Cosmopolitan*. Nancy Trent, the editor-in-chief, famous for pulling off some of the magazine's most iconic shots, knew she had struck gold. Riley Spencer, draped only in Gordon Gabriel jeans, had delivered a moment destined to be remembered. Of all Nancy's celebrated covers, this one was by far the boldest, the most exhilarating, and the one that sent shockwaves through the fashion world.

The phones at Gordon Gabriel rang nonstop, buyers begged for appointments, and the press circled like moths to a flame. By every measure, it was a triumph. Still, underneath all the excitement, something gnawed at David. He couldn't put his finger on it, but the feeling lingered, tugging at him even in his proudest moments. Something was out there, heading his way, he just didn't know what.

On paper, everything looked perfect. He had hired the best in the industry, denim mavens and a sales force that over-delivered season after season. The usual family dramas played out as they always had. His wife spent too much money. Lauren Minkoff was busy redesigning yet another room in their Scarsdale estate, and Alan and Justin remained at his side in business.

None of that worried him. He was used to noise. But this was different. This was deeper. A quiet gnawing settled at the back of his mind, a whisper of warning he couldn't shake. David Rosere, the man with the cold, steel-blue eyes who had stared down competitors and crushed doubt for decades, felt something unfamiliar. Fear.

It was six months later when Riley Spencer's mother, Margot, came bursting into the Gordon Gabriel showroom, tossing her purse onto a chair and declaring, "What's a girl gotta do to get a cup of coffee around here?"

Debbie, the receptionist and the closest thing the company had to a human Swiss Army knife, jumped to her feet. She had dealt with Margot before, the woman who had a habit of ordering dozens of jeans for her friends and family at no cost to her. "They're part of Riley's deal, right, Deb?" Margot would always say. Debbie never knew if that was true, but she had been told to keep Margot happy, and it took everything in her not to tell this ass of a woman exactly where she could shove her jeans.

"Of course they are, Mrs. Spencer," Debbie lied smoothly.

"Oh, and Deb, make it quick, I'm desperate for caffeine," Margot snapped. "And while you're at it, Riley would like a vanilla skimpy treat. Small. Make sure you get a small one for my baby girl."

"Just kill me," Debbie muttered under her breath as she bolted from the showroom.

Trailing behind her mother was Riley herself, red-faced and mortified, wearing Style 1411, the jeans everyone was dying to get their hands on.

"I'm fine, Mom," Riley mumbled.

"Nonsense," Margot barked, waving her off.

Just then, Alan swept in, his smile a little too practiced to be genuine. "Margot! Riley! Come in, come in, sit down. My father will be joining us shortly."

David Rosere opened his office door and gave a quick wave, motioning Alan, Margot, and Riley into the private conference room attached to his office, away from the showroom floor where whispers were already starting.

He had been dreading this talk, but there was no way around it. Gordon Gabriel had called over the weekend, screaming on the other end of the phone. He had been at a dinner party in Fire Island when he overheard a couple of models raving about the "Riley jean."

"Well, that's a good thing, right?" David said with a grin. He thought it was great that models were talking about his jeans, especially on the Fire Island party scene. After all, Gordon's motto was practically legendary— "I don't care if people are talking about me, as long as they're talking about me."

"WRONG!" Gordon screamed into the phone. "It's my goddamn jean, not hers. It's not the Riley Jean, David, it's the Gordon Gabriel Jean, something called brand identity, have you heard of it? Do not renew her contract and cancel the upcoming photo shoots. Do I make myself clear, Rosere?"

David didn't argue. "Crystal, Gordon. I'll take care of it." This fucking business, David thought as he hung up the phone, you couldn't make this shit up. He went to the bar, poured himself a stiff drink, and let his mind drift back to when Riley was their golden girl. James Clive photographed her topless in nothing but the jeans, her hair cascading over her shoulders, a sly, sexy smile that said it all. They all knew it was a big deal, but even they couldn't have predicted the tidal wave it unleashed.

The networks banned the commercials, too provocative, they said. But the ban only poured gasoline on the fire. The jeans weren't just fashion anymore; they were rebellion, independence, defiance. Women weren't buying denim; they were buying freedom. Gordon Gabriel himself sent David a bouquet the size of a small car, the card scrawled with just two words— Well done. But success always came with a price. And this meeting was not going to be easy.

"Please, everyone, sit down." David straightened his tie and leaned forward, all business. "We've got a problem, Margot. Gordon's not happy. He thinks his label isn't getting the brand recognition he's after."

As he spoke, David could feel it, that uneasy feeling he'd been trying to ignore. Riley was everywhere— the magazines, the headlines, the late-night talk shows. People were talking about her, not the jeans. Somewhere along the way, she had stopped being the face of Gordon Gabriel

    - - - B A R B A R A A. D A V I S

and started becoming the brand itself.

Margot narrowed her eyes. "What the hell does that mean? She's on fire! Everyone wants a pair of his jeans," she said, tugging playfully at Riley's leg.

David glanced at Riley. "It means you have done such a great job, sweetheart, that people are calling Gordon Gabriel Jean the Riley Jean. And because of that, we are not going to be able to renew your contract."

"For fuck's sake, David!" Margot exploded, slamming her hand on the table. "You have got to be kidding me, are you all insane?" Get Gordon on the phone. Now. I want to talk to him."

"You know that's not possible, Margot," David said firmly. "The decision's been made. Riley will be paid for the rest of her contract, but the ad campaign is officially over."

At that moment, Debbie appeared, holding a hot cup of coffee for Margot and a small vanilla "skimpy treat" for Riley.

"Not now, Debbie!" David snapped, staring at her like she'd lost her mind.

"No problem," Debbie muttered, turning on her heel and heading out of the conference room. She stopped at Justin's office and set the cup down on his desk. "Here's a coffee for you."

"I didn't order coffee, Deb."

"No problem, it's on Margot," she winked. "The skimpy treat's for moi." She took a big bite, looked at Justin's confused face, and in her best imitation of Margot's condescending tone added, "Oh, and Justin, dear… don't you just love working here?"

Back in the hall, she kept up her sing-song commentary under her breath. "Coffee for Margot, skimpy treat for Debbie. God bless Seventh Avenue."

Margot couldn't contain herself. She shot out of her chair and started pacing around the conference table like a caged animal waiting to strike. "So what you're telling me is, let me get this straight, because the ad did so well, my daughter's out of a fucking job?"

"Correct," David said flatly.

Riley sat motionless, staring straight ahead. She knew her mother's temper. She knew this was about to get very ugly.

"I'll sue you, David! I'll take this whole damn company down; you just watch me!" Margot snapped, her voice rising to a piercing shriek.

David didn't flinch. He let her rant, knowing she didn't have a leg to stand on. "I'm sorry, Margot. This isn't my decision. Gordon's moving on."

"Let's go, Riley." She yanked her daughter's hand and stormed out of the conference room, the sound of their rushed footsteps echoing down the long hallway, past the receptionist's desk.

"Have a lovely day, ladies," Debbie chirped sweetly.

"Fuck you!" Margot shot back without breaking stride.

David and Alan sat back in their chairs, the air between them heavy after the circus that had just unfolded.

"This is a huge mistake, Alan," David yelled, pacing the length of the conference room. "A big, fucking mistake."

It was not a decision he would have made if he were the one making the decisions. The golden girl had just walked out the door, and with her went millions of dollars trailing quietly behind her.

They had already tested the Riley style, quietly rebranded as the Gordon, by shipping it out to Dayton Hudson in Minneapolis. Nancy Hersh, the buyer there, jumped on it immediately. She was sure the new style would fly out of the store and was already working on getting her reorder approved by management.

Meanwhile, Paula Jennings over at Bloomingdale's was hell-bent on locking down the East Coast launch. After a few too many glasses of wine and at dinner at Charlie's, she had Alan convinced Bloomingdale's was the place to debut the "Gordon" in New York.

Within days, 144 pairs of each size were delivered to Bloomingdale's. Paula stood proudly before the racks; the denim displayed like a badge of honor on the fourth floor.

Dayton Hudson and Bloomie's were both ready. The game was officially on. Both stores reported sales that outpaced every other style on their selling reports. Riley Spencer did not disappoint, but Gordon Gabriel couldn't have cared less.

— 16 —

Astrid Peyton adjusted her reading glasses as she sank into her iconic Proust Chair, the centerpiece of her sprawling 5,000-square-foot Central Park South apartment overlooking the park. She flipped through the latest issue of *WWD* with a mixture of disdain and disbelief, her lips tightening as she read about the frenzy surrounding her two competitors, men who, in her mind, had shamelessly stolen what was rightfully hers.

Patents weren't possible in fashion; if they were, Astrid would have secured one years ago. She had always been ahead of the curve, an innovator who blurred the lines between society girl and businesswoman. Unlike most of her contemporaries, Astrid had never needed to chase money; she was born into it and understood it as a certainty rather than a goal. What she craved instead was something money couldn't buy—legacy. She longed to etch her name not only into the social register but also into the very fabric of American style.

Her mind drifted to the empire she envisioned—jeans that bore her name stitched into the pocket, not as mere apparel but as identity. Women didn't just want clothing; they wanted belonging, they wanted status. Astrid had lived her entire life in glossy magazines and society columns, and she intended to keep it that way. Her jeans were never meant for everyone. They were for the very wealthy, the women whose names appeared in the Social Register, not the phone book. Status, privilege, pedigree—that was her world, and she had no interest in dressing the girls from the Bronx.

She looked again at the headlines about Gérard Jeans and Gordon Gabriel, and a thought occurred to her—*denim*. They were just companies selling denim. She, however, was planning to sell a lifestyle. What she had started as a brand was about to get a major upgrade. She would build something so elevated, so untouchable, that neither Gordon Gabriel nor Gérard Jeans would ever come close.

Her gaze shifted to the window, where a few pigeons fluttered onto the sill. She tilted her head toward them, almost amused, and whispered, "I'll show them. No one will ever rise to my level."

"Done!" she declared aloud, the word snapping in the air like a gavel.

She had always been one step ahead of her peers; this time was no exception. Astrid rang for her assistant. "Rita, please join me in the study."

Her assistant appeared within moments, notebook in hand. "Rita, reach out to my attorney. I would like a meeting this afternoon."

Rita nodded briskly, already up and walking toward the phone. Within the hour, Wesley Lord, her family's trusted legacy attorney, was standing across from Astrid as she reclined in her favorite chair, poised like royalty.

"I'm more than a little annoyed with what I am seeing in the papers, Wesley," she sighed, her voice a breathless whisper.

That tone, airy and affected, always grated on him. It was the kind of delivery people might mistake for an act, so exaggerated it almost seemed like parody. But Wesley had known Astrid Peyton since she was a child and recognized it as the inescapable cadence of the Peyton women. The whisper was deliberate; a subtle weapon honed over years to disarm and unsettle.

Astrid did not waste time. She laid out her plan with icy precision — one flagship department store, Bergdorf Goodman, to debut her label, paired with three of her own boutiques carrying nothing but her own designs and household treasures. Her locations were already chosen — an anchor store on the Upper East Side, another in the Village, and one on the Upper West Side.

"There's a vacancy near Charivari, Columbus and 72nd," she said, her eyes glittering. "That's mine. Secure it." Wesley raised an eyebrow but said nothing.

Astrid leaned forward, her voice dipping to a razor's edge. "I will not lower myself to play games with David Rosere, and as for those four brothers who stole my embroidered logo, they are beneath me. Let them enjoy their noisy little headlines while they last. What I am building cannot be replicated. It is something they will never touch." Her smile sharpened. "They scramble after fashion while I invent a legacy."

Wesley knew better than to do anything but nod in agreement. With Astrid, instructions were never requests; they were elegantly stated directives, polished yet absolute. She dismissed him with the faintest tilt of her chin, leaving no doubt that his course was set. Out of respect for her late parents, whom he had dearly admired and still missed, he had promised long ago to look after her. It was a promise made out of loyalty but also affection, for beneath Astrid's imperious charm, he still saw the little girl he once knew. Looking out for her felt natural, almost second nature, though at times, it was anything but easy.

– 17 –

Julie was on the road again, another Gérard Jeans business trip, another city. This time it was St. Louis, a place she had only ever read about in travel magazines. She gathered her order pad, denim swatch cards, and pens, tucking them neatly into her black sample case, almost as big as she was, and stepped out of the Gateway Hotel. The lobby was busy with businessmen clutching briefcases, families snapping photos before heading out to see the Arch, and there was the faint smell of coffee drifting from the café near the elevators. She loved it all.

She paused for just a moment at the revolving doors, catching a glimpse of the Gateway Arch in the distance, before darting across the busy St. Louis street. Her bag rolling over the sidewalk cracks as she hurried toward Famous-Barr to meet Pete Ebby, one of her favorite buyers.

Just as the case was about to fall, Pete came running from the opposite curb, grinning as he rushed over. He grabbed the handle, steadying it with an ease that made her laugh. "Got it," he said, holding the door open for her.

They headed upstairs to his small second-floor office, cluttered with papers and half-empty coffee cups. Julie unbuckled the case like it was holding treasure.

"What do you have in there, dead bodies?" Pete joked, his go-to line.

Julie laughed. She had heard it a dozen times, but it never got old. "Yours will be the first body in if your order's too small," she shot back without missing a beat.

Pete grinned. "Well, we'll just have to see about that, won't we?" Julie carefully laid out each piece from the new line. Famous-Barr had always been one of her favorite stores, beautifully curated and always such a pleasure to do business with. And Pete? He was a joy to work with. There was something about his Midwestern charm that instantly put her at ease, something that reminded her of home, of her own childhood in East Lansing, Michigan.

Julie lifted a new pair of jeans from the rack and glanced at him with a smile. "Do you want me to try this one on so you can see the fit?"

"Yes, please, Missy," Pete said without hesitation. "Let's see it."

Julie slipped behind the makeshift curtain that had long served as her dressing room in his office. She wriggled into the denim, smoothed the waistband, and stepped out, giving a slow turn so he could see every angle.

"You've still got it," Pete teased, leaning back with a satisfied nod.

She gave Pete a playful spin. "Not bad, right?"

"Perfect," Pete said, scribbling notes on his pad.

Julie smiled. She had done this routine a hundred times, but it never felt ordinary. Every time she modeled a pair of jeans like this, she thought of Morris Shaffer, the man who had once taught her how to stand tall to show the strongest lines of a design. His simple lessons had stuck, and now, in offices like Pete's, they made all the difference.

Then came the dreaded part, the "open-to-buy" discussion. Or more often, the lack of one, depending on how last season's styles had performed. But this was where Julie shone. She always came armed with competitive selling reports, a sharp eye on what was moving and what wasn't, and the kind of quiet confidence that buyers respected. She reminded Pete that Famous-Barr's strongest sellers were sizes 10 and 12, not 6 and 8, and this season she wanted him to test GG's newest style with the whipstitch detail. Every order she had written this season included it, because she had made sure of it. The Gérard brothers were paying out big bonuses to move the massive production they had locked in six months earlier, and Julie wasn't about to let them down. The whipstitch jean was on every order.

"Well, it looks like by the size of your order, Mr. Ebby, I won't have to dispose of your body in the black travel case after all," Julie teased. Pete laughed, and she gave him the biggest hug, thanking him warmly for his order. With a dramatic little bow, she scooped up her case and headed back toward the hotel, still smiling.

Beyond the business, Julie relished the travel. The hotels, the new cities, the chance of seeing the world, never lost its thrill. One of her favorite trips was to Jacobson's in East Lansing, Michigan. Most of her childhood friends had long since moved away, but walking those familiar streets grounded her. She would look across at Michigan State University, directly opposite Jacobson's, and wonder what her life might have been if her family had never left Michigan. Attending MSU had once been her dream, like the horse, the canopy bed, and the pool she had wished for as a girl. But, like those dreams, it had slipped away, replaced by others she hadn't even known she wanted.

Julie plopped into a cab outside LaGuardia Airport, exhausted but relieved. She was finally back in New York City after a whirlwind round of store visits, eight department stores in just over a week. Only two last-minute cancellations, which in her business counted as a win. As the cab sped toward Manhattan, the familiar sound of honking horns and the glow of neon lights bleeding into the night sky wrapped around her like an old friend.

There were only a handful of people Julie trusted to keep her life running when work took over, and Nikki was at the top of the list. More than a friend, Nikki had a way of stepping in when Julie needed her the most, no fuss, no questions, just big smiles and no expectations.

They met in a way that a lot of New York friendships start: by accident. A long line at Nathan's, a shared eye roll over how long it was taking, and two hot dogs eaten standing up. Nikki made a joke about how nothing in the city was ever worth the wait except maybe a good hot dog. Julie laughed, and that was the start of their friendship.

When they finally went their separate ways, it felt strange, like leaving someone she had known for many years. Nikki called the next day. After that, she just became part of Julie's everyday life.

Luckily, Nikki was babysitting Pepper. It meant Julie could go straight home, grab something to eat, and collapse into bed without having to walk him.

The cab pulled up to the building, Tristan East, where Charlie, the doorman, greeted her with his usual half smile. "Long week, Miss Julie?" he asked, reaching for her bag before she could protest. She just laughed and shook her head, too tired to explain the details, "The longest Charlie," she said, stepping inside.

Julie picked up Pepper from Nikki's the next morning, and the three of them decided to take a walk through Central Park. It was their favorite thing to do together. The air smelt like fall, and it was one of those perfect autumn days that make you feel alive and glad to be amongst the living. Pepper had become so much more than just a roommate; he was her constant companion, who made even the loneliest days feel full. His quirky personality, those adoring looks, and the way he seemed to understand her moods made every day extra special.

She honestly didn't know what she would do without him. He was her little buddy, curling up beside her for scary movies at midnight when she didn't have a date. She loved their neighborhood walks around the block, which always ended with a stop at the doggy bakery for his favorite treat. He was such a good boy, and Julie adored him. They walked through the park until they found a bench, laughing as Pepper tugged at the leash, eager to chase after squirrels. Julie loved Central Park, especially moments like this that were so simple, easy, and perfect.

There were people from every corner of the world—tourists snapping photos, nannies pushing strollers, couples hand in hand, joggers weaving through the crowd. If only the whole world could be like this, so many countries, so many religions, all blending in one space, in one perfect moment. It felt special. And Julie wished, just for a moment, that it could stay that way. They lingered over lunch at The Boathouse before wandering through the Central Park Zoo, then on to Conservatory Water, which was Pepper's favorite spot. The kids loved sailing their toy boats across the lake, but they always stopped what they were doing to run towards him when they saw him coming. Pepper, of course, adored all the attention, springing onto his hind legs and spinning in little circles to their laughter.

It was one of those uncanny coincidences; both of them had been photographed as little girls in front of the Alice in Wonderland statue by Conservatory Water. Julie sat down on one of the bronze mushrooms beside Alice, pulling Pepper into her lap. She traced her fingers over the dedication plaque—"In memory of my wife, Margarita Delacorte, who loved all children."

"Can you imagine?" Julie said, her voice soft with wonder. "Creating something that lasts through time, something that makes people feel, think, and maybe even see the world differently? How amazing must that be."

She smiled at Nikki. "You know what's funny? I feel just like Alice after she fell down the rabbit hole. Work is completely insane, and the people I work with are so weird and completely unpredictable.

It's like I went from childhood to adulthood at warp speed, thrown in with people just as wild as the ones in that story. Maybe even worse."

Nikki nodded. "You're so right. It is like Alice in Wonderland. We're all trying to make sense of it all, but nothing on Seventh Avenue ever actually makes sense."

Julie sighed. "Exactly. I keep asking myself 'who am I? What do I really want?' But the answer's not coming."

Nikki grinned and crouched down, curling her fingers into whiskers like the Cheshire Cat. "Where should I go?" she said in a mysterious voice. "That depends on where you want to end up."

Julie burst out laughing. "How do you even remember that?"

"College, 1973," Nikki said proudly. "Alice in Wonderland. I was the understudy, and I had to memorize every line. Didn't get to perform but still loved it."

Julie smiled, shaking her head. "Well, I hope the answer comes soon, because honestly, some days it feels like I'm walking around in one big fog of confusion."

"If I ran into the caterpillar today and he asked, 'Who are you?' I would probably just look at him and say, 'It beats me, Caterpillar.'"

Nikki smirked. "Well, at least you're not smoking a hookah."

"Not yet," Julie laughed. "Let's just hope we're both following the right path."

"Yeah," Nikki grinned. "Wonderland was never supposed to feel normal anyway." Then she nudged Julie, eyes twinkling. "Hey, I'm craving a cup of tea all of a sudden."

Julie raised an eyebrow. "Of course you are."

She winked. "Come on, you Mad Hatter, let's get out of here. You used to be much more... muchier. You've lost your muchness."

Julie laughed, shaking her head. "You're insane."

Nikki winked. "Maybe. But at least I still have my muchness. You, on the other hand," she pointed dramatically, "you've lost yours." Julie cracked up, clutching Pepper. "Guess I'll have to find it again."

"Good," Nikki said, linking her arm through hers as they walked off. "We'll start with tea. All good adventures do."

Nikki's path to New York had been a story in itself. A theater major from Ohio State, who had arrived with, as her mother Bunny used to say, "two nickels to rub together." She had pounded the pavement of Broadway, auditioning for everything from a singing monkey to a tap-dancing showgirl, even though she had never tapped a day in her life.

Her mother gave her one year. After that, the safety net would disappear, and Nikki had to find a job, pay rent, and support herself. The year was running out, and panic started to creep in when she spotted an ad posted on the corner of 36th and Seventh for an assistant designer. She had no experience, but she was an actress at heart, and she played the part. To her surprise, she got the job.

Soon after, she found a rent-stabilized apartment on the Upper East Side and learned to live with a carpet of cockroaches that scattered whenever she turned off the lights. Two mischievous Siamese cats, Madame and Turkey, eventually solved that problem. It was while dropping off fabric at a contractor's office that Nikki met Alex. He was an Israeli with a thick accent and a determination that matched his charm. Nikki said no more times than she could count, but Alex was persistent. After a year of dates, long walks, and weekends at Gurney's in Montauk, she finally said yes. Soon after, they married, and before long came Geoffrey, the sweetest little boy Julie had ever known.

As they walked toward Rumpelmayer's for afternoon tea, Julie found herself thinking about what a good friend Nikki had become. In just a short period of time, she had grown into someone Julie relied on. New York was a little kinder when she was around. She was proof that even in a city as overwhelming as New York, you could still find family in the people who chose to show up for you.

— 18 —

Julie stepped out of the cab onto Seventh Avenue, headed to work. She was meeting a new buyer that morning, and the last thing she wanted was to be late. The Garment District hit her all at once, steam rising from the grates, delivery trucks double-parked, men shouting in a dozen languages as racks of samples rattled across cracked sidewalks, construction workers whistling from scaffolds. She tightened her grip on her handbag, weaving past graffiti-splashed subway entrances and a corner newsstand stacked with the latest *WWD* beside *The New York Post*.

The city was still rough around the edges, muggings after dark, trash piled high on the curbs, whole blocks that felt better avoided, but it moved with a kind of wild, unstoppable energy. Mayor Koch's face was on the cover of the *Daily News*, grinning with his "How'm I doin'?" slogan, promising to clean up the city, make it safer, brighter, better. Maybe he would. Maybe he wouldn't. Either way, it didn't matter. Julie had her own life to build, and she was determined to do just that.

She loved the contradiction of it all. One minute she was dodging pickpockets near Port Authority and stepping over homeless people who called the sidewalk home, and next she was walking into a showroom lined with velvet sofas and racks of denim jeans worth more than she could ever imagine. That was New York, gritty and glamorous, dangerous and dazzling, always both at once.

The Gérard Brothers had grown so quickly that they took over the showroom next door for their new sales office. It was tough living through all the construction and renovation, but in six months, the two spaces merged as one. With the expansion, Barry Rubin took over hiring; no one read people better. His team included Karen Singer, who handled all the major East Coast and chain accounts, and Nell Dobbs, who oversaw the West Coast and was forever spotted at The Ivy with the power crowd.

And then there was Tracy Aiello, who spoke as if everyone around her were hard of hearing, but somehow, no one seemed to mind. She was as close to pure sunshine as they came, and she and Julie quickly became inseparable. Tracy's territory was the Southern part of the country, a stretch for a young Irish girl from Brooklyn who had never been farther than Coney Island.

Tracy's distinct New York accent sometimes clashed hilariously with the drawls of her buyers, but somehow, they adored her for it. She had a way of winning them over, blending her straight-shooting Brooklyn attitude with just enough charm to make even the most skeptical southern buyer laugh and sign the order. More than once, Julie had watched Tracy lean across a showroom table, grin wide, and say, "Honey, these jeans will make your customers look so good, they'll come back for seconds before the first pair's even worn out." Delivered with that bossy Brooklyn attitude, it was impossible not to believe her.

Her boyfriend, Brendan, whom Julie was never particularly fond of, loved to tag along, which annoyed her… until the night he introduced her to his college fraternity brother, Davie Rose, at a birthday party he threw for Tracy at Café Un Deux Trois.

  - - - B A R B A R A A. D A V I S

Brendan and Davie had studied abroad together in Rome, and Julie immediately felt comfortable with him. There was something familiar about Davie that put her at ease instantly, though she couldn't quite explain why. He was tall and so handsome, with blue eyes that seemed to shine when he laughed, and a smile that could shift a crowded room into the background. His hair fell in an easy wave, the kind that looked unstudied yet perfect, and his jawline carried the kind of strength that made him look older than he was.

It wasn't just his good looks that drew Julie in; it was the way he talked about the things he loved. Animals, especially dogs, came up often, his voice softening whenever he mentioned them. And then there was the ocean, which he called his truest inspiration, the vision that fueled his drawings late into the night in the cramped Harlem apartment he shared with three roommates just to afford the rent. Julie listened, oddly moved. The way he spoke, and the way his cheeks flushed when he talked about something he cared about, stirred something deep inside her, something she couldn't quite name. It felt strangely familiar, as if she'd brushed up against that part of him before, in another place, another time.

Even though the restaurant was packed with over fifty of Tracy's closest friends, Julie and Davie seemed wrapped in their own world, as if the rest of the room had melted into a soft watercolor blur. They shared a cab ride home. Her apartment was the first stop, and then on to 103rd Street in Harlem for Davie. That destination was never met.

Her plan was simple—he would just come up to meet Pepper, a polite end to a perfect night. Julie knew how much he loved dogs, and that felt like the easiest excuse to keep him close just a little longer. But the second the apartment door clicked shut, the air between them shifted. It wasn't rushed; it wasn't clumsy. It was as if they had both been waiting, without knowing it, for this exact moment. He leaned down, those blue eyes still tracing her face as though memorizing every line, and kissed her.

The world outside fell away, the traffic, the city noise, even Pepper's tiny bark from the corner. All of it disappeared into nothing but the two of them. By the time dawn crept through her window, Julie realized her life had changed. Whatever this was, it wasn't casual. It felt inevitable. It felt perfect.

Davie rolled over to find Pepper perched on the edge of the pillow, staring him down. "Hey, little buddy," he said, locking eyes with his newest and perhaps fiercest rival. Pepper's breath was awful, his dark curls tousled, his head cocked with an inquisitive stare that seemed to say— "What are you doing here? And when are you leaving?"

Pepper was a tough one to win over, but once he decided you were safe, he was your biggest fan, a five-pound bundle of black curls, one bent ear, and a nose that was always twitching for the next scent. Julie had fallen so in love with him. On nights when she sat cross-legged on the floor eating a slice of pizza by herself, Pepper was her crust eater. He was also the reason she could afford her Tristan East apartment, fully furnished, with a tiny kitchen and a big bathroom. All thanks to Pepper. "Thank you, Pepper baby, thank you, Kerry Turnberry," was a phrase Julie said at least once a day, and she meant every word of it.

She laughed now at the sight of Pepper sizing Davie up like a bouncer at the door. Davie just grinned, stretched, and said, "Brunch, anyone?" He was up in a flash. Julie quickly learned the man required six meals a day, minimum, and if any of them were skipped, his sunny personality dimmed fast.

They found themselves at her favorite corner restaurant, Johnnies, ordering omelets and mimosas. Conversation flowed easily. Julie learned that Davie was estranged from his family, though he wouldn't go into detail. She didn't push, though the thought unsettled her. She couldn't imagine being cut off from family like that; it made her ache to call her father, just to hear his voice.

Davie shared lighter things, too. His favorite color was green. He loved traveling, bike riding, sports, and most of all, painting. He admitted he started out in college sketching in black and white, convinced that was his medium, until Europe awakened something in him. Rome had especially changed him. Oils became his new love language, and with them, he chased the colors of Rome's skies, piazzas, and ruins, its beauty and magnificence poured onto canvas.

He had spent the past two years pounding the sidewalks of the art world in New York City, portfolio in hand, going from gallery to gallery. But no matter how many doors he knocked on, none opened wide enough to let him through. Breaking into that world wasn't just about talent; it was about connections, the right last name, the right dinner invitations, the right country club memberships. And those came with a price tag far beyond what Davie could afford.

One night, sitting across from Julie, he let the frustration spill out. "I don't get it," he said, shaking his head. "I'm doing everything I can. But it feels like I'm invisible, I'm not getting anywhere."

Julie nodded, pretending to be fully absorbed in his words, but her mind was already racing. A scenario crept into place. Davie didn't need to wear himself out on cold gallery visits; what he needed was Carol Tanaka. And through Carol, he could meet Kenji, whose name carried real weight in the art world. If anyone could help Davie break through, it was them.

She leaned forward, offering comfort, but inside she was already calculating her next move, sketching the plan that might finally change everything for him.

— 19 —

At 9:00 a.m. sharp, the entire Gérard Jeans team gathered in Times Square for the unveiling of their new billboard. It was a bold creation by their advertising agency, featuring one of Kenji's oil paintings, the very piece the Gérard brothers had commissioned months earlier at Simon Guez's SoHo Art Studio, the show that had changed Kenji's world forever.

"Ten, nine, eight, seven…" The countdown began as the massive white drape was tugged away. The brothers clutched one another in a tight embrace, still not quite believing the whirlwind of success that now surrounded them.

And there it was—perfect. Their vision, larger than life, towering over Times Square. The entire company had turned out to support them, and the energy was amazing.

Julie stood there, watching the spectacle unfold, and couldn't help but think back to her own first time in Times Square. Years ago, she had stumbled off the bus with wide eyes, overwhelmed and unprepared. She had been nearly late for her interview with Morris Schaffer at Phillipe

Leon because she didn't realize Broadway and Seventh Avenue split at a point, sending her in the wrong direction. She remembered wandering in circles, her nerves rising, until she finally found someone who didn't scare her enough to ask for directions.

Back then, Times Square had been a different world, neon lights flashing over peep shows, men whistling from the sidewalks, women with mascara streaked down their cheeks and stilettos dangling from tired hands. It was dangerous and fascinating all at once. She had passed a man dressed as a vampire with a boa, a woman shouting into the air, "I am the son of God!" The chaos was dizzying, so far from the safe, small-town life she had left behind.

She had bitten her lip hard, willing herself to keep moving, to push through the madness. And somehow, she had made it. She arrived at her interview just in time to meet Morris Schaffer, the first step into the world that had changed everything. Now, standing in the middle of Times Square once again, surrounded by friends and colleagues, Julie couldn't help but be amazed at how far she and all of them had come.

The four brothers were hard to explain. They were always yelling, always at each other, each one convinced his vision of the future was the only path forward. Over strong black coffee and endless cigarettes, the conference room would erupt, shouting matches so loud they rattled the walls and distracted everyone on the floor.

More than once, Carol had to storm in and fix it with nothing more than a look. One arched eyebrow, a sharp tilt of her head, and her expression said it all—Enough already. There's a buyer in the showroom, for the love of God.

As fierce as their fights were, there was an unspoken rule— no one else got to cross that line. They could battle with each other all day, but an outsider trying the same thing would be finished. Larry Spencer learned that the hard way. Hired on November 12, fired by November 13, all because he dared to pit one brother against another. That was the one line you didn't cross.

It was a blood pact, born not out of choice but out of blood itself; they were brothers. They could scream, curse, threaten to walk out, but they would never truly break. If that bond was ever severed, it wouldn't be by force. It would only be because one of them chose to leave.

They knew there was no safety net. Every last penny had gone into launching Gérard Jeans, and the banks expected to be paid on time, or they were finished. Julie couldn't help but notice the difference between the Gérard brothers' fight for survival and David Rosere's world at Gordon Gabriel. For the brothers, every stitch, every shipment, every sale, and every movement they made was life or death.

But David? His hunger wasn't survival; it didn't need to be. His wallet was already full. His drive came from something else, something territorial, wrapped in entitlement, as if the game had been won before it even began. It wasn't ambition so much as a proclamation— Sit down, son. The seat's already taken. I own this. How dare you try to compete with me?

The brothers, though, were fueled by desperation. They couldn't afford to fail, because failure meant ruin. Success was their lifeline, and because of it, the work never stopped. The creativity poured out of them like oxygen, because survival depended on it.

After the Times Square celebration, everyone returned to the office, still so excited about how incredible the morning had been. Julie thought it would be a good time to ask Carol for an introduction for Davie to meet Kenji. She nervously went to the showroom to ask her.

It was hard to explain. In the office, Carol was everything Julie could have asked for in a mentor, always there through every question, every problem, every drama-filled situation. But outside of work, when it came to asking for even the smallest personal favor, Carol Tanaka seemed to disappear, as if that version of herself simply didn't exist. Julie found that out the hard way that morning; Carol had no interest in making introductions. "Sorry, Julie. I don't mix business with pleasure."

Julie froze, blinking at her, waiting for a laugh, a hint that Carol was joking. But none came. Carol just stared back, cool and unreadable, as if she hadn't even understood the question.

"But why, Carol? Please," Julie heard herself say, her voice smaller than she intended.

The warmth Julie had always counted on in Carol's eyes was gone, replaced by a cold, almost practiced stare. No explanation came. Carol simply turned and walked away, leaving Julie alone in the showroom with nothing but piles of denim samples to console her.

Carol's upbringing had never allowed for favors. Generational wealth did not work that way. They hung on to every dollar like pearls on a family necklace, passed down but never given away. She had grown up watching her father handle the endless stream of men and women eager to break into his circle of privilege. They came armed with flattery, introductions, and promises, and he would listen with a polite smile, nodding here and there, letting them believe they might stand a chance. But Carol knew the truth. He was only ever weighing what he could take from them. Once he had it, the meeting was over. A firm handshake, a quick dismissal, and they were gone, heads lowered, dreams quietly crushed.

Carol absorbed it all. She didn't just observe her father's way; she learned it, lived it. And so, when Julie asked her for the introduction for Davie, there was never really a chance. For the first time, she felt betrayed by the woman she had admired most.

Julie followed Carol to the waiting car, blinking back the sting of tears after her abrupt dismissal. The black sedan idled at the curb, ready to whisk them to a luncheon at Bergdorf Goodman. Julie slid beside Carol, folding her hands tightly in her lap, willing herself not to dwell on the awkwardness of the moment.

When they arrived, Julie stepped out first, grateful for the rush of cool air on her face. Carol emerged behind her in a sleek Perry Ellis suit, a navy-blue cashmere sweater pulling out the pinstripe in the fabric, every detail immaculate. Julie, always on a budget, had chosen her faithful black dress with the tiny, covered buttons trailing down the back and her black suede boots. Simple, it was her best attempt at fitting in among the fashion elite.

They were met by Melissa, the assistant buyer responsible for Gérard Jeans' selling reports and keeping their third-floor department stocked with the sizes customers needed. It was Carol who saw it first.

The signage gleamed from across the floor—ASTRID PEYTON, framed by her butterfly logo, arching above a pristine white arbor in the center of the first floor, right beside the handbags. Prime Bergdorf Goodman real estate.

Carol stopped mid-stride, her eyes narrowing as she took it in. With the smallest nudge, she directed Julie's gaze toward the gleaming display, then turned back to Melissa with a polite, incensed smile Julie had seen many times before, the kind that masked irritation and signaled insincerity. Underneath the veneer, Julie could feel it—Carol was seething.

"Excuse me, Melissa," she said, her tone calm, even pleasant, edged with curiosity. "When exactly did this little Astrid Peyton shop go up? I must have missed the memo."

Her words were smooth, but Julie caught the faint tightness beneath them. The stacks of jeans were neat and pristine, folded with military precision, every pair lined up just right, as if the denim itself were whispering "buy me." It wasn't flashy, but it was smart, simple, and unmistakably Astrid. Carol wasn't one to show her hand, but Julie knew her well enough by now to hear what went unspoken—How did Astrid pull this off without me knowing about it?

"Oh, isn't it amazing?" Melissa beamed. "We all love it so much. And Bergdorf Goodman is the only department store in the country that will have an Astrid Peyton boutique department."

— — — — —

Wesley Lord had wasted no time after leaving Astrid's penthouse. He had assembled Manhattan's best real estate professionals, secured three prime leases, one of them right next to the coveted Charivari location Astrid insisted upon, and construction crews were already transforming each space. Her vision was uncompromising—she would decide what her stores sold, not some "dim-witted" buyer.

And now here it was, her first coup—the ribbon cutting of her very own Bergdorf department, just this morning. Astrid had kept the entire opening shrouded in secrecy, reaching out only by phone to a carefully curated handful of New York's A-list for private invitations. No advance notice, just a sudden, dazzling reveal. That was why Carol hadn't heard a word of it until she saw it with her own two eyes.

Liza Jones herself had been front and center, scribbling notes, pointing her photographer toward the butterfly logo, ensuring every angle was captured for the society pages.

Astrid's plan was clear, simple, and ruthless. She had no children; this was her baby. And like an overprotective mother, she intended to defend her brand with the same ferocity.

— 20 —

David's wife, **Barbara Sutton-Rosere**, had insisted on keeping her maiden name. Why, he could never understand. To him, it meant nothing. She had grown up poor, with no inheritance attached to the name Sutton. Her father had been in and out of the picture for as long as anyone could remember. It was even rumored he had started another family in Brooklyn, leaving Barbara and her mother to scrape by. She grew up hungry, not just for food, but for love, for validation, for a kind of approval that never seemed to arrive.

She had met David while working at his father's dress business so many years ago. Her mother had taught her to sew, not because she wanted to, but because she had to. Barbara made her own clothes out of necessity, stitching together skirts and blouses from whatever fabric her mother could afford. She was never great at it, but she could get by, and she was smart. It was enough to land her a job stitching the hemlines of the dresses manufactured by Phillipe Leon. The work was steady, the pay was fair, and for once in her life, she felt like she was getting ahead. She even opened a bank account in her own name. Barbara Sutton, the bankbook read. Just seeing her name in print made her happy. For once, something in this life felt like hers.

It was a whim, really, an idea that came to her over lunch. She had bought a thin piece of lace to make herself a scarf, but, bored on her break, she had the idea to stitch it to the hemline of a dress instead. She left the lunchroom, sat back down at her sewing machine, which she had nick-named Mabel, and finished it. She couldn't help but smile at the result. She called the other girls from her sewing line to gather around and asked what they thought.

Their chatter grew loud enough to draw the attention of young David Rosere, the owner's son. The plant manager noticed too, tossing out his usual line—"That girl has a Yiddishe kop." Barbara let it go this time. She knew he meant it as a compliment, but it always rubbed her the wrong way. She was raised Protestant, left abandoned when her father walked out, and she had struggled to believe in much of anything. To her ears, the phrase carried an edge, as if brains belonged only to someone else's faith. Still, she forced herself to take it in stride, because in that moment, all that mattered was that someone had noticed what she did and liked it.

"Hello, ladies," he said, stepping closer. "May I ask what's going on here?"

Barbara proudly held up her lace-trimmed hem. To her surprise, David was very impressed. In fact, he loved it. He walked her straight into his father's office.

"Dad, what do you think?" David asked.

The following season, every dress was shipped with a lace-trim hem. Buyers loved it. So did the customers. Women were purposely crossing their legs and pulling up the hems of their dresses just to show they were wearing the latest style by Phillipe Leon.

The lace hemline had changed everything for Barbara. What began as survival, sewing her own clothes because she had no other choice,

  --- BARBARA A. DAVIS

suddenly became her ticket out. For the first time, she felt valued, even admired. That little piece of lace unlocked something deep inside her. It taught her that standing out wasn't frivolous; it was power. From that moment on, plain would never be enough when she could make it special.

Against his parents' wishes, they married a year later. Barbara was the first Protestant to enter the Rosere family, and the weight of that difference wasn't lost on anyone. Winning them over required persistence, patience, and a promise to raise the children Jewish. But Barbara was nothing if not determined. When David proposed, and she said yes, Barbara Sutton became Barbara Sutton-Rosere, the hyphen not just a mark between names, but a bridge between two worlds, and a symbol of the new life she intended to claim as her own.

Thirty-five years later, they were still going strong. David liked to joke that he had married his very own Nancy Sinatra, thanks to the white patent leather go-go boots Barbara insisted on wearing everywhere, in and out of the house. He never missed a chance to tease her, especially when boxes of clothes or rolls of wallpaper samples from Lauren Minkoff's studio showed up at their Scarsdale estate. With a mischievous grin, he would break into song, borrowing Nancy's tune but changing the words—"These boots were made for spending, and that's just what she'll do."

But Barbara's drive wasn't about frivolity. It was about filling the void she had carried from childhood, the relentless need to prove she belonged somewhere bigger and more glamorous than the life she had been born into. She was a good daughter. As soon as she married David, Barbara moved her mother into what her mother proudly called a "rich-bitch house." Her presence was a constant reminder of where she had come from, and not a day went by that Barbara forgot it.

Their first son, Alan, arrived a year later. Then came Junior two years after, then Karen, and finally Lisa, the baby who cried through infancy and, at twenty-one, still hadn't quite stopped.

Alan, though, was different. He grew into the kind of young man people couldn't help but admire. All four children had inherited David's piercing blue eyes, but Alan carried them with something extra, an easy charm, and a natural confidence that drew people in the way a famous figure might. Adults trusted him instantly, while his friends wanted to be around him, to catch some of his charm. He learned early that doors opened more quickly for someone like him, and he made sure to step right through.

All four children attended the prestigious Talborne School, a 24-acre college-preparatory campus in Westchester, New York that prided itself on fostering "confidence, growth, and practical risk-taking." Barbara couldn't help but find that statement almost laughable, especially the part about practical risk-taking. Her children had been raised in a world so carefully padded and sheltered that it was hard to imagine any of them truly knew what the word risk even meant. Not with so many safety nets stretched beneath them their whole lives. Junior, Lisa, and Karen scraped by on grades that were nearly failing, smoothed over by a generous donation from the Rosere Family Trust.

Alan was the exception. He had the willpower, the drive, the discipline to chase after what he wanted and keep at it until he got what he was after. Harvard, Yale, and Princeton competed fiercely for him, David dangling the promise of a new building like a carrot before all three institutions. Harvard won. Alan thrived there, graduating summa cum laude, valedictorian, the undisputed golden child of the Rosere family. And when he walked off the graduation stage, there was already an office waiting for him at Phillipe Leon. His name gleamed in large gold letters on the back of the door—Alan A. Rosere, President. No slow climb, no proving ground, he had stepped straight into the seat his father had carved out for him, as though it had always been waiting.

His siblings were secretly jealous but never said it aloud. Alan was untouchable. Even Annie, Barbara's beloved dog, acknowledged she took second place.

Junior escaped right after high school. It was a humid, rainy day in August when he sat down in front of his father's massive mahogany desk in the library and announced he wasn't going to college in the fall: he had made up his mind. David had already secured a spot for him at Syracuse University through a business colleague who owed him a favor. In David's mind, everything was lined up exactly how he had planned, except for his son.

What started as a civil conversation between father and son quickly escalated into a screaming match, son against father, hurt against pride. It wasn't just about college anymore. Every hurt Junior carried, every missed baseball game, every withering glare when a report card arrived in the mail, every quiet disappointment came pouring out in a flood of tears.

The words tumbled out before he could stop them, building into anger, hoarse voices, and hurt feelings. And then the noise stopped, replaced by a deafening silence. His son packed a few things and walked out the door. Years had passed since that day, and there was still no sign of him.

Karen had chosen a very different path. Law school lasted barely a year before she traded textbooks for a wedding dress, marrying Justin Weiss, who worked for her father as vice president. Motherhood followed soon after, and she adored the life she had built. In many ways, she was a mirror of her mother, right down to her own white pair of go-go boots. She had married well, well enough at least, and whatever her husband couldn't provide, her trust fund quietly covered without question. Her life revolved around ensuring her children were polished, successful, and scandal-free.

She played golf twice a week at the family country club, summered in Fisher Island at the eastern end of Long Island Sound, and loved nothing more than watching the rocky coastline glow under the kind of sunsets that belonged on postcards. It was a place where manners mattered more than wealth, where privacy outshone nightlife, a life Karen found perfectly suited her.

She threw herself into committees, her favorite being the New York

Public Library board. She never failed to pat the lion's head at the entrance, a small ritual before each meeting that made her feel connected to something lasting. She loved the arts, too, and never missed the opening season at the Met, her name etched onto a seat that came with board membership.

An animal lover at heart, Karen often helped her friend Martha at the ASPCA, though her own family never had pets; two of her children's allergies had seen to that. Still, she was quick to lend a hand when it mattered.

Her days were filled with dinners out, temple on Fridays, galas, luncheons, and play dates that all seemed to blur together into one seamless picture of privilege. Yet she loved it, truly. And in the end, Karen was the only one of David's children who consistently said thank you.

And then there was Lisa. Trouble seemed to follow her like a shadow. Not a day went by without some crisis, some cause, some crusade. The environment and the pollution, she was convinced, were killing everyone, which stung all the more given how much land waste her father's factories were leaving behind. She never wore makeup, never dressed well, and David wasn't entirely sure she bathed on a regular basis. But Lisa was also the kind of girl whose mind wandered into unexpected places, her thoughts skipping like stones across a pond. When she was four, she tugged on Barbara's sleeve as wild turkeys strutted through their backyard. "Mommy," she asked, her eyes serious and wide, "do you think it's the same turkey family from last year, the same mommy and daddy with the same children? Or a new family?" Barbara never had a ready answer, but the question spoke of a curiosity that never faded.

She grew into a woman both rebellious and tender-hearted, ready to fight the world with her words, not weapons, always with love behind her fire. Whether marching with handmade signs or writing letters to city officials, Lisa never shied away from speaking her truth.

She could be found linking arms with students at Columbia, chanting until her voice was hoarse, or standing on the courthouse steps in mid-town, holding her sign high against the drizzle. Barbara would sometimes catch a glimpse of her on the evening news, her hair wild, her voice carrying above the crowd. It seemed Lisa was born with a protest sign glued to her hand, her causes endless, sometimes exhausting, but always carried with conviction.

But they were his, all of them, the Roseres. His responsibility. His creation. Some nights, he wished he could start over, seal all the cracks, rewind time to before things had turned chaotic. But this was his family, the only one he had, and despite everything, he loved them more than he could ever say.

— 21 —

It **had been a hard** week. They were battling on every front, fighting buyers for more floor space, hounding suppliers for extra yardage, pushing their sales team for bigger orders. And on top of it all, the brothers were fighting with each other in a way Carol had never seen before. Even her signature arched eyebrow, the look that usually cut through the noise and pulled them back in line, was losing its power. "Sami, you fucked up. Big time. Big Fuck-up, brother." Jérôme's voice cut through the chaos like a razor. "You're in charge of quality control, every fucking zipper, every fucking grommet, every fucking label, every thread. And you missed it. You fucking missed it."

Phones rang nonstop in the showroom, sales reps shouting over one another. The buyers were livid. Return stickers now, they demanded. The white thread, the thread Sami should have washed and tested before it went into production for their number one projected style, was bleeding all over the blue denim. And not just any style. This was the one, the whip-stitch jean the brothers had agreed would be their home run of the season.

Now, instead of bonuses, the sales team faced nothing but returns. Six hundred gross of defective jeans, piling up like a nightmare no one could wake from.

"What a fucking mess!" Jérôme yelled, slamming his fist on the table. "How could you let this happen?"

Sami sat silent, ash from his cigarette spilling to the floor as the others ripped into him. He didn't move, didn't defend himself, he just stared straight ahead, the smoke curling in lazy spirals above his head. Daniel finally snapped, shoving back his chair so hard it hit the back wall with an explosive bang. He stormed out, unable to leash the fury burning through him, muttering under his breath the many ways he was going to strangle his brother when he got his hands on him.

"You ruined us, Sami, you ruined everything!" were the last words he hurled before the conference room door slammed shut.

Bernard sat back in his chair, the shouting coming at him like a pack of hungry dogs. His eyes drifted past his brothers, past the haze of cigarettes to the oil painting in the lobby, the one they had commissioned from Kenji. It hung there like a reminder of what they had built, bold strokes of denim blues and fiery threads of ambition, four G's woven into the canvas like a signature.

For a moment, the chaos quieted in his head. He buzzed Carol. She walked in, pale, the aspirin bottle still in her hand. She had not been raised in this kind of world, this raw, combustible energy of men who yelled first and thought second. The smoke, the slammed fists, the language, it overwhelmed her.

Her father's boardrooms had been cold, precise places, where decisions were handed down with final words and firm nods, not brawled over like this. Every nerve in her body told her to retreat, but she stood still, her spine straight, even as her temples throbbed. Bernard didn't shout. Instead, he took her arm and led her quietly to the corner where two leather chairs faced each other.

"I have an idea," Bernard whispered, reaching across to take Carol's hand. "Last week in El Paso, Hugo, the plant manager, showed me something. Pumice stones. They're throwing good denim into giant washers with the stones, softening the fabric, fading it into this lived-in blended look. He said it might be the next big thing."

He gave her hand a squeeze, his eyes searching hers. "This might be the answer to our problem, Carol. If everything's washed and faded, then the stitching could look intentional… right?"

"They were working on some samples when I had to jump on a plane to get back to New York. Find out what happened for me."

Carol's eyes widened. She darted out of the room, ducking as an order pad came flying at Sami's head, and returned minutes later, grinning ear to ear.

"I just got off the phone with Hugo," Carol said breathlessly. "I told him your idea about the whipstitch. He said he'll test some of the samples, throw them into the washer with the pumice stones, and send them up to you as soon as they're done."

Bernard's eyes lit up, the fatigue in his face giving way to a spark of excitement. He reached for her hand again, squeezing it tightly. "Carol, this could be it. The answer we need to solve this fucking mess."

For the first time all day, she felt it too. She smiled back at him, her heart racing, hoping this problem might turn into something wonderful. Maybe, just maybe, they were on the verge of something…a new trend the buyers would love.

He shot to his feet, slamming his palm on the conference table, and glared at his brothers. "Merde! Will you two just shut up for one goddamn minute? I have a plan. Someone, go grab Daniel."

He laid it out fast and hard. They would take back every damaged jean, ship the jeans to El Paso, run them through the industrial washer with the pumice stones, and bring them back with a whole new life. The bleeding whipstitch wouldn't look like a mistake anymore; it would look like a new design they had created, an edgy detail no one else had. The plan was simple but daring—turn a disaster into the next big thing. By the time he finished laying it out, even the loudest of them agreed, it was their only shot.

What they didn't count on was this—Bernard's desperate gamble wasn't just damage control. It was a gold mine. The first stonewashed jeans hit the floor weeks later, and women went wild. Gérard Jeans had done it again. They weren't just saved; they were leading the denim war.

$$-\ 22\ -$$

Barbara and David were celebrating their thirty-fifth wedding anniversary over Chicken Kiev and vodka at the Russian Tea Room on West 57th Street, right around the corner from Carnegie Hall. The place glittered with the kind of old-world glamour that made you feel as if you had stepped onto a stage instead of into a restaurant. Barbara loved the Faberge-inspired decor. Red leather banquettes were filled with celebrities and famous artists, samovars lined the walls like jewels, and the hum of conversation carried with it the weight of decades of successes and scandals. Theirs was just one of a thousand stories that had unfolded in that room, but tonight it felt like the room belonged only to them.

Barbara Rosere cut into her chicken, set down her fork, and, in her matter-of-fact way, asked her husband, "So tell me, how many more topless ads of models wearing nothing but jeans before you finally design a white Gordon Gabriel shirt to sell with them?"

It landed like only Barbara could make it land, so simple, so obvious, yet with the punch of a twelve-person think tank. David looked across the table at his wife with that same expression he had worn so many years ago when she held up her lace-trim hemline for his approval. She recognized it instantly—that look that told her she was right.

Barbara knew that before long, there would be a crisp white button-down shirt draped on the "it girl" model of the day, and women everywhere would be rushing to buy it.

"That's a great idea, Babs," he said, using the affectionate nickname that didn't pass his lips nearly as often as she wished it would.

Oh, wonderful, she thought, already giving herself permission to call Lauren Minkoff in the morning to schedule a design consultation. After all, she had earned it. The two glasses toasted in celebration, first to thirty-five years, and a second toast to the white cotton shirt that was destined to be their next home run.

Alan loved the idea. Timing couldn't have been better. Just days earlier, they had fired their head designer, Max, after traces of cocaine kept showing up on his design table in the back room. Alan had confronted him once already, and Max swore it would never happen again. For a while, it didn't, at least not on the cutting table. It happened during the Bloomingdale's presentation.

Paula Jennings and her assistant buyers sat front and center, ready to take notes on the newest styles they believed would work for their department. A new season was about to begin, and this was the moment they looked forward to, the first look at Gordon Gabriel's latest collection. They sat around the showroom table, all excited for the presentation to begin, and watched Max slowly walk toward them, samples draped sloppily over his arm, his walk a little clumsy and unsteady. At first, no one noticed. He launched into the pitch with a burst of energy, gesturing at the racks behind him like a showman selling snake oil.

But Alan noticed. Oh God, he noticed. A thin white dust clung to the bottom of Max's nose. Alan's stomach dropped, a wave of nausea rising in his throat. You have got to be kidding me, he thought. He tried to save it,

       – – – B A R B A R A A . D A V I S

standing behind the buyers, flicking his finger toward his own nostril in a frantic pantomime. Max didn't get it. Or worse, he didn't care.

One of the assistant buyers tilted her head, her polite smile hardening into something secretive. She leaned in toward Paula, whispering just loud enough for Alan to know the damage was done. Paula's face said it all—irritation and that cold annoyance of someone who felt their time had just been wasted.

Justin Weiss, David's son-in-law, caught the whole thing from behind his glass office wall. The look on Alan's face was enough. Without hesitation, Justin strode into the room, slipped into the chair beside the buyers, and tried to wrestle the conversation back. One glance at Max's nose, and his suspicions were confirmed. Alan and Justin locked eyes, a silent agreement between brothers-in-law— this was over.

The presentation limped to a sad finish; the Bloomingdale's team was polite but clearly annoyed and unimpressed. Everyone had expected to be blown away by Gordon's designs. Instead, the only blow at that meeting was found under the designer's nose. As soon as the doors closed, Max was done. No drama, no more chances.

Ann Benton, reliable, talented, drug-free, and endlessly creative, stepped into Max's position as head designer. She wasn't simply asked to design the next great pair of jeans. She was entrusted with designing the missing piece: a crisp white button-down shirt, the perfect counterbalance to the jean Riley Spencer had made iconic. She was thrilled to be head of design for one of the fastest-growing companies on Seventh Avenue and quickly hired Sara Isaacs as her assistant, who had an uncanny instinct for spotting trends before they hit the street.

Ann quickly came to appreciate the way David ran his New York operation, lean, focused, and disciplined. There was no excess or confusion about roles. His son Alan was always at his side, while his son-in-law Justin handled marketing and strategy. Frenchie, his trusted pattern maker, cut every single pattern with an exacting eye. At the front desk sat Debbie

Manning, the no-nonsense receptionist, who ran the office with military precision. Nothing got past her, and somehow, she managed to keep the whole company in line.

Beyond New York, David's reach stretched coast to coast. In Miami, there was Alden Hollings, the heart of the Miami Mart. He ran one of the biggest and most successful showrooms, and while his business was on fire, it was his kindness that everyone talked about. He was called the "Mayor of the Mart," and he wore the title proudly. In Los Angeles, it was Serge Zaris, the spunky, larger-than-life, insanely funny, and endlessly creative style icon. He always had a glint of mischief in his eye and a spring in his step. Serge made selling feel like a party and buyers lined up just to be part of the scene.

Dallas was home to Bert and Ted Givings, two no-nonsense brothers who had a way of keeping buyers laughing even while selling them everything they didn't know they needed. Production was anchored in El Paso, Texas, right down the street from the Gérard brothers' factory. Bolts of denim rolled in and were cut and sewn under the eye of plant manager Jim Morrison, with Ricardo right at his side, keeping the wheels turning.

"What do you think of the blouse sketches?" Ann asked Alan and Justin over lunch at PJ Clarke's, tucked down in the cellar of Macy's. She spread the drawings across the small wooden table, careful not to let the grease from their burgers smudge the edges. After two straight days of sketching and starting over, she was running on fumes, and every bite of that burger was the only thing keeping her upright.

PJ Clarke's was a world unto itself. Dark wood paneling, old photos on the walls, mirrored bar, tin ceilings, it felt like stepping out of midtown chaos and into the charm of old New York City. It didn't matter that floors above them were filled with perfume counters and tie displays; down here, it was history and comfort food. The waiters knew their regulars, the Bloody Marys were strong and spicy, and the burgers were famous. Nat King Cole had once called their bacon cheeseburger the "Cadillac of burgers," and Ann believed it. She bit into hers with the hunger of someone who had just designed the next big thing, or at least hoped she had.

She leaned back, eyeing Alan and Justin as they studied her sketches of the white blouse that was Barbara Rosere's inspiration. "I think I nailed it," she said, wiping her hands on a napkin, her confidence flickering between exhaustion and excitement.

They had agreed that sketch #3 would be the one to launch first, with plans to follow it up with sketches #5 and #7, depending on how sales performed. Alan and Justin exchanged a look, hoping David would sign off when they met with him later that day. As David loved to say, "Then we're off to the races," a nod to Lancelot, his beloved Kentucky Derby winner.

But when the moment came, David surprised them. He preferred sketch #7, and that was the one he told them to launch first. Ann disagreed, though she knew better than to voice it. Quietly, she set to work, directing her assistant, Sara, to source the fabric, buttons, and every detail needed to bring style #1112, sketch #7 to life—the perfect white shirt.

One by one, sales reps crowded Ann's office, each presenting options, plastic white buttons, mother-of-pearl, and many more. Fabric swatches spilled across the desk—crisp 100% cotton, lustrous silk, sturdy polyester blends. It took days of deliberation, but Ann finally made her choice, confirmed by Sara's subtle nod.

With the decision made, Frenchie could begin his fittings. From there, "The Gordon Blouse" would be born, the shirt photographed, splashed across every fashion magazine, and, ultimately, hanging on racks in contemporary departments of stores across America. Style #1112, "The Gordon," had arrived. The buyers went wild. It was exactly what they needed, the perfect addition to break up the endless sea of blue denim. Suddenly, amongst the rows of jeans stood mannequins dressed in the crispest white shirts, belted at the waist, and nothing else. Clean, sensual, and striking. It was an instant hit.

Alan and Justin didn't hesitate. They pushed the other designs Ann had shown them straight into production, but at the very last moment, they decided to add a thin edge of white whipstitching around the collar and cuffs of one of the blouses, a quiet, deliberate middle finger to Gérard Jeans.

When the photographs dropped, the effect was on target. The model stood with her shirt half-open, pearl buttons catching the light, a belt cinched tight at her waist, stone-washed jeans anchoring the look. The image spread across the industry and even graced the cover of *WWD*.

Sara Isaacs was the first to see the sales reports. Sketch #3, the very design everyone but David had insisted should come first, had outsold every other white blouse by a landslide. She allowed herself a quiet laugh. David would never know. And really, who would ever want to be the one to tell him?

The buyers couldn't keep it in stock. Women across the country were rushing to own the blouse. In a season when denim ruled, that crisp white shirt had become the one thing everyone had to have.

— 23 —

Astrid Peyton had no problem saying no. She had promised Bergdorf Goodman exclusivity, and she intended to keep that promise. They would be the only department store in the country to carry Astrid Peyton jeans. The other stores tried, oh, how they tried. Letters arrived daily, flowers piled up in her penthouse lobby, gifts delivered in glossy boxes with handwritten notes.

Astrid's response was always the same— a courteous but simple, "No thank you." Her boutiques were almost ready to launch, timed with surgical precision for the end of October, just ahead of the holiday selling season.

Every item had her name on it. Fragrant candles labeled "Astrid Peyton." Tea towels embroidered with her butterfly logo. Perfumes made exclusively for her by Quest, the famed ghostwriters of fragrance. She had chosen three scents she adored, Monarch, Painted Lady, and Viceroy, each named for a butterfly. Oversized coffee-table books lined with her favorite topics and old Hollywood stars. Audrey Hepburn, her personal idol, greeted customers in every store from the cover of a book displayed on a gleaming glass table near the boutique front entrance.

The interiors themselves were designed to seduce. Stunning over-sized floral arrangements from Renny & Reed spilled out of crystal vases, filling the air with gardenias and roses. Above, a breathtaking Murano glass chandelier from Barovier & Toso, shipped directly from Italy, cast a warm, golden glow across the space. Gilt-framed mirrors reflected every angle of the room, giving the illusion of endless luxury. Cashmere throws were draped casually across velvet armchairs, as if waiting for customers to sink into them. The walls shimmered with hand-painted silk panels, each one brushed with delicate butterfly motifs, a nod to her signature logo. Even the fitting rooms were indulgent, lined with plush carpeting, antique sconces, and mirrors framed in polished brass, each space de-signed less like a changing area and more like a private sitting room.

Monogrammed chocolates, silk scarves, and handbags crafted from the softest Italian leather lined beveled glass display cases, while cashmere sweaters imported from France were stacked in perfect towers of color, shifting with the seasons. Every detail sang with intention— silk-lined display cases, mirrored shelves that made the space feel endless, velvet ottomans in jewel tones where women could pause and admire themselves in the floor-length mirrors.

Astrid stood in the center of her crown jewel, the 72nd Street store, her eyes sweeping the space with proprietary pride. It whispered sophisti-cation, and it was all hers. She was ready to launch.

The final touch was the sign above the door. Astrid had woken at 3:00 a.m., unable to sleep, when the idea struck. In the dark, she scrib-bled it onto her notepad— not simply Astrid Peyton, but Cocoon by Astrid Peyton. The name carried everything she wanted the boutique to stand for.

A woman would step inside still wrapped in her cocoon, and emerge renewed, radiant, a butterfly set free. By morning, she was on the phone with her attorney, Wesley, to secure the rights and set it in motion.

                    – – – B A R B A R A A. D A V I S

The ribbon-cutting took place on the last Saturday of October. Mayor Edward Koch stood proudly at her side, along with her Upper East Side circle, Liza Jones and Crystal Morris, *The New York Times* fashion authority. The cameras flashed, champagne flowed, and Astrid basked in the glow of her carefully orchestrated moment.

When the doors finally opened, she hung back, listening. *Stunning. Unbelievable. Oh my God, amazing.* The words drifted through the air, each one a small victory. With every compliment, Astrid seemed to grow taller, her presence expanding to fill the boutique itself.

In that moment, she realized something she had never dared to admit, even to herself— for years, she had cocooned herself inside a world that existed only for her. The boutiques were more than business; they were her way of proving to the world that she was more than a very wealthy heiress who had lost her family much too young, only to inherit a fortune that felt more like a burden than a gift. Wealth had become its own kind of full-time job, one that demanded appearances and perfection.

But this, this idea of hers, was her opening into a new world. Yes, it was still privileged, but for the first time, she wasn't hiding. She was celebrating who she was. Astrid Peyton was no longer just the sad little rich girl. She was building something of her own. On the ride back to her penthouse, she pulled the velvet curtain across the partition, shutting out her driver's view, and for the first time in years, she felt something stir. She lowered her head and wept, whispering to herself, "I almost forgot what it felt like to feel something, to actually be happy."

She stepped into the private elevator that carried her up to her penthouse. By the time the doors slid shut, the weight of the day hung over her. It wasn't like her to cry, and yet she couldn't stop. The tears felt foreign, almost frightening, because she couldn't even say why. She had faced so many things, most of them alone, and had never let herself break. But this afternoon, in the quiet of her penthouse, nothing seemed to hold her together.

When the elevator doors slid open, Ruby was waiting. Her house-keeper, of more than twenty years, tried to mask the shock on her face at seeing Astrid so upset. "What can I get you, Miss Peyton?" she asked gently.

"I honestly don't know Ruby," Astrid whispered back.

She carried the glossy Audrey Hepburn coffee-table book from her boutique to her bedroom, thinking it might somehow hold her together. Sitting on the edge of her bed, she looked out at Central Park. Usually, that view made her feel grounded, but not tonight. The light felt cold, the trees too far away, and instead of joy, all she felt was emptiness and loneliness closing in.

Ruby knocked softly a few minutes later. "Your attorney is on the phone."

"Tell him I'm resting. I'll call tomorrow," Astrid murmured.

The room was silent again. Silent, but not peaceful. She had built everything, every store, every headline, every whispered compliment, with her own two hands, yet as she sat there, the truth pressed down on her. She was alone in the world, except for the people she paid to stand beside her. No one to share the victory. No one to celebrate with. No one at all.

– 24 –

It was the most coveted invitation on Seventh Avenue, the Black Tie Christmas Ball. Year after year, it was the glittering crown jewel of the rag trade's social calendar, where designers, buyers, editors, and power brokers all jockeyed for a spot beneath the crystal chandeliers at the Waldorf Astoria Ballroom. To be seen there was to matter. To miss it was to risk being forgotten.

Stylists, makeup artists, and New York's most sought-after hairdressers had been booked weeks in advance. Everyone wanted Oribe Canales, the magician of hair, though his waiting list was a mile long. Frédéric Fekkai was the new darling on the scene, and Carol Tanaka had managed to snag a coveted appointment the moment she heard of a cancellation, her instinct always a step ahead of the crowd.

The ballroom was enormous, bigger than anything Julie could have imagined. The ceilings seemed like they were two stories high. Gorgeous floor-length mirrors covered the walls, exaggerating the enormity of the room, making it all seem so whimsical and surreal. Each table had exquisite floral arrangements made up of white roses, lilies, orchids, and green holly with red berries. The gold candelabras, each holding tall white candles, flickered softly and sent a warm glow across the room, as if the whole place had been wrapped in one big, beautiful Christmas bow.

The women shimmered in sequined gowns that glittered as they brushed across the marble floors, and the men in their custom-made tuxedos and monogrammed velvet slippers looked like they had walked straight out of a magazine. It didn't feel real. This wasn't just a party; it was the Christmas Ball, fashion's crown jewel. And somehow, Julie was standing right in the middle of it.

That night, the Gérard brothers made their first appearance. Heads turned as they entered, their presence loud without trying to be, raw in a room that lived for polish. David Rosere spotted them instantly. His eyes followed them around the ballroom like a heat-seeking missile, narrowing as though tracking prey. He had seen their photos in the trade papers, had studied their designs hanging uncomfortably close to his Gordon Gabriel label in department stores. But seeing them in person was different. You could read someone better in the flesh, catch the undercurrents their image never revealed. And what David saw unsettled him.

There was no pedigree, no finishing school polish, no family crest or Ivy League degree to fall back on. Just raw ambition wrapped in an electric pulse of energy. It made his skin crawl. The room suddenly felt smaller, and the music too loud. That same unwelcome feeling swept over him, the one he had tried to ignore for months. Fear.

David gripped Barbara by the arm a little tighter than usual as they made their way through the lavish ballroom to their table in the prestigious VIP circle.

Barbara couldn't help but notice where her husband's attention lay on the newcomers, the Gérard brothers. These were the men who had been keeping David up at night, and for the first time since she had known him, Barbara sensed a weakness in her husband. It unsettled her. She needed him to be strong, not only for his company, but for her.

At David's table sat his eldest son Alan with his wife Francis, his daughter Karen with her husband Justin, and Lisa, the rebel child, who, against all odds, had decided to play along tonight. With Barbara's gentle nudging, she stepped into a stunning black dress, added a touch of make-up, and for once seemed to enjoy the ritual of dressing up.

When Lisa climbed into the Rolls, David nearly dropped his cigar. "Who are you," he teased, squinting at her with mock suspicion, "and what have you done with my daughter?" Lisa rolled her eyes but couldn't hide a small smile. For once, he thought his baby actually looked like she belonged to the glittering world she had spent so long resisting. Rounding out the table were Mayor Ed Koch, Liza Jones, and Harry Lipchin, president of the Black Tie Ball, with his partner, Kenneth Owens. It was a table made for the society pages, and the photographers couldn't resist circling like bees around honey. Champagne flowed, waiters hovered, and every glance in their direction carried a mix of envy and awe.

Across the room, Carol Tanaka felt her face flush. Annoyance prickled under her skin, the kind she usually kept hidden behind a polished smile. She was not accustomed to being tucked away in the far corner of any ballroom, least of all on a night like this. Finding herself seated at a table just outside the kitchen door did not sit well with her. She cared very much for all four brothers and had enormous respect for them, often wondering if she could have accomplished the same in so little time, without help or connections.

Her own path had been the opposite— every door had swung wide open for her; she had never even needed to knock. Her place was at a table like David Rosere's, where the mayor of New York, Liza Jones, and the president of the Ball, Harry Lipchin, held court. She tried to brush it off, but the sting of exclusion burned. It was not just the seat in the back corner; it was the symbolism of it. It was a reminder that, despite her success, her connections, her reputation, someone else had decided where she belonged tonight. Carol despised that feeling. She glanced at Julie and forced a smile, but her mind was already calculating how she would ensure this would never happen again.

Even though Carol was far from pleased with the seating arrangement, her gaze softened when she looked at Julie, sitting quietly beside her. Julie's eyes were wide, full of wonder at the beauty of the room, and Carol reached over to give her a warm hug. She was genuinely happy for her. How sweet it must be, Carol thought, to take it all in for the first time.

"I wish Davie could be here," Julie whispered. Davie was away at an artists' retreat in upstate NY-something he had ben looking forward to for months.

"You've got me, Toni, Barry and four of the most unforgettable brothers this Black Tie Ball has ever seen." Carol smiled, giving her hand a squeeze. "Come on sweet Julie, let's hit the bar and get ourselves a drink."

She left Carol at the bar and excused herself to freshen up. She couldn't help but laugh quietly to herself as she glanced over at the men holding court at the bar, so alike in their tailored tuxedos, a class of high-pedigree penguins competing for bragging rights on who had caught the biggest fish. In the middle of them was David Rosere, his presence magnetic. Just as she passed, he looked her way. He nodded at her and to Julie's dismay started walking toward her.

"Julie," he called, his voice cutting through the music. "Please, wait a second."

She was unsure if she wanted to face the man she had once stormed out on. Yet something inside her told her not to move, to stand still and meet the gaze she had once been too afraid to look at.

"Hello, Mr. Rosere," she managed, her voice even. "How are you?"

"Well, I'm just fine, Julie Glass," he replied smoothly, almost too smoothly. "And how have things been for you?"

"Very well, thank you."

He reached for her hand, his grip firm, his blue eyes catching hers

     — — — B A R B A R A A. D A V I S

with an intensity that made her pulse quicken. "Julie," he said, his tone uncharacteristically measured, "I'm very sorry things ended the way they did between us. I never had the chance to wish you well… so, Julie, I wish you well."

But David's apology wasn't entirely selfless. As he stood there, studying the young woman who had once put him in his place, another thought pressed at him. Julie had become important, too important, to the buyers who also bought his line. They respected her and trusted her. That kind of influence was power, and David knew power when he saw it.

In his mind, the calculation had already begun. If Justin could talk her into joining Gordon Gabriel, it would not only be a direct hit to Gérard Jeans, but also bring her talents under his roof instead. He masked the thought behind a faint smile, but the idea lodged firmly in place. This was not just a hello. It was an opening move. The chess game had begun. And with that, he released her hand, turned, and walked back toward the VIP circle, his posture as commanding as ever.

Julie was confused, her mind reeling. What in the world was that all about? David Rosere's apology, if that's what it was, had left her un-steady, her mind racing for an answer. She needed a moment to breathe, to collect herself. She made her way through the crowd of people to the ladies' room, her new, inexpensive high heels slipping against the marble floor. Inside, the air was cooler, and the smell of powder and expensive perfume filled the air. As she moved toward the sinks, trying to shake off the moment, a voice, low and unmistakably distinctive, rose from behind her, carrying across the tiled walls.

Julie's heart stopped. She knew that voice before she even saw the woman. And then, as the stall door opened and the figure stepped out, there she was, Barbara Walters. Her idol. The very woman she had pretended to be during those long nights in her Seton Hall dorm room with the yellow floral bedspread, practicing interviews into a hairbrush microphone. The gasp escaped before she could stop it. "Barbara Walters!"

She had always carried Barbara Walters in her imagination as something larger than life, an untouchable superstar she admired from afar. But seeing her there, stepping out of a bathroom stall like any other woman, shattered the illusion she had built around her. Suddenly, she wasn't just the voice on the evening news or the name in the headlines; she was a real person. Flesh and blood. She was human. If Barbara Walters could become Barbara Walters, why couldn't Julie Glass become… And there it was, that was the problem. She didn't yet know what she wanted to become, only that she needed to decide on something. Was the fashion business really what she wanted to do? Was this her path in life?

The newscaster turned then, gracious and composed as ever, a faint smile lifting her lips. "Yes, my dear," she said warmly. "How can I help you?"

Julie swallowed hard, her throat tight, and managed a small, trembling smile. "You have," she whispered. "In so many ways already… you have." And for the first time that night, the background noise around her seemed to fade, leaving her with the quiet, steady certainty that possibility was real. For the first time that night, Julie felt the swirl of chaos around her fall away.

Across the ballroom, Jérôme had caught the moment David Rosere had walked towards Julie. His sharp eyes, always scanning, landed on Julie and David just as their brief exchange ended. His first thought was— What the fuck was that all about? He needed details, and he needed Carol to find them for him.

But even as the question formed, another thought pushed its way in, quieter, more unsettling. For the first time, he really noticed how extraordinary Julie was, the tilt of her head, the warmth of her beautiful smile, and the effortless grace in the way she carried herself. It caught him off guard, making him feel something he didn't care to name. The look he shot Carol said it all, a silent directive sharpened by instinct—*find out what Rosere said to Julie.*

   — — — B A R B A R A A. D A V I S

Barbara's head tilted slightly toward her husband, her voice dropping to a sly whisper. "Don't you find it interesting that the Gérard Jeans logo—GG—could possibly be considered a trademark infringement? GG could also stand for Gordon Gabriel, could it not?" She swirled the ice in her glass as if it were an afterthought.

David set down his glass of Macallan, staring at her as if he were seeing her for the first time. How had he missed it? Across the table, Alan glanced over, sensing something important had just happened, but wisely kept silent.

"That's a thought, Baaabs..." David drew out her name slowly, each syllable hanging in the air as though it carried the weight of something dangerous yet brilliant. Barbara didn't need him to say more; she could already see the wheels turning behind his calculating steel-blue eyes. She leaned back, satisfied. Another small victory. Another reason she decided to book a fresh appointment with Ingrid, her personal shopper at Bergdorf's.

— 25 —

On the way home in the cab, Julie stared out the window. The Ball had been more than she ever imagined. It had started to rain, and the smell of it hitting the sidewalks of New York was one of her favorites. She rolled the window down, breathing it in deeply. There was something about the freshness, the way the air carried the scent of wet pavement and possibility, that reminded her that New York was now home. She loved everything about it. The mix of it all. It was as if God had scooped up the world in his hands, given it a shake, and dropped the whole insane bunch right into the heart of the city.

The cab turned toward 57th Street. Pepper, would be waiting for her, one last walk, and then bed. But as she opened the door to her apartment, she felt it. Something was wrong. Pepper always knew when she was coming. Usually, she would hear the frantic bark, the scratch of paws against the floor, his little curly body bursting with excitement to cover her in smelly-breath kisses.

"Pepper?" Julie called out, flicking on the light. And there he was.

The tiniest ball of fur, curled beside his favorite stuffed ladybug. Still. Too still. Julie's heart dropped.

"Oh no, Pepper, please… please, baby, be okay." She dropped to the floor, scooping him into her arms, but there was no movement. No sound. Just silence.

The noise that tore out of Julie was unrecognizable, a primitive scream, raw and guttural, the kind that starts in your toes and claws its way out of your chest until you don't even recognize it as your own.

It was late, but the walls in Tristan East were thin. Her neighbor, Sherry, heard the cries and cracked her door. From across the hall, she saw enough to know.

"Julie, dear… Julie, come sit with me," Sherry urged gently.

But Julie couldn't move. She felt numb; the world crashed down around her. She sat on the floor, hugging and rocking Pepper in her arms, her sweet baby she had mothered for two years, every second of it joy.

It felt like hours before she felt a hand on her shoulder. Kerry Turnberry. Sherry had called her; she had remembered where she had tucked Kerry's number away, in the back of her kitchen drawer. Kerry was Pepper's mommy, too.

Kerry knelt beside Julie, trying to be strong, but the moment she saw Pepper, guilt shattered her. She had been the one to leave him behind, and now here she was again, saying goodbye.

The two women stayed there, side by side on the floor, tears slipping quietly as they whispered their favorite Pepper stories. The little dog who had filled their lives with so much love, so much happiness was gone.

Finally, Kerry moved. She had brought a blanket, soft and pale, and wrapped Pepper gently inside with the ladybug tucked close. Frank, her boyfriend, was waiting in the car downstairs; they would take her to the vet that was open through the night.

Julie kissed Pepper's little head one last time. "Goodbye, my baby. I love you Pep, thank you Pep she cried."

     – – – BARBARA A. DAVIS

The door closed, and silence rushed in. Julie sank to her knees, her voice breaking as she whispered into the empty apartment—"Mother Mary, please help me," she prayed as she cried herself to sleep."

She woke up knowing she needed to shower, get dressed, and head to work, but she couldn't do it. All she could hear was Carol's voice in her head—"Isn't it funny how everyone always seems to get sick on a Friday?" Julie stared at the ceiling, then finally picked up the phone and told the receptionist she wasn't coming in.

When Jérôme heard the news, he immediately called Carol into his office. "I saw her talking to David Rosere last night," he said, lowering his voice. "Do you think she's making a move to Gordon Gabriel?"

Carol shook her head firmly. "Julie? Never. She can't stand him." She told Jérôme the portrait crasher story, how Julie had stormed out years earlier, and that was enough to put an end to his suspicion. Relieved, Jérôme waved her off, and Carol excused herself.

But she wasn't entirely at ease. She walked down the hall to Toni's office and leaned in the doorway. "Can you give Julie a call, see if she's okay?"

Toni frowned. "Why? What's the matter?"

"She called in sick," Carol said carefully. "I just want to be sure that's the real reason, and nothing more."

Toni nodded, grabbed her coat, and walked out of the building. She passed Harry's Coffee Shop, slipped around the corner to a pay phone, and dialed Julie's number.

"Julie? Are you okay? You seemed fine last night. What happened?"

Julie tried to answer, but the sobs made her words almost impossible to understand. Finally, in broken pieces, the story came out.

"Oh, Julie…" Toni's voice softened, thick with tears of her own. "I'm so sorry. What can I do for you?"

Her heart broke. Everyone loved that little dog. Julie had even brought Pepper to the showroom in the early days, when they were just moving in. Pepper had been the showroom mascot, curled up on fabric swatches, soaking up everyone's affection.

Toni blinked hard, promising Julie she would bring dinner over that night, knowing Davie was still away. After she hung up, she marched straight into Harry's, bought a black-and-white cookie the size of a dinner plate, and ate the whole thing, crumbs and all, before she got back on the elevator.

It was her condolence cookie. The one she wished she could have shared with Pep, he had always loved the vanilla part. And before she knew it, the tears came again.

– – – – –

It was Saturday morning when the lock on the apartment door jingled, and Davie walked in. He was smiling, ready to surprise her, but the expression vanished as soon as he saw Julie in bed, her eyes swollen, her face puffy from crying.

"Jules… what's wrong, honey?" he whispered, stepping closer.

She opened her mouth, but the words caught. Finally, she managed, "She's gone, Davie. Pepper died Thursday night."

For a moment, he just stood there, stunned, his breath leaving him in a heavy sigh that seemed to fill the room. He glanced toward the door, half-expecting Pepper's little paws to come skittering across the floor, but the silence told him everything.

Without another word, he kicked off his shoes and climbed into bed beside her, wrapping his arms around her as if he could hug the pain away. Julie buried her face into his chest, and together they let the exhaustion take them, drifting into sleep still holding on to each other.

It helped, just having him home. She loved him, and in that quiet, grief-stricken moment, she knew with all her heart that she never wanted to be without him in this life.

                    – – – B A R B A R A A. D A V I S

— 26 —

Davie woke up first, turned to face Julie, and announced, "Let's get out of the city." He thought getting her out of the apartment, where Pepper's absence hurt too much, might be a good idea. Rhinebeck came to mind—a walk through the galleries, some fresh air, maybe lunch, and a weekend away at The Beekman Arms & Delamater Inn. It was one of his happiest childhood memories, vacations and dinners with his family when he was a kid, and he wanted to share it with her now.

They caught the Amtrak at Penn Station, the train hugging the Hudson River as sunlight danced across the water. Julie leaned into the window, and Davie could feel her spring back to life. Ninety minutes later, when the train doors opened, it was like stepping into another world.

Davie knew Rhinebeck like the back of his hand. A short taxi ride brought them into the center of town, Montgomery and Market Streets, with their cozy cafés, antique shops, galleries, and bookstores. Julie didn't know where to look first; she caught herself smiling, really smiling, for the first time in days.

"Let's eat," Davie grinned. Julie didn't argue; she knew better than to stand between him and food. He had the appetite of a baby on a strict two-hour feeding schedule and keeping him fed meant keeping him happy.

He pushed open the heavy wood door of The Beekman Arms Restaurant, and Julie was instantly taken by its charm. The low-beamed ceilings made her feel as though she had slipped back into colonial times. The air was thick with the aroma of roast beef, so mouthwatering her stomach growled loudly enough for Davie to laugh.

They were seated at a small table for two, a flickering candle shielded by a hurricane lamp between them. The stone fireplace crackled in the corner, wrapping the room in a warmth so comforting it made Julie feel immediately at ease. She caught herself beaming across at Davie, thankful for him, thankful for this moment.

Something came over her. Before she could stop herself, the words slipped out. "Why don't you talk to your family, Davie? What happened?"

Davie swallowed hard, then looked back at her with a kind of softness she rarely saw. She realized how little she really knew. She knew that he never read a newspaper, didn't care about the gossip columns, or world events. It was as though, when he had closed the door on his family, he had shut out everything else, pouring all of himself into his art and now, into her.

Over wine, she pressed gently, each glass giving her more courage. He didn't resist. He told her how much he loved being raised Jewish, not just for the traditions but for the sense of belonging it gave him. He loved Shabbat dinners because everyone gathered around the table together to celebrate what really mattered in life. He loved the holidays, each one tied to a story of survival and resilience, lessons that had quietly shaped him even as a boy. And most of all, he loved the music and the prayers that felt older than time, that made him feel part of something ancient, much larger than himself.

Yes, he had siblings. No, they didn't speak anymore. Yes, he only ever wanted to paint; nothing else mattered to him. It was the way colors spoke to him, how he could mix ten shades of blue until it perfectly matched the summer sky. Painting was where he felt most himself, where time stopped, and the noise of the world disappeared. He loved how a blank canvas dared him to begin, until he filled it with something that had never existed before. For Davie, painting was simply what made him happiest, the one place where everything felt right.

Julie leaned back in her chair, listening to Davie talk, every word landing like something she had been waiting to hear for a long time.

"You really know," she said quietly. "What you want to do. Who you want to be."

Davie shrugged, almost embarrassed, "I guess I do. It just feels right."

"That must be amazing," Julie said. "To be that sure."

He studied her for a moment. "You'll get there, Jules."

She smiled, "Maybe, right now it just feels like all the questions are still spinning around in my head."

"That doesn't mean you don't have answers, Julie, it just means you're still trying to figure it all out. You are in the middle."

Julie looked at him puzzled, "The middle of what?"

"The middle of your journey," he said. "The beginning of anything is very exciting; everything is new. And when your journey ends, there's usually some kind of big celebration. Job well done kind of thing, You made it," he smiled at Julie. "But the middle? That's the most important part."

Julie listened, completely still, taking in every word.

"That's where you're challenged," he continued, "where you're tested. Where you grow. Not knowing exactly what you want to do with your life isn't a failure, Julie. It's the opposite. It means you're exactly where you're supposed to be, at exactly the right time."

She wrinkled her nose. "It doesn't feel that way, Davie."

'It never does," he said gently, "That's why people quit in the middle. They can't see the finish line, so they stop running." He leaned forward. " The ones who get there are the ones who don't stop. The ones that stay in it even when it's hard."

Julie searched his face. "You really believe that?'

"I do," he said without hesitation, "and I believe that's what you're going to do to. You may not know exactly where you are headed yet, but the middle is where you become who you need to be to get there. That's where the real reward is found."

Julie let out a quiet sigh, 'I hope you're right."

He smiled. "Just wait and see."

The conversation lingered there, circling between fear and uncertainty, until finally Davie laughed and lifted his glass. "Alright, enough philosophy. Let's talk about something I actually understand, the wine."

He swirled it, savoring the color, steering them gently back to lighter ground. Julie smiled, but she tucked the moment away. It had felt like a small window into a part of him she had not yet been allowed to see, and though she didn't know why, it struck her as important.

— 27 —

There was a note taped to Julie's apartment door when she returned from their trip to Rhinebeck. Even before she unfolded it, Julie recognized Kerry Turnberry's beautiful handwriting, and her heart sank. All the lightness she had carried back from the weekend seemed to vanish in an instant. She already knew what it would say.

"You know I adore you," the note began, "and I can't even begin to tell you how grateful I am that you took such loving care of my Pepper. But Julie, darling, there's no longer a reason for me to keep the apartment. The lease ends in three months, and I wanted to give you plenty of time to make arrangements. The furniture is yours, the kitchen too, in fact, anything not nailed down is yours. I want you to have it all if you would like it. I will forever be thankful to have known you. Hugs and kisses, Kerry."

She sank onto the brown corduroy couch, her legs folding beneath her as if the weight of the letter had drained every ounce of strength from her. Now what? The thought echoed sharply in her mind. Her salary was decent, yes, but New York rents were impossible. She knew she would never again be able to afford a place like this one.

Her eyes lifted toward the ceiling. "Mom," she whispered, her voice fragile, "I need you. I know you're there, even if I can't see you. I don't know what to do, Mom."

Julie closed her eyes and tried to picture her mother sitting across from her, the way she always had, always ready to listen, always ready to talk about every problem that came her way. "Please, Mom," she whispered. "I just need to talk to you."

Only silence answered. And yet, slowly, something else seemed to fill the room, a warmth, as if invisible arms had wrapped around her shoulders in a quiet embrace, easing her worries. The faintest trace of Shalimar, the only perfume her mother ever wore, drifted around her, as though she were right there again. Julie breathed it in, holding it close as if it were a gift.

She wiped the tears from her cheek and took a breath. The ache was still there, but she pressed it down into that quiet place deep within her, the place that holds pain for another day.

   - - - B A R B A R A A. D A V I S

— 28 —

Davie ran up the five flights of stairs to his Harlem walk-up on 103rd, whistling the tune they had heard in the cab ride back from Rhinebeck. It was light and carefree, the kind of melody that stayed with you. It matched exactly how he felt, how Julie always made him feel. Alive. Inside, all three roommates were home, which almost never happened.

"Catch!" Paul called out, lobbing a football just as Davie came through the door. It ricocheted off his backpack and spun straight into Brendan's lap. Laughter broke out as Davie dropped his bag onto the couch.

Keith, the one whose name was on the lease, was perched at the kitchen counter surrounded by legal briefs, a pencil tucked behind his ear. He was the only one of the four with a nine-to-five job, working as a law clerk at a high-powered Wall Street firm. His hours were brutal, his commute worse, but he liked the grind. The research, the writing—he thrived on both, despite a boss famed for relentless demands.

Paul, by contrast, was larger than life in every sense. He sold advertising space for an Italian magazine and had a knack for telling stories that kept everyone entertained. The fifth-floor walk-up nearly killed him; he cursed those stairs daily, but once inside, it was all worth it because of the brotherhood that existed.

And then there was Brendan. Davie's favorite. He had been the one to introduce him to Julie at Café Un Deux Trois two years ago, a night that had changed everything. Hard to believe it had only been two years. Time was racing, and for the first time in ages, Davie felt like life was finally pulling him forward.

That brotherhood meant everything. Harlem was a tough but vibrant mix, brownstones with peeling paint, fire escapes lined with laundry, kids running in the streets, while men argued over dominoes at card tables on the sidewalk. Money was always tight, but inside those walls, Davie had something he had not felt in years— a second family. The late-night debates, the laughter echoing down the hall, the records playing, the meals shared—it filled the emptiness left by the family he no longer spoke to.

"Hey, Davie, I forgot to tell you," Paul said through a mouthful of pizza as the four of them sat crowded around the kitchen table. "Some guy came by looking for you."

Davie looked up mid-bite. "What guy? What did he say?"

Paul shrugged. "Didn't say much. Just left his card. It's on the counter."

Davie set down his slice and walked to the counter, picking up the card. His back was to his roommates, so they couldn't see the color drain from his face.

Robert Preston

Estate Manager

Rosere Residence

Beneath it, a phone number. A number Davie knew by heart, because once, it had been his.

"Do you know him?" Brendan called from the table, competing with all the yelling going on around him.

Davie paused for half a second, the card still in his hand. Then, without turning around, he slid it smoothly into the pocket of his jeans.

"Never heard of him," he said calmly, sliding his chair back in and picking up his slice of pizza like nothing had happened. He took a big bite, but it might as well have been a piece of cardboard, no taste, just air. He chewed, even forced a grin at one of Paul's jokes, but his mind was already a million miles away.

Robert Preston was more than an estate manager; he was the Rosere family's butler, their compass, passed down from Davie's grandparents to his parents, the way other families pass down a Bible. He carried their history in silence, guarding every secret as if it were his sworn duty. And now, he was the one who held the card that forced Davie to face what he least wanted to admit—Barbara Rosere had finally found her son.

She had never stopped searching. The private investigator she hired had finally earned his keep, tracing the trail of a boy who had changed his name to Rose, wandered Europe painting, and slipped quietly back into New York two years earlier. His name wasn't on a lease, which made him harder to pin down, but not impossible.

The memory slammed into him before he could push it away— his mother's voice calling after him, running after him on the gravel driveway.

"Junior! Please! Wait, darling, please wait!"

He had loved her enough to stop running, to turn and face the only ally he had ever known. She was the one who hid his failing report cards from his father, who defended him through thick and thin. She hugged him so fiercely, he thought one of them would break.

She slipped a folded piece of paper into his hand, her voice trembling. "Before you go, darling, please call Mark Hawks. Tell him I told you to call. Transfer the money from this account. You're eighteen now. This belongs to you. Take it before your father has his lawyers freeze it. If you must leave, I won't have you on the street. Please, baby, promise me."

Davie had done the first thing—he had taken the money. But he never told her where he went. It broke her heart, he knew, but it protected her. When his father asked her if she knew where he was, she could look him in the eye and say she truly didn't know.

Barbara could still hear the slam of the receiver the next morning, her husband's voice bellowing down the halls—"God damn you, Davie!" Rage shaking the house. But Barbara held on to one truth— that because of her, he wasn't going to be living on the street, cold and hungry.

Now, years later, standing in his Harlem kitchen with his roommates laughing behind him, the card in his pocket felt heavy. Too heavy. His past had finally caught up to him.

- - - B A R B A R A A. D A V I S

— 29 —

"**David threw the first punch.** It came as a leak to *WWD*—"Gordon Gabriel takes its intellectual property very seriously and will defend the prestige of the line to the fullest extent of the law."

"What the hell does that even mean?" Sami asked, his voice low, the production pad slipping from his lap as the brothers huddled around the table.

No one answered. The room fell silent, the kind of silence that comes before bad news. It didn't last long. Within days, the official complaint landed, straight from the Southern District of New York, the epicenter of fashion disputes. The charge was clear—trademark infringement and dilution. Gérard Jeans, GGGG, was, according to David's lawyers, weakening the prestige of Gordon Gabriel's brand.

"This is bad," Daniel muttered, pushing the papers away as if the words themselves might burn.

"It's more than bad," Sami said, rubbing his forehead. "What the fuck of fucks is going on?"

Carol didn't bother answering. She knew they were in way over their heads. Within minutes, she had grabbed Barry Rubin, the brothers' so-called fifth sibling, hauled him out of his office, and flagged down a cab on Seventh Avenue. Twenty minutes later, the two of them were sitting in front of her father.

Bob Reynolds listened in silence, his fingers steepled under his chin, while Carol laid out the situation as clearly as she could. The words felt heavy in her mouth— lawsuit, infringement, dilution. When she finished, the room was so still she could hear the tick of the brass clock on his desk.

Finally, Bob leaned back. "Give me a minute."

He disappeared into the hallway, returning with the company's attorney, George Ahrens, at his side. He didn't like getting involved in other people's messes. Bob Reynolds never strayed from his own lane, but for his daughter, this was different. It took a few tense days before the attorney finally found himself seated in the Gérard brothers' conference room, the air heavy with smoke, panic, and silence. The brothers had barely spoken to one another since the news broke, the sales reports abandoned on the long glass table. Carol stood off to the side, arms folded, her eyes fixed on the man who had been brought in to steady the storm.

The attorney laid the thick complaint folder on the table, flipping it open like a priest preparing scripture. His tone was professional, almost surgical. "You have four options," he began, scanning the brothers one by one. "Option one—fight. We dig in, argue that GG is distinct from Gordon Gabriel, and that your logo, the four Gs for four brothers, has no likelihood of confusion. But litigation like this is not cheap. We are talking hundreds of thousands in legal fees, maybe more. And David Rosere has deeper pockets than all of you combined."

Sami shifted uneasily in his chair, muttering Merde under his breath, each time a little more forceful than the last.

"Option two—settle. Negotiate a licensing deal or co-existence agreement. That means you keep using GG but maybe with restrictions.

                    — — — B A R B A R A A. D A V I S

Certain markets, certain categories. You give him something to make him go away."

Bernard slammed his palm on the desk. "Why should we give him anything? He's the one who is afraid of us."

The lawyer didn't flinch. "Option three—rebrand. You walk away from GG. Painful, yes. Costly, absolutely. But it might save you years in court."

"No way," Jérôme snapped. "We built this company with the GG logo. It's our name."

"Then there's option four." The lawyer leaned forward now, lowering his voice. "Counterattack. File for declaratory judgment. Say you were first in commerce with GG and that his claim is overreach. But understand, this escalates the war. Once you go down that road, there's no turning back."

The brothers fell into an exasperating silence. Carol crossed her legs, her face unreadable. Barry stared at the floor, knowing what this meant—money, time, blood, war!

George Ahrens finally broke the quiet. His voice was calm, but firm. "Whatever you choose, understand this—David Rosere did not come after you because he thinks you're weak. He came after you because he knows you're a threat."

The room went still again, the weight of those words settling heavy on every shoulder. Everyone but the four brothers got up and left the conference room. The heavy door clicked shut, leaving them trapped with the nightmare that now demanded an answer. No one spoke. They all knew it. Rosere had the money, the lawyers, the power. They didn't. A court battle would crush them before it even began.

Jérôme had been pacing for hours, wearing a path into the carpet while smoke and frustration filled the room. He heard the phone ringing in the background, but the idea that was slowly forming in his head started picking up speed, racing faster and faster. A grin tugged at his mouth as he turned back to his brothers.

"Wait… hold on. I think I have come up with an idea. "What if we don't fight him in court? Jérôme continued. "What if we fight him on the streets of Seventh Avenue? Here me out," His voice was hoarse but strong. "We go to Paula at Bloomingdale's, we let it slip, casually, that Rosere is trying to take us down. Then we ask her to steer us toward *WWD*. She's got the connections, and the papers would kill for a story like this."

He paused, letting it sink in.

"But it can't come from us,' Jérôme added. "Not directly. It has to look like a leak. That's how it gains traction. That's how it grows legs."

Silence followed, thick with understanding. This wasn't a legal battle anymore. It was a street fight, and Jérôme knew exactly how to play it.

He reached for Bernard's shoulder across the table, his voice dropping into a near growl. "Let's show Seventh Avenue what a bâtard David Rosere really is." Jérôme leaned forward, eyes narrowing. "The press loves an underdog. Little guy versus the giant. That's the story." The fear that had paralyzed them was released, replaced by something brilliant. A plan. A counterattack.

Jérôme stopped pacing, planted both hands on the table, and looked at each of his brothers. "Rosere thinks he's Goliath, the giant man who wants to destroy us, and maybe he is. But even Goliath fell. We will use Goliath's own sword to defeat David Rosere."

The next morning, Jérôme raced to Paula's office, under the pretense of a check-in, the kind that happened all the time during Market Week. He took a moment with her assistant, asked about the kids, cracked a few jokes about buyer fatigue, then pushed open the door like he belonged there.

Paula looked up from a stack of orders and broke into a genuine smile. "Jérôme," she smiled. "Perfect timing. I was just thinking about you."

"Thought I would see how you were holding up," he joked lightly.

     --- BARBARA A. DAVIS

"This week always takes years off our lives."

She laughed and waved him in. "Sit. Tell me what's going on.

They talked about business, the buyers, the mood on Seventh Avenue, which brands were overperforming, and which ones were struggling. Jérôme listened, nodded, and played like he truly cared about what she was telling him. Only when the conversation began to lull did he pivot, just slightly, leaning forward as if something had only then occurred to him.

"There is one thing," he said carefully. "Off the record."

Paula's smile faded, replaced by something sharper. "Go on."

— — — — —

He didn't dramatize it. He didn't rush. He laid out the lawsuit calmly, almost clinically, what Gordon Gabriel was claiming, how aggressive the filing was, how quickly it had escalated to something they could no longer ignore. He framed it not as outrage, but as concern not only for himself, but also for the buyers carrying his brand. Jérôme knew that was the lever, and Paula realized immediately what was at stake.

She listened without interrupting, her expression unreadable, already thinking several steps ahead.

Jérôme sat back, shoulders heavy, his eyes fixed on something in the back of her office. "It feels like David versus Goliath," he said. "Hard to know who's going to be left holding the slingshot."

By the time Jérôme stood to leave, he had not asked for anything. He didn't need to. The seeds were planted. And seeds, he knew, when left alone, had a way of finding their own path to the light.

Hours later, Paula picked up her office phone, pressed it to her ear, and staged a conversation with nothing but the dial tone. Her gossipy assistant was close enough to hear every word, exactly as Paula intended.

"Really? That's insane!" Paula exclaimed, her voice sharp with outrage. "How could Gordon Gabriel stoop so low? Anyone can see those G's don't stand for Gordon Gabriel; they stand for the Gérard brothers. All four of them! This is David versus Goliath, and everyone deserves to know it. She slammed the receiver down for dramatic effect, and then, without missing a beat, returned to her papers.

— — — — —

The following day, the words Paula had planted were everywhere. And splashed across the front page of *WWD* in bold letters:

DAVID VS. GOLIATH — THE DENIM WARS

It was Bernice Greyson, the sharp-eyed fashion reporter from *WWD*, who called for their side of the story. One by one, the brothers laid it out for her, how Gordon Gabriel had come after them, how they were being portrayed as thieves instead of dreamers, men simply trying to make their mark. Bernice listened, her pencil flying, never once interrupting. By morning, her piece had dropped, and the story moved fast, spreading far beyond anything they had imagined.

The buyers whispered, assistants gossiped in elevators. Everyone had an opinion, and everyone seemed to relate. The underdog always won the sympathy vote. Gérard Jeans — 1. Gordon Gabriel — 0. The brothers had won the first battle.

It was waiting for him in the back seat of his Rolls-Royce; Robert Preston made sure of it. The coffee rested securely in its holder. *The New York Times* and *WWD* stacked neatly on the leather seat beside a tissue box, in case the ink bled onto his fingers. David had barely taken his first sip of morning coffee before his eyes froze on the bold headline — DAVID VS. GOLIATH — THE DENIM WARS. He read the article once. Then again. Slowly. As if the words themselves were loaded, carrying more weight than newsprint should ever hold. He laid the paper across his lap as though it was something fragile, almost sacred.

"Well played," he murmured under his breath, the corner of his mouth tightening. "Well played." Then his gaze hardened. The next move would be his. David knew what was coming. The phone rang through the center console of the Rolls just as his driver turned the corner onto Seventh Avenue.

"Go around the block, Bradley," David ordered with a flick of his hand. He wasn't ready to be dropped off, not with this call.

"David!" The voice on the other end roared over the static phone line. "Gordon Gabriel here." Even half a world away, calling from a Paris hotel suite while sourcing fabrics for his next couture line, his outrage cut through the phone.

"I assume you have seen the *WWD* headline," Gordon snapped. "David vs. Goliath? Do you realize what you have done? You have dragged my name into a circus." He paused, his voice turning icy.

"Let me remind you, Mr. Rosere, the license agreement is explicit. Any actions that damage my brand or its goodwill constitute trademark tarnishment. You are in breach of contract."

He drew out the words with legal precision, each one landing like another nail in the coffin. David clenched his jaw. Breach of contract. The words hit harder than he expected.

"You have twenty-four hours," Gordon continued, "to turn this around. Otherwise, your license is revoked. Gordon Gabriel Limited will cut ties with you permanently. Do you understand? I will not allow your public brawl with a handful of denim street rats to taint my name or the reputation I have spent decades building. Everything falls under the Gordon Gabriel umbrella—couture, fragrance, accessories, and global licenses. I will not have a perfume launch derailed because you can't control your narrative."

The line crackled again, but the authority in Gordon's voice was unmistakable. David felt like a schoolboy being reprimanded, caught with his hand in the cookie jar. It was a role he didn't recognize, one that twisted his stomach. He was always the one in command. Always the one issuing orders. Now he was being lectured, threatened, and given a deadline. David opened his mouth to respond, to claw back even a shred of control, but Gordon's voice cut through like a whip.

"Do you hear me, David? I want this stopped. I want this fixed, now, goddammit." And before David could get another word out, the line went dead. The silence in the car was deafening. The driver circled the block again. David leaned back against the leather seat, his chest tight, his fingers drumming restlessly against the folded newspaper still on his lap—David vs. Goliath—The Denim Wars.

This wasn't just bad press. This was survival. Justin, his son-in-law, spotted him first, David striding down the hallway toward the showroom, shoulders squared, the look of a man on a mission.

"Alan," Justin called, "your father's here."

Without needing instructions, the two slipped into David's office and closed the door behind them. This was not a casual conversation; this was triage. They leaned in together, orchestrating their move like chess players, each weighing the consequences two, three steps ahead.

By the time the clock edged toward lunch, the decision was made. David himself would make the call. Straight to Bernice Greyson, the very reporter who had splashed the David vs. Goliath story across *WWD*. He would insist he had no idea how the lawsuit had been filed, that it was a misunderstanding, already corrected. Gordon Gabriel, he would claim, had filed a notice of voluntary dismissal, legally retracting the suit, erasing it as if it had never existed.

It was the only way out. No trial, no headlines dragging on for weeks, no further damage to Gordon's name, or his own. In a matter of weeks, David knew it would fade into yesterday's news.

Still, as he settled back in his chair, the weight of it pressed in. The so-called "King of Seventh Avenue" had been forced to fold his hand. And nothing infuriated David Rosere more than retreat. He had the next move on the chessboard, and already the pieces were sliding into place. What he needed now was a strategy, something underhanded, quiet, but effective. A play that would cut deep without leaving his fingerprints behind. The wheels were turning. The idea hadn't revealed itself yet, but David knew it would. It always did. You could bet on that.

– 30 –

Davie excused himself, slipped out of his Harlem apartment and into a corner phone booth. The city noise surrounded him, taxis honking, sirens wailing in the distance, but inside the booth, it was just him and the gnawing pull of his memory. He knew Robert's schedule. Back at the estate, this was Robert's quiet hour, when no one dared to disturb him. But tonight, would be the exception.

He fed the coins into the slot, his hand trembling against the cool steel buttons. For a moment, he just stood there, staring at the keypad, breathing hard. Then, with a deep breath, he pressed the numbers he still knew by heart.

"The Rosere residence. Robert speaking. May I help you?"

The voice nearly undid him. Familiar and so kind. Davie swallowed hard, guilt pressing down on him. He had always liked Robert, always trusted him.

Leaving without saying goodbye had been one of the many things that he had felt bad about.

"Robert…" His voice cracked before he steadied it. "It's me."

A beat of silence. Then, softly, warmly, "Well, hello, Master Davie. It is very nice to receive your call." There was no judgment in his tone, no hesitation. "Your mother would love to arrange to see you. May I tell her you can accommodate her wishes?"

Davie's chest tightened. The words were there before he even thought them through. "Yes, Robert. Can you ask her to meet me downtown? This Thursday evening. The SoHo Art Gallery. Eight o'clock."

"Of course, Master Davie," Robert replied. "She will be delighted." Then, after a pause that carried years of unspoken loyalty, he added quietly, "Oh… one more thing. I have missed you, sir."

Davie closed his eyes. For the first time in a long while, he let himself feel it. He had missed him, too. As he hung up the receiver, his reflection stared back at him in the scratched glass of the booth, caught between two worlds. His past had just merged with his present, and for the first time in years, the lines between them blurred. He hoped and prayed they would not collide.

The thought of his mother seeing his paintings hanging under the gallery lights filled him with something else entirely, pride. She would be proud of him. And for once, maybe that would be enough for his father too.

— 31 —

Davie spent the entire next day apartment hunting with Julie. She had called in sick. Carol and Toni would just have to survive without her, because weekends in New York were madness, and she wasn't about to compete with a thousand other desperate renters. Still, the weekday search was no easier. Hours slipped away as they trudged up endless staircases to fifth-floor walk-ups, stood in lobbies where doormen barely glanced up from their betting sheets, and were met with the same dismissive refrain—"Hire an agent." By the time noon rolled around, Julie's feet ached, and her patience was frayed.

Davie noticed before she said a word. He caught her arm, grinned, and tugged her across the street into a little coffee shop in Chelsea.

"Again?" Julie teased as he ushered her toward the booth. "Are you really hungry already?"

"Always," he said, sliding in beside her, placing his arm around her shoulders. He pressed an exaggerated kiss on the tip of her nose. "I love you, Julie Glass. Do you know that? I absolutely love you."

Julie's laugh bubbled out despite herself. "Well, right back atcha, Davie Rose."

That was him; he could take the most impossibly frustrating morning and turn it into something wonderful. Over plates of eggs and endless cups of coffee, they fell into the kind of conversation that flowed easily from one topic to another, laughter spilling between them. And then, suddenly, it hit him. The answer had been there all along, clear as daylight.

He set down his mug and looked straight at her. "Julie, let's move in together."

Her fork froze midair. She stared at him as if he had started speaking another language. "Move in together? The two of us?"

Davie burst out laughing. "Of course, the two of us! Who else are you planning to invite?"

Julie jumped up without thinking, nearly knocking over the table as she scrambled onto his lap. She threw her arms around his neck, her voice breathless against his ear. "Yes. Yes! I would love to live with you, Mr. Rose."

The waitress passing by shook her head, muttering something about young love. But Julie didn't hear her. For the first time in days, she wasn't thinking about lost apartments, Gérard Jeans lawsuits, aching feet, or even Pepper. She was thinking only of this moment, of Davie's arms tight around her, of the simple, perfect truth—they belonged together.

Julie's address was about to change from Trident East to Dryden East, 150 East 39th Street, New York, NY 10016. Davie had spotted the listing in the paper and wasted no time setting up an appointment. It was a one-bedroom with a generous bathroom, sunshine pouring through the windows, and parquet floors that glowed in the afternoon light.

Best of all, the kitchen had just enough space for a small table for two.

Julie rushed over to see it after work and fell in love instantly, until she saw the price tag—$950 a month. Her heart sank.

Davie, though, was ready for this. He had rehearsed the conversation in his head, word for word. "I'll cover most of it, Jules. You'll only pay what you were paying at Trident. Nothing more."

Julie blinked, quickly doing the math. Something didn't add up. She knew Davie sold the occasional painting, one had sold last night at the SoHo gallery, but it wasn't nearly enough to bankroll an apartment like this.

Where was the rest of the money coming from?

She hesitated, weighing her words carefully. The last thing she wanted was to ruin this perfect moment. "But Davie…" she began. "Where—"

He pressed a finger softly to her lips, silencing her before she could finish. Then he lowered himself onto the parquet floor and patted the spot beside him.

Julie sat down, her knees brushing against his, waiting.

"You know I never talk about my family," he said quietly, his eyes fixed on Julie's questioning stare. "It brings me back to a place I don't want to go. But before I left for Europe, I withdrew all my money from the bank to make sure I would be ok. I lived frugally, staying at hostels in Europe, having cheap meals, and splitting rent with roommates in Harlem. I still have a lot left. Enough to support the two things I love most— you… and painting." He stopped there.

No names. No details. No explanations for the questions she ached to ask.

Julie felt her words stick in her throat, but she ignored them. For now, she would take what he offered. A glimpse into a past he kept locked away. A reassurance that, at least for the moment, they were safe. And for Julie, that was enough.

— — — — —

Davie woke up Thursday morning with a knot in his stomach. Tonight, at eight o'clock, he would see his mother for the first time in years. He had no idea what words would come, or if the years apart could ever be bridged. The weight of it left him restless, unable to decide how to fill the long hours before meeting her. In the end, he did the only mindless thing he could think of to take his mind off it; he started packing his things for the big move to Dryden East.

It seemed as good a distraction as any. He folded the few belongings he planned to bring to the new apartment, letting the packing keep his thoughts from spinning too far ahead. His roommates wandered in and out of his room, offering a hand with boxes or just lingering in the doorway. They were sad to see him go. They were losing a friend, but they were happy for him too. Everyone liked Julie; she and Davie fit together in a way that made sense.

The move-in date was set for next week, and Julie had already thrown herself into paint swatches and color charts. She would be bringing everything from Kerry's apartment with her, dishes, furniture, even a few of Pepper's things she still couldn't bear to give away. Davie reassured her gently that it would take time. He knew it wasn't just about Pepper; he sensed it was something deeper, something Julie herself didn't yet understand.

Since her mother's passing, goodbyes had cut Julie more sharply than most. When her best friend Nikki moved back to Columbus to care for her father, Julie cried for days, even knowing Nikki would return eventually. "I'll be back soon, Julie, don't you worry," Nikki had promised as the yellow cab sped off toward JFK airport. The last thing Julie saw was Geoffrey's little face pressed to the back window, blowing her kisses as the taxi disappeared down the street. She stood on the curb, still waving long after she had lost sight of the cab. She couldn't stop herself. The wave felt almost like a lifeline, her way of holding it together. If she let her hand fall too soon, she feared the fragile grip she had on her sanity might break loose.

Loss of any kind crippled her. She devoured books on grief, memorized the so-called "steps" of mourning, but books couldn't teach her how to live with absence. The enormity of her loss had settled in for good, and some days just staying upright felt impossible. Each goodbye stacked onto the last, the layers of loss piling up like heavy blankets, pressing down until she thought she might collapse beneath them.

There was sadness woven so deeply inside her that it sometimes made it impossible to breathe. How do you go on, she wondered, when the person you loved so completely is no longer there to hug you back? How much more time would it take to reach a place where remembering didn't end in tears? Anger and bitterness rose unexpectedly, catching her as she stood alone on the curb waving goodbye to her dearest friend. She knew she needed to walk towards happiness again, but the road ahead kept throwing her detours and potholes, and she wasn't sure which way forward would finally lead to a brighter place.

Still, she promised herself she would try, for Davie, and more importantly, for herself.

— 32 —

The subway doors slid open, and Davie stepped into the packed car, reaching up to grab one of the overhead straps. He didn't bother looking for a seat; rush hour riders piled in too quickly for that. He checked the sign above the door—the 6 train. Good. It would carry him from the 103rd Street Station down to Spring Street, a straight shot to the gallery on Sixth Avenue.

He arrived early, around 7:30 p.m. He didn't want to risk being late.

Inside, the air smelled faintly of varnish and wine. Simon Guez, the owner, gave him a firm pat on the back. "There's someone here who recognized your work," Simon said with a knowing look. "Someone who wants to meet you."

Barbara Rosere had also arrived early, though for her, the anticipation was almost unbearable. Of all her children, Davie had been her favorite, her tenderhearted one. She wandered slowly through the gallery until she stopped to look at a painting that she couldn't stop staring at. On the white card beneath it, in simple type, read—By Davie Rose, NYC Artist.

Her hand trembled slightly as her finger traced the name on the card before she gestured to Simon. "Please wrap this up," she told him, her voice soft but barely steady. "My driver will collect it."

A moment later, Simon guided Davie toward her. "Mrs. Rosere, may I introduce you to our newest artist, Davie Rose." He slipped away, leaving them face-to-face.

"Davie," Barbara gasped, her eyes shining. "Look at you, my handsome boy. Davie, Davie..." She repeated his name like a prayer; she couldn't stop hugging him. It felt as though they had only been apart since breakfast, all the years apart dissolving in a rush of motherly love.

Davie hugged her back just as tightly. For a moment, he couldn't speak. Being in her arms again felt like coming home. He had not realized how much he had missed her until now.

They decided to walk across the street to a small bar, an unlikely choice for Barbara, which made Davie laugh. "Really, Mom? Is this place okay?"

"Yes," she smiled. "Anywhere with you is okay."

They talked for hours, Barbara listening more than speaking, her eyes fixed on him as though she were half-deaf and needed to read his lips. She wanted every detail. He told her all about Europe, and how it had changed him as an artist, how his sketches had given way to colorful oils, how he had returned to New York two years ago and fought to break into the art world.

She listened with quiet pride, hanging on every word, not even sure she was breathing. It was one of those rare moments in life when the world seemed to stand still, when the only thing that existed was right in front of you. She loved the confidence in his voice and the light in his beautiful eyes as he spoke to her. All it would have taken was a single phone call. He had chosen the harder road. That was her Davie.

Finally, he saved the best part for last. "I've met someone, Mom. Her name is Julie. We're moving in together next week. I really love her,

Mom."

Barbara's face softened, her smile spreading without her even realizing it. He hesitated before adding, "She doesn't know anything about our family."

"That's all right," Barbara said gently, reaching for his hand. "That's between us, sweetheart. You tell me what you're comfortable sharing, and I'll follow your lead."

"So… how's Phillipe Leon these days? And Dad, he's still working?"

Barbara's eyes widened in surprise as the truth hit her all at once; her son knew nothing about what had happened to the family business. He had no idea that his father now sat at the helm of Gordon Gabriel Jeans, one of the most powerful fashion companies on Seventh Avenue. She drew in a breath, steadying herself.

"There's so much that has happened since you left Junior," she said gently. She hesitated, then smiled, reaching for his hand. "But not today. We don't need to get into all of that right now, sweetheart."

He looked at her, searching her face. "Are you sure, Mom?"

"Yes, absolutely sure . I want to go back to the gallery with you and see more of your beautiful paintings."

His expression eased, "Okay, there are a few I really want to show you."

Barbara nodded, relieved. This was not the time to talk about family business. This was her time with her son, and that was all she wanted to talk about.

"So what does Julie do, sweetheart? Is she an artist too?"

"No," he laughed. "She works as a sales executive for Gérard Jeans."

Barbara wasn't quite sure she heard him correctly, the words hitting her like a sudden chill. She steadied herself with a sip of her drink, willing her expression to stay smooth. There was no way she would ruin this moment, not now, not when she had her baby back.

"Mom? Are you okay?" Davie asked gently, his eyes full of concern.

She forced a laugh, tapping the rim of her glass. "Wow. They certainly make a strong drink at this fine establishment." But even as she smiled, her right eye began to twitch uncontrollably. They made plans to see each other again soon. Barbara was still pinching herself as she sank into the backseat of the limo on the ride home. She had her son back. After all these years, she had Davie again. And yet, beneath the joy, there was a girl named Julie, and that could be a problem. The next shoe would surely drop and drop very soon. It was only a matter of time before she had to tell her husband that their son's girlfriend worked for his number one rival, Gérard Jeans.

This life, she thought to herself as the car turned toward home. Barbara carried Davie's carefully wrapped painting inside and set it gently in the foyer while slipping off her coat. David passed by, drink in hand, his tie loosened, his mood sour.

"What've you got there, Babs?" he asked, pausing only for a glance.

"Do you really want to know?" she teased lightly, forcing a smile.

"Probably not," he snapped, and without another word, he climbed the long winding staircase to bed.

The next morning, David shot out of bed with an energy Barbara had not seen in years. She lifted her eye mask, still half-asleep.

"What's gotten into you?" she mumbled from her side of the bed.

"I think I know how to destroy Gérard Jeans," David announced, his voice electric. "I've got a brilliant idea."

Barbara rolled over, twisting her face into the pillow so he wouldn't see the strain she couldn't hide. "Let's talk about it over breakfast," she suggested carefully.

"No, Babs, listen." He slid back onto the bed beside her, eyes gleaming. "Carol. Carol Tanaka is the key. If I steal her away from them, they've got nothing. Nothing."

Barbara knew he was right. Carol was their North Star, but she was sick to death of it. The endless tit-for-tat, the childish vendettas between the so-called denim kings of Seventh Avenue. She loved her husband, but there were days when his hunger for control and power felt unbearable.

"Why can't you just play it straight?" she asked softly. "Whoever has the better designs, whoever sells the most, let that decide who wins the season. Is that so bad?"

But David was already lost in his scheme, his mind miles ahead. Barbara sat silently at the edge of her bed, her thoughts racing. She couldn't allow this, not now. Not when she had just started to mend the cracks in her family, not when Davie was back in her life. If David pulled this stunt, it would blow everything apart. Davie would hate him for it. She needed her own secretive plan that was quiet, steady, and strong enough to stop him.

– – – – –

Barbara spent the entire morning deciding what to wear. By the time she left her dressing room, half her closet lay in a heap across the bed, abandoned to the maid. Today had to be perfect. This wasn't just lunch, it was strategy. She had a mission, and failure was not an option.

She had dialed Astrid Peyton directly, one of the few numbers in New York that cut straight through layers of assistants and housekeepers. Astrid had answered on the second ring.

"Barbara, my dear, how have you been? It feels like ages since I've seen you. Was it at Tootsie's 80th birthday? No, no… wait, I remember, it was the Lawrence's wedding at The Breakers. You looked stunning that night, that's how I recall it."

Barbara smiled politely into the receiver, though inwardly she was annoyed. With Astrid, it was always impossible to tell if a compliment was sincere or one of her well-practiced jabs. Stunning that night, as if it were the only time she ever had been. Still, she let it go. She had bigger things on her mind.

The two agreed to meet for lunch at BG, Bergdorf Goodman's restaurant perched high above Fifth Avenue. Barbara had chosen it deliberately. It would be discreet and familiar enough to Astrid that her guard would be down.

When she arrived, Astrid was already there, every detail flawless, from the tilt of her hat to the way her Hermès scarf draped just so across her shoulders. Barbara slid into the private banquette Astrid had secured in the back corner, grateful for the seclusion. They belonged to the same country club, moved in overlapping circles, but Astrid had a way of always reminding Barbara of the social gap between them. Barbara had wealth, but Astrid carried pedigree, and she never let anyone forget it.

The meal began with the expected small talk. Where they had traveled recently. Which Upper East Side penthouse Lauren Minkoff was re-designing. Which children had been accepted into the Ivy Leagues, and which marriages were quietly crumbling behind manicured hedges. After a glass of rosé, even the divorces were traded like juicy morsels, wrapped in knowing smirks.

Barbara kept her smile in place, nodding at all the right moments, though her mind was elsewhere. She waited patiently, letting Astrid fill the silence with her usual blend of arrogance and detail. Timing was everything. At last, she set down her fork, dabbing at her lips with the napkin as if preparing for something more delicate than the salad she had barely touched.

"So," Barbara began smoothly, her tone casual though her heart was pounding. "How are your beautiful Cocoon boutiques? I imagine you must be very pleased with all your recent success."

Astrid's eyes lit at the prompt, her vanity engaged exactly as Barbara had planned. She launched into an elaborate account of expansions, design choices, and exclusive contracts, every detail as tedious as Barbara had expected. Barbara sat back, feigning interest, nodding slowly while her mind ticked ahead to the next move in her scheme. Her right eye twitched. She blinked it away quickly, praying Astrid hadn't noticed.

"So, darling Astrid," Barbara said lightly, leaning forward as if sharing a secret, "how in the world do you manage everything and keep up with such a busy social schedule?"

Astrid gave a small, dramatic sigh, the kind that made every movement feel choreographed. "Oh, Barbara, you are quite right. There are days when it all feels so overwhelming. I have missed wintering in St. Moritz, two years now, if you can imagine, all because of these endless business obligations. It simply is not sustainable."

She looked Barbara squarely in the eye, her cadence breathless, her wide-eyed expression both vulnerable and practiced. "But where would I even begin to look for someone to help me, someone I can trust? How does one even find the right person?"

Barbara's pulse quickened. It couldn't be this easy, she thought. But it was. She took a slow, deliberate sip of her drink before unleashing her plan. Her voice softened, carrying a touch of honey that sweetened the weight of her words.

"And you know, Astrid, I do not even have to mention this, I know it goes without saying, but just for old time's sake, let us keep what I am about to share with you between us girls." She added the faintest Southern accent to her last line, as if to lighten it, keep it playful rather than serious. "After all, it does put me in a rather awkward position, considering my husband's company… and the competition among the denim houses."

Astrid waved a hand as though brushing lint off a sleeve. "Oh, dear girl, really, competition?" Her laugh was low, almost indulgent. "Don't you worry a hair on that little head of yours. I have already moved past all that."

She raised her glass, taking a slow sip to mask the smirk tugging at her lips.

Astrid smiled politely, but behind her steady gaze, she thought—

What a foolish woman. What competition? She had already elevated herself above the street fight. She was not even playing the same game anymore.

Barbara slid a folded card across the linen tablecloth, Carol Tanaka's name and number written neatly in her hand. "This is your person, she said. "You can thank me later."

With that, the two women nodded their approval and raised their glasses, toasting to wintering once again in St. Moritz, a quiet acknowledgement that certain social circles took care of their own.

— 33 —

There's a package on the kitchen table for you, sweetheart."

"What did you do, Kenji?" Carol smiled at her husband. They had been married for just over two years, and she still had that puppy-love crush for him.

"No, not me. Looks like you've got a secret admirer." The box was marked *hand delivered from Tiffany's*.

"Must be Father then," Carol said as she made her way toward the kitchen table. The coffee smelled amazing. Kenji had already poured them both a cup, and he handed her a pair of scissors.

She opened the envelope first, scanning the neat script before looking up at her husband with a puzzled expression.

"What does it say?"

"It's from Astrid Peyton," Carol said slowly, then began to read aloud.

> *Dearest Carol,*
> *It would give me the greatest pleasure to have you join me*

Carol carefully untied the white ribbon and lifted the lid of the iconic blue box. Inside, nestled in velvet, was the tiniest crystal butterfly, Astrid Peyton's trademark

"Hmmm," she murmured. "This should be interesting."

Kenji studied her face; no need for words between them. He knew exactly what she was thinking. They both knew what this meant.

"Well," he said finally, downing the rest of his coffee in one swallow, "looks like I'll be painting a butterfly very soon."

Carol laughed softly, shaking her head as she cradled the delicate crystal in her palm. What a day, she thought. And it's not even nine o'clock.

There was no easy way to do this. Carol knew what it would mean to all of them, especially Jérôme, whom she had the most love and respect for. After several cups of coffee with Kenji, she rambled, circling the point, pretending for a while that she had not already made up her mind. He listened quietly, letting her talk it through, though she knew he could already see the outcome written across her face. Finally, after hours of discussing the pros and cons she looked at her husband across the table.

"I feel like I helped them when no one else would, Kenji. I was there for them from the beginning; I set them on their path to success. But now...I need to find my way back home. I'm not the type of girl who can just wait around.

Someday, someday soon, Gérard Jeans will be sitting at the VIP table at the Christmas Ball. I just don't want to wait that long. Cocoon by Astrid Peyton has my name written all over it."

Kenji watched her, his dark eyes steady, his hands folded around his

    — — — B A R B A R A A. D A V I S

mug.

"And besides," Carol added softly, her fingers tracing the rim of her coffee cup, "we've built our own little cocoon here, you and I. And soon…" she paused, her eyes brightening as a tender smile spread across her face, "…soon our own little butterfly will emerge, about seven months from now."

Carol's words hung in the air, and for a moment, Kenji just blinked at her.

Then he tilted his head, puzzled. "What do you mean?"

She reached across the table, took his hand, and placed it on her stomach. "You're going to be a daddy, honey. The doctor called me yesterday with the news."

For a long moment, he was speechless. The man who had always been ready with a quick word and a sarcastic remark had nothing to say. His throat tightened, and then in seconds, he was out of his chair, wrapping her in his arms. He had wanted children from the moment they were married, and now, here it was, his dream, their future.

The phone calls came quickly, parents on both sides crying happy tears, voices breaking with joy. It was an extraordinary morning, an ending, a beginning, and a new life stirring in more ways than one.

— — — — —

The dinner with Astrid had been everything Carol hoped for. Over a dry martini for Astrid, and a club soda with lemon for Carol, they mapped out a path forward for Cocoon, Astrid listening intently, never once flinching when Carol named a salary so high even she worried it sounded unreasonable. By the time dessert arrived, it was settled. Carol would be joining Cocoon in two weeks.

She hummed all the way home, a lightness in her step she had not felt in a very long time.

Carol lay in bed as the reality of her decision played out in her mind. She had been up for hours, staring at the ceiling, replaying the moment she would have to say the words. The thought of walking into the business she had helped launch, facing the four brothers who had come to rely on her, made her stomach turn. This was not going to be easy.

She decided the sooner the better. Letting it linger would only make the goodbye harder. As she walked towards Jérôme's office, her knees started feeling weak, but she pressed on, knowing what needed to be done. At the doorway, she paused, took a steadying breath, and leaned in.

"Jérôme," she said quietly, her voice softer than usual, "I need to speak with you and your brothers. Can we meet in the conference room this morning?"

He gave her a curious look but nodded. "Sure. Give me a minute to round everyone up."

Daniel was in El Paso overseeing production, so when Carol opened the conference room door, it was Jérôme, Bernard, and Sami waiting, their faces bright with the usual expectation that she was about to unveil a new idea or campaign. Out of habit, she took her familiar seat to the right of Jérôme.

"What's this all about?" Sami asked, half-smiling, glancing between his brothers.

"She probably has another campaign idea," Bernard said with a smirk.

But Carol didn't smile. She felt as if she was holding a grenade and in minutes, she would be pulling the pin that would blow up their world. All her training had taught her to separate business from pleasure, to keep emotions out of the room. The only thing that mattered was the bottom line.

She had done her job; more than that, she had set the brothers on their way. But now, something deeper pulled at her. Maybe it was the pregnancy hormones, she thought, remembering the dog-eared copy of *What to*

     - - - B A R B A R A A. D A V I S

Expect When You're Expecting on her nightstand.

She couldn't hold it in any longer. The words came out in a rush.

"I need to leave you all, I need to leave Gérard Jeans." Her words hit like a punch to the gut.

Jérôme blinked, confusion clouding his face. "What do you mean… leave? For a vacation? For…what?"

Her lips trembled. "No, Jérôme. Leave the company."

Sami caught it immediately, the truth plain on her face. He leaned back in his chair, shaking his head slowly, disappointment written all over his face.

Jérôme leaned toward her, his voice soft, almost pleading. "Carol… why? Did we do something? Did something happen?"

She looked at him then, she looked around the table at all of them, her chest aching. In a way, Jérôme had been like the brother she had never had, and the loyalty in his eyes made what she had to say even harder.

They were all in shock, unwilling to believe what was coming next.

"It's time," Carol said, her voice sad but steady. She looked around the table at the faces she knew so well, knowing this would be the last time. "I can give you two weeks' notice, but I think it's best if I say good-bye today. I have been offered a position to run Cocoon by Astrid Peyton, and it's something I want and need to do at this point in my life."

Sami stood and, without a word, stormed out of the room. He didn't trust himself to speak; he didn't want to say anything he'd later regret. Carol had been his rock, and now she was leaving. The disappointment in his eyes said more than words ever could.

Jérôme and Bernard remained seated, stunned. Jérôme broke the silence first. "Carol," he said slowly, each syllable heavy, sinking between them like a weight that couldn't be lifted. "Thank you for everything. For what you have done for us personally, and especially for this company. I will always be indebted to you." He lit a cigarette, drew in the smoke, and leaned back; his eyes fixed on her. It looked as though he was reaching for more words, but none would come.

Carol sat still, trying to stay composed. One more thing, she thought to herself. If she stayed here, she would be harming her unborn child with the constant haze of cigarette smoke that lingered in every corner of this office. The thought gave her the strength she needed to stand.

"Please, Jérôme," she said softly, but firmly, "don't say anything more. It's too hard. I know you are all on your way to the very top. Sales are soaring, profits through the roof, you don't need me anymore. "I accomplished what you hired me to do, and I am very pleased about that." She swallowed, fighting the lump in her throat. "I will call with a list of people who I think would be a good replacement."

Jérôme's eyes filled with sadness. "There's no such thing as a replacement for you, Carol. But we wish you well. And please… know you will always be welcome back."

That was it. No more words left. They all rose, slowly and reluctantly, and Carol Tanaka walked out of the conference room for the last time. At the elevator, she paused, turning back for one last look at the office that had challenged her, and made her part of something she would always be proud of. The doors slid open. She stepped inside, placed her hand on her stomach, and as they closed, she whispered to her little one, "Let's go home, baby. Daddy will be waiting for us."

Jérôme broke the news one by one. Julie could hear it ripple through the office, the sharp gasp from Toni's doorway, followed by Barry's thunderous bellow—"Are you fucking serious?" Julie straightened in her chair, bracing herself as Jérôme appeared in her doorway.

"Carol's decided to leave," he said carefully. "She's going to explore other options."

Julie's throat tightened. She forced herself to nod, her voice soft but steady. "Don't worry, Jérôme. You'll find someone else, someone amazing."

He lingered a moment longer than he needed to, not wanting to be

   - - - B A R B A R A A. D A V I S

by himself. He gave her a faint, grateful smile, but as he turned away, she saw the heaviness in his shoulders. They both knew what an impossible task lay ahead. Carol was irreplaceable.

Later that afternoon, her phone rang. Davie's voice came through warm, steady, grounding her even before she spoke. She was still reeling. "She didn't even say goodbye to me," Julie whispered. "She was… she was my person, Davie. Almost like a second mother. My work mother."

"It's okay, Jules," he said gently. "These things happen. I'm sure she will call soon, explain everything. You should be happy for her. If she walked away from Gérard Jeans, it must be one hell of an opportunity."

He could hear how quiet she was and knew the way goodbyes of any kind affected her. He jumped in quickly, offering her a lifeline. "How about Hannibal's tonight? Barbecue ribs, potato salad, and a glass of red wine. We'll celebrate Carol, talk it all through."

The mention of Hannibal's forced a small smile from her lips. It was their spot, the place they went when the world got too heavy. Comfort food, comfort company. For the first time since she heard the news of Carol leaving, she felt like she might just be okay.

— 34 —

Julie was curled up on the sofa of her new apartment, lost in Stephen King's *Cujo*, when she heard a large crash that made her jump. Something had slammed into the window. "What was that?" Davie called from the kitchen, thinking she had dropped something heavy.

Julie rose slowly, her eyes catching the faint smear of red splattered across the glass. Her hand shot out to grab his arm. "Davie… I think it was a bird. I need to see if it's okay."

"What? Jules, of course, it's not okay," he said, bewildered. But she was already halfway to the door, not waiting for him to put on his shoes.

She flew down the stairwell, skipping the elevator. "Pete!" she called to the doorman as she burst through the lobby. "Did you see a bird on the ground?"

Pete blinked, confused, as if Julie had started her Saturday night a little early. "No, Julie, nothing."

But then she spotted it, nestled in the bushes near the sidewalk. The tiny baby bird trembled, its chest rising unevenly as it fought for breath.

"Davie, over here!" she cried.

He approached cautiously, like a man inching toward someone on the edge of madness.

"It's still alive," she whispered, her voice breaking. "I need to say the prayer."

"What prayer, Julie? What are you talking about?"

Her father had taught her the words long ago; he adored animals and passed that passion down to her. Kneeling beside the bird, she closed her eyes and spoke softly— "Little one, I honor your life and your spirit. May you return to the sky from which you came, free, light, and at peace. Thank you for reminding me of the fragility and beauty of life."

She stuttered, the last line slipping away, then it came back to her. "May your journey be swift, and may you soar in eternal rest." She looked up suddenly. "Go find a flower, Davie."

"A flower?" he repeated, glancing around the concrete sidewalk in disbelief.

Pete, watching from the lobby, understood. He darted inside, returned with a single bloom plucked from a floral arrangement that was just delivered, and pressed it into Davie's hand.

"Can you believe this woman?" Davie muttered.

Pete only winked. "She really is something special."

Davie passed the flower to Julie. With trembling fingers, she laid it gently across the bird's still body. For a moment, the busy city around them hushed, and the small ceremony on the sidewalk felt like the only thing that mattered, one fragile life, now in God's hands.

Pete gave Julie a small nod of respect as Davie laced his fingers through hers and guided her back toward the elevator. The ride upstairs was silent, heavy with the weight of what had just happened.

Inside the apartment, Davie led her to the kitchen table, pulling out a chair and gently easing her into it. He crouched beside her, his hand still holding hers.

"Jules," he said softly, searching her eyes, "I know you feel like the smallest thing can split you wide open right now. But I really don't think what you're feeling is really about this little bird. You've been through so much in such a short time, your body and your mind haven't had the chance to heal. It's like a scab that's almost closed, but you keep bumping into things that make it break open and bleed again.

"Just think about it, Julie. You lost the most important person in your life, your beautiful mother, just a few years ago. Then came losing your dream of becoming Barbara Walters. Losing Pepper. Losing the apartment you loved. Nikki leaving for Ohio. Carol walking out of Gérard Jeans without a goodbye. And now, this tiny bird that crashed into our window. You hold on to every goodbye and every loss and stack them one on top of the other, until the weight of it all feels too heavy to carry."

He paused, his voice quiet but steady. "How do I help you with this, Julie?

This is life; goodbyes are a part of it. The hardest part. We can't hold on to everything or everyone, no matter how much we want to, or how much we try. All we can do is love them while we have them and be grateful for the time we're given. That's what makes the letting go bearable. Because the love doesn't disappear when they do. The love stays with us. It changes shape, but it stays."

He reached for her hand, his thumb tracing small circles against her skin. "You don't have to stop feeling the loss," he said gently. "You just have to learn to live with it. I'm here for all of it, Jules. You don't ever have to go through this alone."

He hesitated, his voice becoming even more gentle. "But sweetheart… Maybe it wouldn't hurt to talk to someone. Maybe someone who could help you where I can't."

She was quiet for a long moment, staring down at their joined hands. He was right, of course, he was right. She would think about it. She had never gone to therapy; it wasn't something her family did. But for Davie, she would think about it.

— 35 —

66 Just a few more shots, Casey, and I promise you we'll be done."
James Clive's job was never easy, but today it felt impossible. He
had been tasked with creating an image that could surpass Riley Spencer's
iconic photo, the one that had launched a million pairs of jeans. But Casey
Jordan was no Riley Spencer. That wasn't his business to say aloud, but
the thought gnawed at him as she pouted, sighed, and refused to follow
even his simplest instructions.

She was a drama queen, through and through. "Head a little to the
left… just a touch more." And that was it. Casey declared herself finished
for the day, brushing off his direction with a flip of her hair. Better luck
tomorrow, James thought bitterly as he lowered the camera. Why in the
world had they gotten rid of Riley? He would never understand the rea-
soning behind that executive decision. Why Casey had been chosen out of
all the gorgeous models in New York remained a mystery to him. But that,
too, was none of his business. She swept out of the studio, her long legs
stretching across the pavement as she rushed to meet her new boyfriend
for drinks, and maybe dinner. Depending on how the evening went, he had

asked her to join him at "21" CLUB.

By the time she reached 52nd Street, the irritation of the shoot had vanished, replaced by a kind of charged anticipation. "21" CLUB wasn't just another Manhattan restaurant; it was a world apart. She had only been there once before, years ago, on the arm of her then fiancé. The line of brightly painted metal jockey statues stood guard at the entrance, gifts from the Mellons, Vanderbilts, Whitneys, Phippses, and other storied families, each painted in the racing silks of their stables. Over the decades, they had become as iconic as the club's legendary wine cellar.

Inside, the air carried a hush of reverence. This was a place where presidents dined, where celebrities whispered over martinis, where titans of industry and international socialites mingled under the guise of casual conversation. Simply walking through its doors felt like stepping into another level of existence, where velvet ropes and whispered introductions quietly determined your place.

She spotted him immediately. A small wave, a smile, the maître d' nodded to follow him to a private table tucked discreetly in the far corner, hidden from the rest of the room. He rose as she approached, pulling her in just a little closer than what was considered polite.

He wasn't hungry. At least, not for food.

Dinner became an afterthought. Their focus was on each other, eyes locked across the table, lips brushing between stolen words, legs entwined beneath the linen tablecloths. The waiters moved in and out like ghosts, unnoticed.

Over dessert, he finally asked, "So... how did the photo shoot go?"

"It went very well," she said, tracing the edge of her spoon through the caramelized top of her crème brûlée. "But we're shooting again tomorrow."

"Maybe I'll stop by," he teased, a grin tugging at the corner of his mouth.

She tilted her head, amused, her voice soft but edged with daring.

"Well, after all, it is your company, Mr. Rosere."

He smiled, basking in the moment, but in doing so, he forgot two things—two things that would matter more than anything else. In New York, the city was smaller than it looked when you traveled in its most elite circles. And second, he was still wearing his wedding ring.

It was the following day, at the second photo shoot, which was going just as badly as the first one had the day before, that James Clive was nearly at the end of his rope. Three hours in, and Casey Jordan had given him nothing but rehearsed poses and forced pouts. A few frames had come close, but not close enough. Then, without warning, something shifted. Casey's eyes flicked upward, her lips parting, her face softening into the first genuine expression of the day. The shutter clicked furiously. This was the shot.

"Thank God," he muttered to himself.

James lowered the camera, turning to see what had transformed her so suddenly. It was Alan Rosere, standing just beyond the lights, watching her with stars in his eyes.

Now it all made sense. James let out a low laugh under his breath. Casey Jordan wasn't just the next cover girl. She was something more.

"Hello, James." Alan's voice carried that easy confidence as he stepped into the studio. "How's our new model doing?"

"Oh, just wonderful, Alan," James lied smoothly, lowering his camera.

Alan smiled, eyes flicking toward Casey. "And tell me, how do you think she compares to Riley?"

The question caught James so off guard, the words sticking in his throat. "Well… ah… hard to say. Very different kind of mood."

"Exactly!" Alan exclaimed, clapping his hands together. "That's what we're going for. A different kind of appeal, a different kind of mood. Perfect."

James forced a tight smile. *If bitch mood was what you wanted, then yes, bullseye,* he thought. But aloud he only repeated, "Perfect. I'll have the photos on your desk by the end of the week."

Alan winked at Casey, his smile lingering longer than it should have, before turning on his heel and heading back to the office, ready to tell his father that they had found their next superstar.

– – – – –

Francis, Alan's wife, loved her job, and she was excellent at it. A striking woman often compared to Ali MacGraw, with her long brown hair and warm, inviting eyes, she carried herself with a kind of natural ease that drew people in. She had always been top of her class, the sort of person others gravitated toward, that elusive "it" quality wrapped in quiet confidence.

Her agency, Take Two, which specialized in representing models over forty, had become her pride and joy. She had cornered a niche no one else had thought to touch, and with absolutely no competition, she ran the business with the same poise she carried into every room. Her client list was impressive, her reputation impeccable, and she had built a wide circle of friends, one of whom had introduced her to Alan more than eight years ago.

At first, she hadn't been entirely sure about him. He was handsome, wealthy, and polite enough. But he didn't make her laugh. He lacked that easy sense of humor she valued so deeply. Early in their marriage, Francis tried everything, playful pranks, little setups she thought would break through his serious exterior, moments designed to coax out even the smallest laugh. But Alan remained Alan—steady, serious, humorless. It hadn't taken her long to realize you can't teach someone the importance of laughter if they were born without a funny bone.

Francis drove the ten minutes to her in-laws' house; the unease she was feeling was unbearable. She couldn't shake it; something wasn't right with Alan, and she needed to talk to Barbara.

"Something's off, Barbara," she said at last, her voice quiet, hesitant.

She loved her mother-in-law dearly and trusted her instincts more than anyone's. "I thought maybe it was work, and that's why he's been so distant lately."

Barbara shook her head gently. "I don't think so, Francis. David's never been happier, and Alan's been right there beside him. They went over sales projections by forty-five percent. I heard him talking to Justin about it the other day."

Francis frowned, still uneasy. "Can you talk to him? Maybe find out what it is?"

"You know it's probably nothing, sweetheart," Barbara said, her tone calm, reassuring. "You know men... maybe his team lost, or something silly like that. I'm sure it's nothing." She rose and took Francis's hand with a warm smile. "Come on, let's go out to the garden and take a walk. It's a beautiful day."

— — — — —

There were only two things in this world James Clive detested more than anything—a bad meal and a disloyal partner. For over twenty years, he had lived with his soulmate, William Payne. Sure, there had been ups and downs, but loyalty was never one of their problems; it was the foundation of their life together.

James had known Francis Rosere through Take Two, her wildly successful model agency. He had been hired for several shoots in recent months and had always been struck by her professionalism. Francis treated him with respect— respect for his time, respect for his work. She was a gem, and it bothered James to think she might be the one being played.

"You're not even sure if anything is going on," William yelled, watching James pace the apartment. "Please, James," he added with a weary sigh, "mind your own business. Who cares anyway?"

James shook his head, unable to let it go, but William had already grabbed his racket bag, heading out for a few matches of racquetball at the Racquet and Tennis Club on Park Avenue. The conversation was over, at least it was for William.

James stood by the window after William left, still restless, still unsettled. To him, loyalty wasn't a detail you ignored. It was everything. And something about Francis's situation really bothered him, no matter how much William urged him to let it go.

— 36 —

Justin hesitated before knocking softly on David's office door. Delivering bad news to his father-in-law was never easy; David thrived on yeses, not noes, and what Justin had to say was most definitely not a yes.

"Carol has already accepted a job as president of Cocoon, Dad," Justin said carefully once he stepped inside, easing into the chair across from him. "I called her at home yesterday, but she wouldn't even listen to what I had to say. She's on board. Starts next week."

David looked up, his face falling into the rare expression of defeat.

"Really?" was all he managed before rising from his chair. He began walking around his office, his hands clenched behind his back, his gaze drifting toward the massive stallion portrait that dominated the wall behind his desk. Horses had always been his obsession. To him, they were pure power, animals that gave you everything they had, nothing held in reserve, every stride as if it were their last.

"I used to be like that," he muttered, almost to himself. "Nothing ever got in my way. I ran every race to win." He turned then, his sharp eyes cutting toward Justin, who was fidgeting under the weight of David's stare. "That's the difference between people, Justin. Everyone thinks they are owed the same thing in life. But only those willing to do what others can't, or won't, ever reap the real rewards."

Justin wasn't sure if he was supposed to respond, so he stayed quiet. The sound of the ticking clock was suddenly too loud in his father-in-law's massive office.

David stood still for a long moment, then shook his head, as if coming to some grim conclusion. "I don't know if that still lives with me."

Without another word, he strode to the door, told his secretary to call for his driver Bradley, and left. Justin remained seated, staring up at the painted stallions on the wall. They seemed to be laughing at him, or worse, judging him. Especially Lancelot, whose flared nostrils seemed to mock him.

— 37 —

Carol's first day at Cocoon was beyond anything she could have imagined.

Her office wasn't just beautiful, it was exquisite. Plush oriental carpets softened every step, and in the center stood a black Chinese writing desk, its glass top freshly cleaned. She eased into the chair, ran her fingers along the polished edge, and pulled open the small drawer on the right. Inside, a discreet plaque caught her eye—a signed edition, only 250 ever produced.

Carol let out a quiet laugh. "Now this is more like it," she whispered to herself, leaning back with a satisfied smile. She had told Astrid she was expecting a baby at their dinner meeting at Le Cirque, and to her immense relief, Astrid was ecstatic. "That's wonderful news, dear," she said, her voice light with genuine excitement.

The phone rang in Carol's office. Astrid's breathless cadence carried through the receiver, her words tumbling with energy. "Carol, I have a brilliant thought I want to share with you. I want you to do some research for a children's line. Newborn only. We will call it Mon Bebe for Cocoon by Astrid Peyton.”

Carol smiled into the phone, her mind racing with the possibilities. “I love it, Astrid.”

— 38 —

It was midafternoon when David arrived home. Hearing the front door open, Barbara looked up in surprise and leaned over the sweeping staircase in the foyer. "David? Is that you?"

"I'll be in my office," was all he said, his voice low, his shoulders heavy as he walked past Robert, his butler, without meeting his eye.

"Would you like some lunch, sir?" Robert offered gently.

"No, thank you, Robert. Just… just to be left alone. That would be perfect. Please tell my wife I'm resting."

Robert raised an eyebrow ever so slightly. *Resting?* he thought. *When does David Rosere ever rest?* But he gave a polite nod and let it go.

Moments later, Barbara descended the stairs, dressed impeccably for a day of shopping in the city. "Where's David, Robert?"

"He said not to be disturbed, madam. He said he was resting."

"Resting?" She scoffed. "Well, that's ridiculous." She swept past Robert as she made her way down the long hallway, through the library, and straight through to the French doors of David's office. Without hesitation, she pushed them open. There he was, seated at his desk, pen in hand, his head bowed. He didn't even look up as she entered. But her eyes focused on the envelope lying before him, already addressed. On the front of the envelope, one single word was written— Junior. She heard her heart pounding in her chest.

Barbara lowered herself into the chair opposite his desk and said softly, "David… please. Talk to me. What is going on?"

At last, he looked up. For a moment, Barbara saw not the formidable man who ruled Seventh Avenue, but her husband, tired, worn, and looking much older than usual. The look in her eyes seemed to soothe him, to remind him that someone still cared, maybe even loved him. Gratitude shot across his face.

"I don't know, Babs," he said finally, voice rough. "It's hard to explain, and I don't want to scare you. But these past few months… something isn't right." He paused, as though searching for words. "The best way I can describe it is, I feel a sense of doom. Like something is coming for me, and I can't stop it."

Barbara sat upright, her whole body tense, the hair on the back of her neck prickling. "But why, David? Business is thriving, you told me yourself just last week, it's better than ever. You have your family working beside you. You're surrounded by people who respect and admire you."

He shook his head, holding up the envelope in his trembling hand. "Except for Junior." If something happens to me, I want you to give this to him. I want him to know that…" His words faltered, and then the tears began.

Barbara rushed to him, slipping behind the desk, pulling his shaking frame against her chest. In over thirty-five years of marriage, she had never seen David like this. Never. She had no words, only the instinct to hold him, to rock him gently, as if to a song only they could hear.

"David, it's okay," she whispered.

But he pulled back, his face wet, his tone suddenly fierce. "No. No, it's not. I was wrong, Barbara." He tightened his grip on the envelope, his

     - - - B A R B A R A A. D A V I S

voice breaking into something raw and unguarded. "I want him to know I am sorry. That no matter where he is, no matter what he's doing, I will always be proud to have called him my son."

Barbara slowly let go of him and told him to wait for her. She rushed up the steps to her bedroom, opened her closet doors, and pulled out the brown-wrapped paper package with the SoHo gallery label neatly adhered to the front of it. She moved like a soldier on a mission, steady, deliberate, knowing exactly what needed to be done. This was as good a time as any to tell her husband about Junior. She had been feeling uneasy for weeks, carrying the weight of a secret this big. Five minutes later, she was back, the package clutched tightly in her hands. She held it out to him. David looked up, confused.

"What's this?" he asked softly, the words carrying more weariness than curiosity.

"Open it, sweetheart," Barbara said, her voice low but steady. "We need to talk."

The brown wrapping paper slid to the floor, landing in a soft heap. David stared at the painting; he couldn't quite understand why Barbara thought now was the time for a gift. He forced a smile, trying to ease the heaviness in the room.

"This is very nice, Babs. Thank you," he said, his voice low, assuming it was her way of cheering him up.

Barbara leaned closer, her eyes steady. "Look at the artist's name, David."

He bent toward the lower right-hand corner, squinting at the faint scrawl. "Hard to read," he murmured, until suddenly, it struck him.

"Davie Rose," he whispered. The name lingered in the air, fragile as glass.

He looked up, confusion breaking into something sharper. "Davie Rose? Who is Davie Rose...?" He stopped mid-sentence. His face went pale. "Is this Junior, Babs? Is this our son's painting? Is Junior, Davie

Rose?"

Barbara's eyes filled. "Yes. Yes, it is. He's living in New York City, he's back home."

Something released inside her, a dam that had been waiting years to break. The words poured out of her, how she had hired a private investigator, how it had taken seven years to find him, how it had nearly killed her, not knowing if her son was safe. She told David everything Davie had shared with her— his travels through Europe, the hostels he stayed in to save money, the odd jobs, the moments of loneliness, the way those years had shaped him as an artist.

And then she added the part she had held closest. "It was me who told him to call the bank and withdraw the money. I gave him the account number. I needed to make sure he would be okay." She stared at her husband, unflinching, her voice firm. "He's my son too, David."

Her breath trembled as she recounted the moment that had changed everything for her. "When I hugged him for the first time… when I held our boy in my arms again, my heart felt whole for the first time in years."

David's shoulders slumped as the truth cut through him. Not only had he driven a wedge between himself and his son, but his actions had broken the heart of the person he loved most in this world, his wife.

Her voice steadied as she added, "And there's one more thing. Davie is in love."

"That's wonderful. I'm so happy he has someone in his life."

Barbara held the rest back, knowing the truth would come soon enough.

He stood and crossed the room, stopping in front of Barbara. With tear-filled eyes, he promised her that he would fix the mess that he created all those years ago. "I'm so sorry, Babs, I'm so very, very sorry, I'll make it right."

— 39 —

I'm over here!" Julie called out, waving as Davie made his way through the lunchtime crowd at Lou Siegel's, her favorite deli in the Garment District. She loved everything about the place, from the constant noise of the waiters screaming at one another to get out of the way, to the clatter of plates, and the smell of fresh rye bread warm from the oven. Toni had brought her here years ago, and from that first visit, it had felt like her spot.

Davie slid into the booth across from her, still carrying the faint scent of oil paint on his jacket from that morning. He had just dropped off a few of his new canvases at the SoHo gallery, hopeful they would sell as quickly as the last few. Simon Guez had even called earlier, saying there was a serious fan wanting to meet him, and eager to buy more.

Julie leaned forward to kiss him across the table, but before their lips met, she caught sight of a man hurrying toward her. The first thing she noticed was the silk ascot knotted at his throat, and in that instant, she knew without a doubt, the man rushing toward her was none other than her Frenchie.

"Frenchie!" she cried, springing to her feet and throwing her arms around him. She hadn't seen him since the day Mr. Rosere announced he was selling Philippe Leon, the day she'd bolted without even saying good-bye. Yet here he was, coming toward her, as charming as ever. His eyes lit up as he walked closer, his familiar smoky breath surrounding her as he pulled her into a tight embrace, holding her close as if not a single moment had passed between them.

Davie sat perfectly still, the name echoing in his ears. Frenchie. His mind flew back to childhood, his father's office at Phillipe Leon, the warm buttery croissants waiting for him whenever his mother brought him to visit. He couldn't move. He couldn't speak. How many Frenchies could there possibly be that work on Seventh Avenue?

Overjoyed, Frenchie slid into the booth beside Julie, chatting away, not even looking across the table. Julie, beaming, reached to stop him, ready to make introductions. Frenchie turned his head, his eyes landing on Davie. A look of pure shock crossed his face as he saw the young man sitting across from him.

"Junior?" he whispered, then louder, his voice breaking. "Junior, is that you?"

For a split second, Davie was back there—Frenchie holding him up in the air, playing rocket ship when he was a little boy, came flooding back to him. But just as quickly, the warmth gave way to panic. He felt like a rabbit caught in a trap, nowhere to run, no hole to dive into.

Julie sat stunned. Davie stared at her, the name Junior crashing into the middle of their table like a stone through glass. Her eyes darted between them, searching for answers. "How do you know Frenchie?" she asked, her voice edged with suspicion.

And then, almost in unison, both she and Davie turned to each other, their voices stumbling over the same question,

"How do you know Frenchie?"

For a minute, they just stared at each other, Julie blinking, Davie's mouth half open, like the world had tilted sideways. None of it made sense.

Frenchie broke the silence, his grin wide, his eyes locking on Davie. "Junior, Juleee was my number one fitting model at Phillipe Leon he said proudly. "The best!"

"What?" Davie stammered, shaking his head. "Julie, you? Frenchie?" He glanced between them, his voice rising. "This doesn't make any sense."

Frenchie laughed, waving a hand. "Those were the good old days," he said fondly, reminiscing about fittings, long days, and the crazy deadlines that needed to be met. Unaware of the tension at the table, he hugged them both goodbye, then rushed out into the street, a brown paper bag swinging in his hand.

Davie leaned forward, his voice low. "Julie… I know I'm not losing my mind. You never mentioned working for anyone but Gérard Jeans. Seton Hall to Gérard Jeans, that's what you told me. So why the missing pieces?"

Julie steadied herself, drawing in a breath. "Because I never tell anyone I worked for David Rosere, who I guess is your father, right?" She gave a queasy smile. "Let's just say I didn't exactly leave on the best of terms. My grand entrance into his office the day he announced he was closing Philippe Leon knocked him back against the wall, and the portrait of the horse came crashing down to the floor." She gave a small weary sigh, "I was even given a nickname from it, 'The Portrait Crasher.' That was my goodbye."

"Still trying to absorb it all, Julie shook her head. 'So your last name isn't Rose?" she asked, her voice catching. "It's really Rosére? Davie Rosere?"

The name felt unfamiliar as she said it out loud, heavier somehow, as if it carried a history she had never been meant to know. For a moment, she just stared at him, her thoughts spinning, trying to make sense of what it all meant for him, for her, for everything they thought they understood. Her head began to ache; under the weight of it all.

Davie watched her carefully, concerned that this would all be too much for her to deal with. The image of Julie, standing her ground while the portrait of Lancelot and his family shattered around them, was almost too much to imagine.

But then, to Davie's relief, Julie's voice softened, her eyes searching for his. "So… do I call you Junior? Or do you still prefer Davie?"

A faint smile tugged at his lips as he shook his head. "Jules, I love and adore you."

Just then, the waitress stepped over with two cream sodas balanced on her tray. And as she set them down, Julie looked over to find Davie on one knee, holding out an onion ring as a makeshift engagement ring.

"Will you marry me, Julie Glass, and make me the happiest man in this crazy, upside-down world?" he asked, his voice steady but his eyes full of hope.

"Of course, yes, yes, yes… of course!" she cried, laughter and tears spilling over as the restaurant seemed to disappear around them

— 40 —

The Rosere's sat together on the back veranda, enjoying their favorite cocktails, trying to come up with a plan to extend the olive branch to Junior.

The sun was sinking low over the expansive green meadow, casting a golden glow across the gardens now bursting in full bloom. It was the kind of evening that gave the soul hope that life could start over, that old wounds could heal, and families might be whole again.

She turned to him, her voice steady. "Leave this to me, David Rosere. Promise me you are going to leave this for me to fix."

She woke the next morning, dressed quickly, and had a small bite of breakfast before asking for the car to be brought around. This time, she wanted to drive herself into the city. The open road stretched ahead, and for once, she felt she was steering more than just the car; she was taking hold of her life again.

At noon, she was meeting Davie at the SoHo gallery. She knew he would feel comfortable there, and she wanted the setting to soften what she had to say about bringing everyone together. It had gone on far too long.

When she arrived, he was standing at the front of the gallery, studying Kenji Tanaka's newest painting. For a moment, she lingered at the entrance, watching him. Her baby boy. How she had missed him. Not a day passed without worrying about him. Silvia, her psychic, had reassured her time and again that he was fine, urging her not to imagine the worst. But how could she not? The visions kept coming, her son stranded on some lonely roadside, in need of her help.

So many nights she had jolted awake, her body drenched in a cold sweat, screaming into the dark, "I'm here, sweetheart, I'm here." David would stir beside her, asking what the dream was about. She would smile it away, blaming it on too many glasses of champagne.

But now, here he was. Standing before her. Back in her life. Her son had become a successful New York artist without any help from anyone, earning his place in the art world with nothing but talent and determination. She was so proud of him, prouder than words could ever say. And she vowed, silently and fiercely, that this time she would make sure he never left again.

"Come," he said to his mother with quiet pride. "Let me show you a couple of my new paintings that were just installed."

He led her toward the canvases, standing tall as he gestured to his latest work. It felt so nice to have his mother back; the comfort of her around him still steadied him.

"Oh, Davie," she breathed, her eyes sweeping over the canvases. "They're absolutely wonderful, darling."

She loved his work. It was abstract, yet each canvas hinted at shapes you could decipher if you looked long enough. His use of color was bold, almost daring, and it left her feeling strangely invigorated.

Then she heard it, his stomach growling. The familiar sound made her smile; how many times had she heard that same rumble when he was a boy, forever hungry, forever reaching for another snack?

                            – – – B A R B A R A A. D A V I S

"Still eating every two hours," she teased warmly.

"Some things never change, Mom." He grinned. "How about I treat you to lunch today? Besides, you're not going to believe the story I have to tell you."

Crossing the street together, they entered the little restaurant where she had first met him, weeks ago.

Inside, Barbara reached across the table to cover his hand. Davie leaned forward, his eyes bright with excitement. "Mom, I have to tell you something." He told her about the chance meeting with Frenchie at Lou Siegel's, how their two worlds had overlapped. How Julie had once worked for Philippe Leon, how, the day she stormed out, the portrait of Lancelot came crashing down.

"She even had a nickname for it..." Davie paused, searching his memory as he tried to remember. "It was... um— I can't remember, but anyway."

Barbara knew before he finished the sentence.

For a split second, the room felt like it was spinning. The clink of silverware, the low hum of voices around them, all of it faded as the pieces slid into place with sickening clarity. Julie, Davie's Julie, not just the woman now working for her husband's fiercest rival, was the same Julie, who had once walked out, slamming the door behind her. Davie's Julie was the Portrait Crasher. She felt a sudden lightness in her chest, as if the air had thinned. She pressed her fingers more firmly against Davie's hand, grounding herself, willing the moment to pass without showing on her face.

"Yes," Barbara said quietly, forcing her voice not to shake. "I think I remember your father telling me the story."

He looked up, then back at her, hardly able to contain himself. "She said yes, Mom"

"Yes to what, dear?"Barbara asked, her brows lifting.

"Yes... to marry me. We're going to get married."

For a moment, Barbara simply stared at him. Then she grabbed his hand again, shaking it up and down on the table, her throat tightening as she fought back tears of happiness.

Barbara caught the waiter's eye and lifted her hand. "Champagne, "your best. We're toasting the future groom."

When the glasses arrived, she raised hers. "To my darling son, who has always followed his own path, with courage and with passion. May this next chapter bring you everything you deserve.

They clinked glasses, the bubbles tickled her nose. Barbara let the warmth of the moment linger for a few moments before her expression softened, more serious now. She set her glass down and leaned closer, her eyes looking straight at him.

"Davie, please help me with this," she began softly. "Your father is looking for a way back into your life."

She spoke of second chances and do-overs, of fathers and forgiveness, but one truth remained: the woman her son loved had once brought a portrait crashing down—and that mattered.

— 41 —

The brothers were still reeling from Carol's abrupt departure. Jérôme, Daniel, Bernard, and Sami couldn't agree on whether to bring in someone new to replace her or to divide her responsibilities between Barry, Toni, Julie, and the sales team.

Jérôme leaned back in his chair, arms crossed. "We can divide her responsibilities. Barry can handle the numbers, and Julie, well, Julie's sharp enough to pick up the rest." His tone softened almost immediately when he said her name. Daniel noticed, though he said nothing, filing the moment away in the back of his mind.

Bernard shook his head. "That's patchwork. Carol held everything together. Splitting her job three ways will only create chaos. We need Barry to concentrate on running the company, not clients."

Sami, quiet until now, exhaled slowly. "Maybe. But bringing in someone new? That takes time and trust. Do we even have that kind of time?"

The room fell silent for a moment, the weight of Carol's absence pressing down on all of them.

Jérôme was the first to break it. He leaned forward, his voice measured but firm. "We can't afford to stall. The business doesn't pause for us to figure this out. Bernard's right, Carol kept everything moving. But Sami's right, too; we don't have time to search for another Carol. There isn't one." He tapped the table lightly. "So we decide now— do we spread the load or gamble on finding someone new?"

The vote was three to one to spread the workload between Barry, Julie, and the sales team, with Daniel and Sami also adding to the load. Jérôme buzzed the receptionist to set up a meeting with Barry, Toni, and Julie to announce the changes, but Toni and Julie were out to lunch, so the meeting was scheduled for two o'clock that afternoon.

It had been Toni's idea to get out of the office instead of ordering in, which they usually did to save time. There was always so much going on that you had to be there just to keep up. So they slipped out and walked up 39th Street to The Birdcage at Lord & Taylor.

Julie looped her arm through Toni's as they headed inside, smiling at the memory of their countless afternoons there. "Remember when you couldn't believe I didn't have a gynecologist?" Julie laughed.

"My, how things have changed," Toni teased, nudging her. "Almost-married lady."

Julie giggled, but her smile faded as she remembered the seriousness of what she needed to share. She had to talk to Toni, had to tell her the truth about Davie, about who he really was. After her conversation with her father last night, she knew there was no avoiding it. He had been firm—the brothers needed to know as well. After all, he had said, she was about to marry the son of their number-one business rival.

They slid into a corner booth, the waitress recognized them immediately and brought over their usual two iced teas with lemon. Toni stirred her iced tea with a straw, glancing up at Julie. "You've got that look," she said. Spill it."

Julie hesitated, twisting her napkin in her lap. "Toni, there's something I have to tell you. It's about Davie."

Toni leaned in, curiosity written across her face. "What about him? Don't tell me the almost-married lady has cold feet already."

Julie shook her head quickly. "No, it's not that. It's who he is. Who his family is, Toni." There was no easy way to say it, so she took a gulp of iced tea and blurted out, "Davie, my Davie, is David Rosere's son."

Toni looked up at her, eyes wide. "What? Did I hear you right, Julie? Your fiancé is the son of the man who owns Gordon Gabriel Jeans? You've got to be kidding me!" She leaned back, still stunned. "When did he tell you? And why didn't he tell you right away, knowing who you work for?"

Julie sighed. "You know him, he never pays attention to what's happening in the world. Never picks up a newspaper, never watches the news. He thought his father still ran Philippe Leon until a few days ago. I had to fill him in on the denim wars, the day I stormed out and quit, the portrait of Lancelot crashing to the floor, and the look in his father's eyes as I slammed the door and left."

Julie's hands tightened around her glass. "From day one, Davie told me there were certain things he didn't want to talk about. Well… this is what he meant. He had a huge fight with his father and took off to Europe. He only came back to New York two years ago. Then he met me, and the rest, you already know."

She lowered her voice, leaning closer to Toni. "It all came out because of Frenchie," Julie exclaimed.

"Our Frenchie," asked Toni, "Frenchie from Phillipe Leon?"

"The very one Toni, can you imagine?" We were having lunch at Lou Siegel's when he suddenly came running over to say hello. I turned to introduce him to Davie, and for a second, I honestly thought Davie had food poisoning; he was so pale and looked like he was going to throw up. And then, Frenchie was hugging him too, hugging Davie, calling him 'Junior'—our minds were absolutely blown.

"At first, it almost felt funny, like some surreal mix-up. But then the weight of it hit us all at once. Everything came together at that moment because of Frenchie. Davie had known him from visits to Philippe Leon when he was a kid, and when we pieced it together, we were both in total shock. Imagine Toni, what an amazingly small world it turned out to be."

Toni's lips parted, but no words came out. When she finally found her voice, she asked, barely above a whisper, "So, David Rosere is your future father-in-law? You've got to be kidding me, Julie. Honestly, who on earth would believe that story? You can't make this stuff up. This is better than my soap opera!"

Julie reached across the table, her voice soft but urgent. "So, dear friend… tell me, what am I supposed to do next?"

— — — — —

On their way back to the office, they paused on Seventh Avenue to watch the Popemobile roll slowly past, carrying Pope John Paul on his visit to America. The streets were lined up shoulder to shoulder. Garment workers leaned from windows tossing paper confetti, turning the moment into a kind of religious ticker-tape parade.

Julie's heart raced when the vehicle passed close enough that she swore she could almost touch it. "God bless you, Pope John Paul!" she shouted over the roar of the crowd. She longed to follow the motorcade to St. Patrick's Cathedral and hear him speak, but she knew they were already late. With one last glance at the sea of waving hands, she pulled at Toni's arm, and the two of them hurried back toward the showroom as the sounds of the city swallowed up the cheers behind them.

By the time they pushed open the glass doors, Jérôme's voice was already booming from his office—"Meeting at two o'clock!"

On his desk, the latest selling reports had just arrived, and nothing pleased Jérôme more than seeing how well the line was selling. Reorders were coming in by the hour, the phones ringing nonstop. The buyers were

   — — — B A R B A R A A. D A V I S

in good spirits too; their own performance was measured by the success of sales, and for the moment, everything pointed in the right direction.

The brothers had finally been accepted as key players on Seventh Avenue. They worked hard and played just as hard—especially Sami. Bernard and Daniel walked into Jérôme's office, worry written all over their faces.

Daniel closed the door behind them before speaking.

"I'm really worried about Sami," he said quietly. "He doesn't know when to stop. Too many parties, out every night, he looks like hell, Jérôme."

"It's that bitch Kelly Laurent," exclaimed Bernard. "She's nothing but trouble."

Sami had been dating Kelly Laurent, a rising movie star who had just broken through Hollywood's inner circles and landed a role in the next big blockbuster. He loved the lifestyle, thrived on the attention, and with Kelly on his arm, the doors of every exclusive party seemed to swing open. But to keep up with it all, he started to love something else too, the little white lines that seemed to appear everywhere he went with her. He loved the way it made him feel, how all his insecurities seemed to vanish the moment it hit.

I'm in control, he kept telling himself. *No problem.*

Kelly, though, was a full-blown addict. She couldn't get through the day without a few lines. For her, it started the moment she woke up; it was the sugar to her coffee, as natural and necessary as breathing.

Sami strolled into Jérôme's office, his grin wide and uneasy. Daniel noticed immediately that his pupils were blown wide open, impossible to miss.

"Hi, brothers," Sami said brightly, teetering on the edge of nervous laughter. "What's going on?"

The brothers glanced at one another, their eyes darting back and forth like some silent game of Whac-A-Mole. Each look carried the same unspoken question—What's up with Sami? The worry was written across all their faces, but no one wanted to be the first to say it out loud. Not now. Jérôme broke the silence by asking the receptionist to buzz Barry, Toni, and Julie to meet in the conference room at 2:00 p.m.

Julie felt weak as she pulled out a chair and sat down next to Toni. She had always looked forward to the meetings held in this room and was so grateful to have a seat at the table, but not today. She loved working for these crazy brothers and respected them deeply. Especially Jérôme. She idolized him. Brilliant, driven, with boyish good looks, those kind green eyes, the dimples, and that irresistible French accent. He was the kind of man who could make a woman forget her own name.

She glanced around the table at the others as they waited for Barry to finish his phone call. Daniel. Sami. Bernard. How would they take the news? How would they react when she told them she was about to marry the son of the man who had once tried to destroy them?

Her stomach churned, queasy, and even the faint taste of her own breath made it worse. Toni had been firm—"Tell them everything from the beginning. You have no choice, Julie. You didn't know, and now you do. They need to hear it straight from you."

Julie knew she had to speak before the brothers shared anything of their own. Slowly, almost painfully, she raised her hand. "Excuse me," she said, her voice unsteady. "I would like to say something."

Toni glanced her way and gave an encouraging nod. Barry nudged his wife under the table, signaling his confusion. Jérôme looked up, surprised, but there was warmth in his eyes as he regarded Julie, unaccustomed to seeing her speak up like this.

"I want to start by saying I have always felt so lucky to have a voice in this room," Julie began. "I am so proud to be part of Gérard Jeans, and I hope what I have to share won't change that." Julie drew a shaky breath.

"Well… first, the good. I'm engaged."

For a moment, the room came alive. All the brothers, except Jérôme, broke into smiles, clapping, voices overlapping in excitement. They

   - - - B A R B A R A A. D A V I S

seemed ecstatic for her.

Julie laughed nervously and lifted her hand as if to show it off, then quickly added, "I don't have the ring yet, but it's coming."

Jérôme felt as if he had been gut-punched, the air knocked from his chest. Still, he forced a smile that felt brittle, ready to crack at any moment. "Congratulations," he managed, the word sounding empty even to his own ears.

Then her voice softened. "And now...."

With her hands trembling, she told them everything, every detail of her relationship with Davie. She paused before finishing, her throat tightening. "I had no idea he was David Rosere's son, and he had no idea I worked for his father at Philippe Leon. And that brings us to today. I only hope my story does not end here."

For a brief moment, Jérôme flashed back to the Christmas Ball.

Something about the way David Rosere had spoken with Julie that night had left him questioning whether she was being entirely honest. But he shook the thought away. After all, this was Julie, and Carol had already filled him in on her abrupt exit from Phillipe Leon.

Before anyone could respond, Sami shot to his feet, screaming in French, "Salope!" His face twisted, his hands clawing at his hair. "You traitor, you fucking traitor! How dare you spy on us? How dare you betray us?"

The two lines of cocaine had finally hit. Daniel lunged for his brother's arm, but the cocaine gave Sami superhuman strength. He tore free and hurled himself across the table toward Julie.

"Enough!" Jérôme's voice thundered.

"Bernard, grab him!" Daniel shouted. But Sami whirled, his rage blinding, and with all his strength, he swung at Daniel. His fist connected, sending his brother crashing to the floor, blood pouring from his nose.

Barry, Toni, and Julie sat frozen in their chairs as chaos erupted. It took all three brothers to drag Sami out of the room, his French curses echoing down the hall.

"Holy shit," Toni whispered, staring at her husband in disbelief. "What the fuck was that?"

Julie broke down, tears spilling, tears of fear, of anger. It wasn't her fault. Nothing had been done on purpose. What hurt the most was how quickly the trust she thought she earned could disappear in a single moment.

Barry quickly grabbed the two women, wrapping protective arms around them, and rushed them into his office.

Jérôme screamed over Sami's shouting, his voice cracking with urgency. "Bernard, Daniel, take him home! Get him something to eat and don't leave his side. I'll call you later. And don't let him run away, do you hear me?"

When the door finally slammed behind them, Jérôme collapsed into his chair, his mind still unable to comprehend what he had just witnessed with his own eyes. The thought of Julie being engaged, Sami acting like a wild man, so out of control, so unlike the brother he knew and loved, it was all out of balance. Shouts, the crash of Daniel hitting the floor replayed in his mind, pieces colliding too fast to hold still. He pressed his palms to his temples, trying to steady himself, but the weight of it all only bore down harder. For once, he didn't know what to do, and that terrified him.

But he couldn't stay stuck. Not now. He drew in a long breath, forcing his hands down flat on the desk as if to balance himself. His mind landed on a news story he had seen just last week, the Betty Ford Center in Rancho Mirage. A place for people like Sami. A lifeline.

Jérôme reached for the phone, then stopped, his hand hovering above it. If he made this call, there was no going back. No more excuses, no more pretending his youngest brother just needed to "slow down." This would mean admitting the truth, that Sami was in trouble, deep trouble. He closed his eyes, exhaled, and lifted the receiver. His voice was shaking as he spoke. "Operator, get me the number for the Betty Ford Center in

Rancho Mirage, California, please."

Within an hour, a counselor was on the line with Sami on his home phone, asking to schedule his intake, background information, medical history, substance use details, and, of course, insurance arrangements.

Sami kept screaming into the receiver, "I'm not going!" until the poor woman on the other end could barely make out a word. Finally, Bernard stepped in, filling in the missing details that Sami refused to provide.

Back in his office, Jérôme booked the flights. Barry, Toni, and Julie waited anxiously for word from him, but instead it was his assistant who appeared at the door. Her tone was careful, almost apologetic. "Maybe it's best if you all go home tonight," she said. "Jérôme would like to meet again tomorrow morning."

Gerard had made the arrangements. The three brothers would be leaving for California soon. And with them, the unspoken fear that Sami might not be coming back.

— 42 —

It **was a short walk** home for Jérôme, just the way he had planned it. When he had first met with his real estate agent, he had been clear—I need to be no more than a ten-minute walk from the office. It was the first time Jérôme had been without his brothers since arriving in New York over two years ago. He never thought he would miss those early days, days filled with nervous energy and the uncertainty of what might happen next.

They had been through so much together, weathering the ups and downs this insane business had thrown at them. And they had made it. Against all odds, they were now a household name. Their slogan, "I'm a Gérard Girl… How about you?" was splashed across billboards from coast to coast, even lighting up Times Square. They were so proud of what they had built, of how far they had come.

The hallway outside his apartment seemed endless, each step heavier than the last. By the time Jérôme reached his door, his shoulders sagged beneath the strain of the day. The key slipped once, twice, before he managed to unlock it.

Inside, the silence struck him first. No phones ringing, no arguments, just the quiet stillness of the walls. He turned on the light, its glow harsh against the darkness, and moved toward the bar like a boxer defeated in the ring, shoulders heavy, steps unsteady. The crystal decanter that Sami had bought him sat on the bar, reminding him of happier times. He reached for it, his hand trembling, and poured himself a large glass of Cognac. Jérôme stared at it for a long moment before taking a large swallow; the burn he felt was a poor match for the ache inside him.

He slowly made his way to the leather sofa and leaned back, closing his eyes. His thoughts drifted back home to Roubaix, to a time when they were all so young and life was so much simpler. As the oldest, he had always been the one in charge of his brothers. With both parents working long hours at the textile mill, responsibility had fallen to him. He liked being the one they counted on, the one they adored. It had never felt like a burden. And up until this afternoon, he had been so proud of the brother he had always tried to be for them. But now, that pride was gone.

"I failed you, my brother," Jérôme cried, his voice echoing against the walls of his empty apartment. "I'm so sorry, Sami. I'm so, so sorry." Sami. Sami, Sami… what have you done?"

The next morning, Jérôme arrived at the office early. He had always loved mornings. Even as a boy, he was the first one awake in his family's home. His mother would find him curled up in front of the white enamel gas range, waiting for her to start breakfast. The kitchen was always alive with comforting smells, warm milk, and freshly baked bread. A red straw basket, her favorite that she had bought from the market years ago, was always filled with golden baguettes. He loved dipping a slice, thick with butter, into a steaming bowl of café au lait or hot chocolate. Those mornings were simple, but to Jérôme, they were perfect.

Now, as he stepped into the office, the showroom was still, the air heavy with what he knew was coming. His footsteps echoed faintly as he found himself drifting toward Julie's office, the weight of his decision pressing harder with each step.

   - - - B A R B A R A A. D A V I S

He pushed open the door and slipped inside. The room felt different without her there. Slowly, Jérôme lowered himself into her chair. The leather was cool at first, but then he caught it, the faint trace of her perfume. He breathed it in, closed his eyes, and in that moment admitted the truth he had been denying.

From the first day he had met her, something about Julie had moved him. She had unsettled him, challenged him, made him feel alive in a way he hadn't expected. And now she was walking toward another man, toward Davie Rose, and if he stayed silent, she would never know.

Two truths pressed against him, demanding action. The first—he needed her to stay with the company. The second—before she walked down the aisle, he had to tell her how he truly felt.

He had a decision to make. Bernard and Daniel had told him it was his call about Julie. She had been one of the first hires after Barry and Toni, and from the beginning, her work ethic impressed him. He remembered once telling Bernard, half-joking, "That girl reminds me of me." She was sharp, reliable, and her buyers loved her.

Julie was surprised to see Jérôme waiting in her office, but she assumed he was just dropping off yesterday's sales reports. "Good morning, Jérôme," but she noticed right away how exhausted he looked. Wanting to ask about Sami but unsure how, she held back, giving him space to speak first.

"I'm so very sorry about yesterday, Julie," Jérôme began, his voice low. "My brother has some serious problems he's working through. He will be out of the office for a few months, but I know when he gets back, he will want nothing more than to tell you how sorry he is. And I'm sorry too, Julie. Please… forgive us." For a moment, Jérôme tried to picture the company without her, but what cut deeper was trying to imagine his life without her.

Julie stepped into the middle of the office, and Jérôme walked toward her. When she drew closer, he asked softly, "Close the door, please."

The building was still, the workday not yet begun, leaving them alone in the silence. For a moment, he just stood there, the quiet stretching between them. This was his chance, and he wasn't going to waste it. Jérôme didn't circle around what needed to be said.

"Julie, I want you to stay with the company. I trust you completely, and I would be so pleased if you continued with us. We've decided to replace Carol's position by dividing the responsibilities between Barry, Toni, you, Daniel, and it was going to be Sami, but now Bernard. You belong here, with us."

He paused, then looked deep into her eyes. Julie felt her cheeks begin to feel warm. Why does he make me feel this way? Her stomach knotted as his gaze held hers, as if searching for something more.

"There's something else I need you to know," he continued, his voice lower now, steadier. "Before you make your decision to stay with the company."

Julie looked up at him, confused. Her mouth was dry, her body leaning toward him almost against her will.

"I need you to know that I have fallen in love with you, Julie. I know you're engaged, and I'm sorry, the timing is not right for this, but I couldn't keep it to myself any longer. What I really need to ask is this." He hesitated, his voice breaking, "Is there a chance?"

She looked across at his perfect face, those sincere, beautiful eyes. For a long moment, the words stuck in her throat. Why am I hesitating? Why is this so hard to say? The silence surprised even her, as if her own heart was testing her before she spoke. Finally, in a voice soft but steady, she said, "I will miss you, Jérôme. I will miss you all, but especially you. I want you to know that I have learned so much from you—to never give up on your dream, to fight even when you are battling giants, to believe in yourself no matter what people say."

Her eyes lingered on his, filled with conflict. "I will always remember you with fondness… and maybe even with love… And who knows,

Jérôme, maybe this isn't goodbye forever. I'm so confused right now." She stepped closer, closing the space between them, and pressed a gentle kiss to his cheek. For a fleeting moment, Jérôme closed his eyes, holding on to the warmth of it, as if he could keep it with him.

Before she turned to go, she slipped her hand into his and leaned close, her whisper brushing his ear. "I think Jérôme, you will always be my what if." Then she turned, walked to the door, and left. She didn't look back. If she had, she knew she might never leave.

His instinct was to run after her, to stop her, but instead he gripped the arms of her office chair and sat motionless, watching the woman he loved slip out of his life.

Julie leaned against the elevator wall, barely able to process what had just happened. The ding of the bell as it passed each floor on the way down to the lobby became her only comfort, a sound to hold on to when her thoughts were in a state of total confusion.

The doorman glanced at her with concern when the doors opened, but he kept his eyes forward, his silence almost a kindness. Julie stood in the lobby, alone, not sure where to go next. She didn't want to go home. Davie might be there, and she couldn't bear to explain any of this, not now. Not to anyone. Finally, gathering what little strength she had, she pushed through the revolving glass doors and out onto the sidewalk.

The street was crowded, people rushing past, wrapped up in their own challenges and problems. No one noticed her. No one saw the emptiness in her eyes. She turned and walked toward 37th Street, to Holy Innocents Church. She had prayed there before, right after she had slammed the door behind her at Philippe Leon and walked away from everything she thought she once wanted. That day, she had prayed the Gérard brothers would take a chance on her.

Now, inside the quiet church, Julie lit a candle in front of the altar. It was her way of telling her mother she was here, still praying, still holding on. She had started the candle ritual that first Sunday after her mother passed, right before Mass began, as if to say, I'm here, Mom. Please be here too.

She knelt, hands tightly pressed together, whispering to her mother, to Mother Mary, Mother Seton, and Mother Teresa, every mother she could think of. *Please, help me,* she begged. *Please, help me find my way.* Then she bowed her head deeper, her voice breaking as she prayed to God— *make me love only Davie, help me forget about Jérôme, and please, please God, help me find a job.*

Her mind raced as she tried to imagine what she could possibly tell Davie. The truth was not an option. She would tell him that the brothers asked her to leave because David Rosere was to be her future father-in-law. But was he? The thought hit like ice in her veins as she imagined it, David Rosere, her father-in-law. The very idea gave her a splitting headache. Was this the family she wanted to marry into? She couldn't let everything unravel.

She would have to find another way. The only option was the lie that the brothers had asked her to leave because of David Rosere. A lie that might be strong enough to hold her world together, at least for now. As she sat praying, Jérôme's face slipped into her thoughts unwanted, yet undeniably there. His steadiness, the quiet strength in his voice, the way his eyes softened when he looked at her. It was wrong, she told herself, impossible. And yet the thought lingered. She bit her lip until it hurt, anxiety twisting deeper inside her.

Julie, she told herself, *maybe Davie is right. Maybe I do need to talk to someone.* Her heart pounded as the words echoed in her mind. *I need help.*

— 43 —

He wasn't happy. David paced back and forth in his office, furious at the numbers spread across his desk from J. Walter Thompson. The latest Gordon Gabriel advertising campaign had performed at barely half of what Riley Spencer's campaign had pulled in. With a meeting scheduled with Gordon later that afternoon, David had called in his son and son-in-law to discuss the dismal results.

"What's going on here, boys?" he demanded. "The way forward in this business is to increase the public's awareness of the brand. These numbers are a disaster. And who the hell is this model, anyway?"

He barked toward the door. "Debbie! Get Bernice Greyson from WWD on the phone for me now!" Within minutes, the phone rang. David snatched it up. "Yes, David," Bernice replied smoothly. "How can I help you?"

"Question," David shot back. "What do you think of our newest model, Casey… what's her name?" He looked at his son-in-law for help.

"Casey Jordan," Justin snapped.

"Jordan," David repeated into the receiver.

There was a pause, long enough to sting. Finally, Bernice answered. "I don't think anything, David."

David huffed. "What the hell does that mean, Bernice? I want your honest opinion."

Her voice was sharp. "Well, it's a little late for that now, don't you think? Perhaps we could have discussed this before you spent hundreds of thousands of dollars on a pale-faced, anemic excuse for a model. Sorry, David." And with that, she hung up.

Alan shifted uncomfortably in his chair, eager to change the subject. "Do we have the sales reports back from the New York majors?" he asked his father. "I didn't see them on my desk this morning."

"Not yet," David snapped, his temper still hot from the newest ad's poor performance. He slammed a hand onto the desk. "And I want to sign off on the next model we hire for the next campaign. Obviously, you two idiots don't know how to pick them. She's one and done, make sure her contract is terminated, God damn it."

Alan swallowed hard, exchanging a glance with Justin. Justin shifted in his chair, clearly upset but wise enough not to argue. Alan nodded stiffly, masking his frustration, both men knowing better than to push back when David was in this mood.

– – – – –

This was not going to be a fun conversation, Alan thought to himself as he pulled out a chair for Casey to sit down.

"Can we order champagne for lunch, honey?" Casey asked, her eyes bright with mischief. She was loving the life Alan had created for her, a tiny studio in Chelsea and a credit card with no limit.

For more than eight months now, they had been sneaking late-night dinners and stolen weekends away. She had even tagged along on a few business trips, though she was never allowed to leave the hotel room. Alan always made up for it when he returned, showering her with gifts, promises, and attention. Casey knew perfectly well he was married. She just didn't care. She was the Gordon Gabriel Girl, the face of the brand, and she was reveling in every delicious, wonderful minute of it.

"When's my next photo shoot, love?" Casey asked, her eyes wide with expectation.

Alan studied her for a moment. To him, she was the most beautiful girl he had ever seen. He couldn't understand why the campaign numbers weren't stronger, why the world didn't see her through the same lens he did.

"Casey, sweetheart," he began carefully. "Yes?" she leaned in, smiling.

"The numbers came out this morning and... sweetie, they're not great."

Her smile vanished. "What do you mean?" she shot back, surprised. "You told me I was going to blow Riley's numbers out of the water."

"Yes, yes, I did say that. That's what I honestly thought. But unfortunately, the numbers don't lie. And at our breakfast meeting this morning... my father, well, he decided to terminate your contract." He reached for her hand quickly. "But that doesn't change anything. In fact, it changes nothing between us."

She jerked her hand away, staring at him as if he had grown two heads. "Are you crazy? That changes everything about us!" She shoved her chair back so hard it screeched against the floor. Heads turned from nearby tables, but Casey didn't care.

"You promised me, Alan!" she hissed, her voice rising. "You told me I was the one, that I would be bigger than Riley. Do you have any idea what this campaign meant to me?" "It meant everything."

Alan held up his hands, desperate to calm her. "Casey, listen, listen sweetheart, this doesn't have to change us, we're still us."

"Doesn't change us?" she cut him off, laughter sharp and bitter. "It changes everything! Do you think I want to sneak around in a Chelsea studio while you play house in Westchester with your wife F-R-A-N-C-I-S? Without this contract, without the spotlight, I'm nothing! And you," she jabbed a finger into his chest, "you lied to me."

Alan's face drained of color. He opened his mouth, but no words came. Casey grabbed her purse, slung it over her shoulder, and stormed out, leaving him alone at the table, staring at the untouched champagne glasses between them.

Just a few feet away, James Clive kept his head low, half-hidden behind a menu at the table directly behind the not-so-lovey-dovey couple. He had heard every word that came out of the mouth of the bitchy little model named Casey.

"Good fucking riddance," he muttered to his partner, William. "I won't have to suffer through another disastrous photo shoot with that husband stealer."

The two men clinked their glasses in a quiet, bitter toast as Alan slipped out of the restaurant, looking like a little boy who had just struck out with the bases loaded.

— 44 —

Mach 2 speed—it didn't matter how many times it was explained to Astrid Peyton, it simply wasn't in her wheelhouse. All she knew was that it took only three and a half hours for the Concorde to fly from JFK to Paris, and for that she was forever thankful. She was finally back to her old travel schedule since Carol had come aboard, and she couldn't have been more pleased. Carol was professional, sharp, and worked at a pace that astounded Astrid. Cocoon by Astrid Peyton had exceeded even her own expectations, and with Carol in charge, she could finally watch from the sidelines, free to return to the life she had missed so much while she built her brand.

The children's line was a runaway success, adding an extra tier to her freestanding boutiques and quickly becoming Bergdorf Goodman's number one infant line. Each purchase came with a butterfly notecard tucked inside for gift-giving, a delicate touch that customers loved.

Astrid loved flying the Concorde; it was sleek, glamorous, and filled with people who thought they belonged there. The difference was that Astrid knew she did. She always insisted that her travel agent book her in the first ten rows. The agent had explained more than once that the plane didn't have an official first-class section, but old habits were hard to break. The rear cabins might have been quieter and less crowded, but Astrid had no interest in compromise.

She loved the luxury and the near-royal attention she received from the flight attendants—pampering that bordered on excessive. The Concorde was the ultimate status symbol of the champagne-drinking elite, and Astrid felt perfectly in her element as the jet sliced through the sky toward JFK. Coming home had never looked or felt so good.

"Look at you, my dear…" Astrid's eyes sparkled as she took in Carol, now in her eighth month and, to her delight, showing only the smallest baby bump. "You look wonderful, darling. How are you feeling?"

Astrid's affection for Carol went far beyond the professional. She was the daughter Astrid had never had, and with Kenji by her side, it felt like life had handed her the family she once thought she would never know. Carol filled a void Astrid had carried for years, and in moments like this, she felt anything but alone.

She hugged Carol tightly, then bent to pat her belly, slipping into an exaggerated baby voice. "Auntie Astrid brought you back a little present, my precious angel."

Carol beamed, glowing in every sense. "Oh, Astrid, honestly, you didn't have to do that. You're spoiling this baby before he or she even arrives!" she laughed. "Come, let me show you the new designs that were just delivered. I think you're going to love them. And the new home fragrances arrived last week. Oh, and so did the new jean designs for your approval." Her excitement spilled out in a rush. "We tested the high-waisted, straight-leg cut in the Upper West Side shop, and it sold out in one weekend!"

Astrid chuckled, reaching for her bag as she hurried after her. "I'm coming, my dear… I'm coming," she said, trying to keep pace with Carol's infectious energy.

   - - - B A R B A R A A. D A V I S

Carol went over everything with Astrid. Three months was a long time to be away, and though they had spoken on the phone almost daily, it was comforting to have her back in the office.

"I wanted to ask what you thought about hiring a full-time sales associate, Astrid?" Carol said carefully. "Angela is wonderful, but she has so many responsibilities. When she's visiting the stores, she's gone all day, sometimes for two. Especially with the baby coming, I think I'm going to need more help."

"Whatever you need, Carol," Astrid replied. "Check with my attorney, Wesley, for the salary we can offer. Do you have someone in mind?"

"Yes," Carol said, a smile tugging at her lips. "And she will be perfect. We worked together at Gérard Jeans. Her name is Julie Glass, and Astrid, you are going to love her."

"Done!" said Astrid. "I'm going to excuse myself, darling. This jet lag is a bit much for me. I'll ring you tomorrow. Let's have lunch." And off she went.

— — — — —

That same morning Julie left Gérard Jeans, she called Carol from a phone booth after leaving the church. "I need a job, Carol," was the first thing she heard when she picked up the receiver.

"What happened, Julie? You loved working at Gérard Jeans. When I left, you were at the top of your game."

"I needed to leave, for personal reasons. Carol, can I meet you for dinner? I need to fill you in on a few things."

Carol had not reached out to Julie since she left Gérard Jeans. Although she had kept her friendship with the brothers, she felt it best to cut ties with everyone else. Still, she missed the old group, and when Julie called, it tugged at her memory and her heartstrings immediately.

"Well," Carol said, smiling into the receiver, "I have a little something to share with you, too, Julie Glass." She could hardly wait to show off her baby bump.

They met that night for dinner on the Upper East Side at Jackson Hole. Carol was craving a hamburger, and she loved the French fries there. Julie was already seated when she spotted Carol walking in, that unmistakable, beautiful smile lighting her face. Overcome with happiness, Julie jumped up to hug her, then froze as she felt something in the way.

She pulled back, eyes wide. "Nooo… Carol, you're going to have a baby?"

"Looks that way, my Julie!" Carol laughed.

They hugged again, laughing and glowing in the middle of the crowded restaurant. Over burgers and fries, Julie spilled out her story, careful to leave out the part about her feelings for Jérôme. Carol listened, stunned.

"Your Davie is Gordon Gabriel's Davie?" she said at last. "Hard to believe."

"I know, Carol," Julie kept repeating, shaking her head.

"Well then," Carol leaned forward, her smile growing again, "how would you like to work with me? Astrid will be back soon, and I know she's going to love you. There's no rival to worry about; Cocoon has no competition. It's a brand, not a label. I'll speak with her, and then it's up to you when you would like to start."

"The sooner the better," Julie shot back quickly. Carol laughed softly. "Well, some things never change, do they? And Julie…" Her voice warmed. "I missed you. I'm so happy to have you back with me."

— — — — —

Julie's first day was nothing short of magical. Carol had arranged a little office for her, complete with fresh flowers on her desk and a view of the park. "Amazing," Julie whispered as Carol showed her around. The space was exquisite—antique pieces mixed effortlessly with striking pieces of modern art. A bold painting by Andy Warhol of Astrid's butterflies hung in the marble foyer, greeting everyone who entered the office.

"It's certainly a step up from denim, wouldn't you agree, Julie?" Carol teased.

Julie nodded, though a pang of guilt flickered through her. She didn't want to feel as though she were mocking Jérôme. "This is certainly the life," Carol beamed.

"Astrid, I would like you to meet Julie Glass, my new sales associate, the one I told you about."

"Oh yes," Astrid said, looking up with a bright smile. "Lovely to meet you, my dear. You will be in very capable hands with Carol guiding your way." She gathered her things with practiced elegance. "Now, please excuse me. I am off to Palm Beach for a ladies' fundraiser luncheon at The Breakers tomorrow. You two beautiful girls behave. Bye for now."

Julie watched her go, struck by the effortless grace with which she seemed to glide across the room. Even the breathless way Astrid spoke impressed her—it made everything sound urgent, important, and somehow a little more glamorous. Astrid wasn't just the name on the label; she was the embodiment of the brand— polished and dazzling. Julie couldn't help but feel both admiration and curiosity about the woman who had built all of this.

Julie had been so completely absorbed in her first day at the new job, so intent on taking everything in, memorizing every detail, that she lost track of time altogether. The marble floors, the art on the walls, and the way the past and present lived side-by-side in the showroom all demanded her full attention. By the time she glanced at the clock, it was already past one.

"Where are you, my dear friend?" Toni laughed when Julie finally picked up the phone. "Have you forgotten about me already? This is supposed to be your congratulations on your new job lunch. Where are you?"

Julie groaned. "Toni, I'm so sorry. I got swept up. I'll be there in a few minutes, just order my usual for me, please." She slammed the office phone back onto its cradle, called out to Carol that she would be back in an hour, grabbed her bag, and rushed for the door.

Lunch with Toni at the Birdcage always felt like home to Julie. She loved all the memories the two of them had shared there, sitting across from each other over tea sandwiches and the best desserts in the city.

"It's hard to explain," Julie said, stirring her iced tea. "It's like working in a museum, but it's a showroom. Absolutely incredible." She couldn't stop gushing. She told Toni about the marble foyer, the Warhol on the wall, the antiques mixed with modern art, and how wonderful it was to see Carol again.

Then her eyes lit up. "And Astrid Peyton, oh my God, Toni, have you ever met her? I've never met anyone like her. She's from another world, yet she lives on the same earth as we do. Crazy wealthy, crazy talented. Honestly, I feel so out of my league there."

Toni leaned in, smiling at her friend's excitement. "Well, it sounds wonderful to me, Julie. And please tell Carol how happy I am that she's going to have a baby! Can you imagine how adorable that little bundle will be, with Carol and Kenji as the parents?"

They both laughed at the thought, then hugged each other tightly before heading off in different directions, for the first time, on their own separate paths.

— 45 —

Davie was so caught up with his new art installation at the gallery that he didn't notice the change in Julie's mood, at least not until dinner, when the warm glow of her brown eyes seemed dimmer than usual. "Jules, everything okay?" he asked, setting down his fork.

She drew in a breath. "I think we need to talk about the elephant in the room, Davie. We're getting married, and you have met my father, my sister, and my brother several times. But I only know your father from a very unfortunate and extremely awkward time. And I have met Justin and Alan professionally, but that's hardly the same as knowing them as family. Why aren't you talking to me about this? How do you think this is going to work?" Her voice wavered with frustration.

"Are you planning to just ignore the fact that this is about as close to impossible as it gets? Help me with this, please. I need you to talk about what you want to do about it, Davie. I'm not comfortable pretending everything is fine when it's not."

Davie leaned back, rubbing a hand over his jaw. "Jules… I don't know what you want me to say. I have spent years trying to get away from him, from all of that. Every time I think about going back there, about facing him, it's like a wall goes up. I'm not ignoring it, I just…" He broke off, shaking his head. "I don't know how to deal with it." He met her eyes, his voice softening. "The only thing I do know is that I love you. And I don't want him, or anyone else, to ruin what we have."

He hesitated, then added quietly, "You know I told you that I met with my mother, she told me he wants to apologize. I just don't know if I'm ready for that."

Julie set her glass of wine down, staring at it before lifting her gaze to his. Her voice was steady, but full of urgency. "It's time, Davie. I want it to be time. I want you to be ready."

Davie knew she was right and knew what had to be done. He sat motionless for what felt like forever to Julie. Finally, he picked up the phone and dialed, waiting for Robert Preston's familiar voice to answer at the other end.

"The Rosere residence, Robert Preston. May I help you?"

"Hi, Robert."

There was a pause, then the warm reply, "Master Davie, sir, how can I be of assistance?"

"Is my mother at home?"

"Yes, of course. Please hold on."

A moment later, her voice came through, full of affection. "Darling, is that you?"

"Yes, Mother, it's me."

Across the table, Julie sat stunned. Was Davie really doing this? Really following through instead of finding a way to avoid it? She knew how much this moment could cost him and how much it could change everything.

"I would like you to meet Julie," Davie said, his voice steady but firm. "And… I think it's time we talked about Dad. Is that okay?"

"Of course, Junior. You just tell me when and where, and I will be there. And please, darling, tell Julie I can't wait to meet her."

Julie felt relief and a spark of hope all tangled together inside her. For so long, she had begged Davie to face this moment, to stop pretending the past didn't exist. Now, at last, he had taken the first step. She reached for his hand across the table, her eyes searching his, hoping to see some peace there, but all she saw was fear.

– – – – –

It was Barbara's idea. After much thought, she called Junior and asked if they could meet with him first, just the family, and then bring Julie into the mix a little later.

"Where do you want to meet?" Davie asked cautiously.

"Would you like to come to the house? We can have dinner together." Barbara offered. "I'll have Veronica make all of your favorites."

Davie let out a long sigh, thinking of Julie. "When should I stop by, Mom?"

"Tomorrow evening," she said softly.

When Barbara hung up the phone, she hurried into David's study and happily announced, "Junior is coming to dinner tomorrow."

David sat up straight, his eyes happy with something close to hope as he looked lovingly at his wife. "Thank you, Babs. It's time."

Barbara had sent the car to pick up Davie, and now she waited by the front door, peering through the seeded glass for any sign of approaching headlights. She had been there nearly ten minutes, unable to sit still, pacing between the foyer and the front steps. Every sound from the driveway made her heart pound. Her hands kept tugging at her hair, though there was nothing to fix.

It had been so many years since he had come home, so many nights she had lain awake wondering if this moment would ever come. A part of her feared he might change his mind before the car turned in, but another part, a mother's part, clung to hope, to the image of her little boy, grown but still hers, finally stepping back into her arms.

Davie sat back as the car rolled up the long, winding driveway, his mind replaying what had happened the last time he was home. He blinked the vision away, forcing himself to stay hopeful about what he was about to face. He was doing this for Julie—that was the only reason he had agreed. His nerves were frayed as he stepped onto the front path and into his mother's waiting arms.

"Sweetheart, it's so good to have you home," Barbara whispered, holding him tightly.

Behind her, Robert Preston stood smiling warmly. "Hello, sir. May I take your coat?"

"I'm good, Robert, thank you."

And then he felt him before he saw him, the familiar weight of his father's presence. David Rosere walked toward him, those steel-blue eyes fixed on his, carrying years of regret and unspoken words.

For a moment, no one spoke. Father and son simply stood there, face to face, their silence saying everything—the years lost, the wounds still raw, and the possibility, however fragile, of something new beginning.

To Davie's surprise, his father broke down in tears. Stunned, he couldn't move. He had never seen his father cry before, and the sight unsettled him to his core.

"Hi, Dad," was all he managed to say.

"Junior…" David's voice cracked. "Please, come in. Look at you, my boy, you're a man."

And with that, he pulled his son into his arms and held him for a very long time. When Davie finally stepped back, he was shaken. His father, one of the strongest men he had ever known, suddenly looked older, vulnerable, even a little weak. It felt as if someone had replaced the man he once feared with a shadow of him.

"Dad… it's so good to see you," he whispered.

Barbara stood just in front of Robert Preston, the two silent specta-
tors, at what felt like the event of the season. They shared a smile as her
two boys made their way toward the dining room together. He was home
at last.

Dinner went better than anyone could have hoped. Veronica brought
out her famous macaroni pie, rotis, stewed chicken, homemade coleslaw,
and of course, her fiery hot pepper sauce sprinkled in for good measure.
Davie ate like he had not had a good meal in years, and Barbara loved every minute of watching her two men catching up on old times.

They swapped stories about their favorite teams, arguing over who
looked good this season, the conversation rolling easily between them.
David told his son how much he admired the painting now hanging proudly in his office. Davie, in turn, asked about what it had been like to sell
Phillipe Leon and start Gordon Gabriel.

"I had no choice, Junior," his father admitted honestly. "Women ar-
en't interested in wearing dresses anymore. Everyone wants jeans today,
except for your mother. Maybe if Chanel rolls out a pair. But even then…"
They all laughed, the room filled with warmth and the kind of ease that
only came with family.

It was Davie who brought up the subject weighing most heavily on
his heart. "I'm sure Mom told you about Julie, Dad. I need to hear how
you feel about her. I love her, and I need you to know I won't let anything
hurt her."

David set down his fork and studied his son for a long moment.
His eyes seemed far away, searching back through decades of memories.
Slowly, he nodded, as though retrieving the right words from somewhere
deep inside.

"Son," he said at last, his voice steady, "the Talmud tells us that a
man must love his wife as himself and honor her more than himself. It
seems like you have found the girl you want to do that for. How wonderful
is that, my son." He reached across the table and put his hand on Davie's

shoulder, his voice carrying a quiet strength. "And I promise you, I will be by your side, making sure Julie is treated as a Rosere."

"Does Julie have a last name?" he added lightly.

Davie looked at him, surprised his father was asking. Surely Mom had told him who Julie was.

"It's Julie, Dad. Julie Glass."

The smile didn't last. The color drained from David's face as the name landed between them, heavy and unmistakable.

Across the table, Barbara felt a sharp flutter behind her eye, an involuntary warning she recognized all too well. She had not told David that Julie was the same Julie who had worked for him and also was working for Gerard Jeans. She had been afraid he would refuse to meet her, shut it down before it ever had a chance to exist. It had felt like the better plan, to let it all come out at once, but now she wasn't so sure. This was Julie. The one whispered about. Barbara's fingers curled tighter around the stem of her wine glass as she shot her husband a look sharp enough to stop him cold. Whatever he was about to say, he thought better of it.

To her astonishment, David pushed back his chair and rose to his feet, lifting his glass. "To the future Mrs. Davie Rosere," he said.

Davie felt his chest loosen, the tension he'd been holding finally releasing. He swallowed hard. "Thank you, Dad," he said quietly. That means more than you'll ever know."

Barbara glanced between them, her eyes shining, knowing this was a moment she would freeze in her memory forever. On cue, Veronica waltzed in carrying a tray of Davie's favorite dessert, homemade nutmeg ice cream, and sugar cake.

"Well," David laughed, "we all know who the VIP is in Veronica's eyes, don't we, Miss Veronica?" He winked at her, making everyone smile.

Barbara took the opening to chime in. "Davie, what do you think would make Julie feel comfortable? I was thinking maybe dinner at the country club, with the whole family. Alan, Francis, Karen, Justin, Lisa…

that way it takes some of the heaviness off a one-on-one meeting with just your father." She tried to sound casual, but her right eye had already begun to twitch again at the thought.

"I like that, Mom," Davie nodded. "Let me check with Julie and get back to you. I know she has a road trip planned with Cocoon."

"With whom, Davie?" Barbara asked, startled.

"Julie just accepted a job working with Carol Tanaka at Cocoon by Astrid Peyton." David leaned back, a faint, knowing smile tugging at his lips, the kind that said, *Here we go again*.

— 46 —

The family had been alerted, warned, and threatened to be on their very best behavior. Barbara made it clear this was a special moment for Davie, and nothing less than their best would do. Julie had just returned from a business trip with Carol, scouting new locations on the West Coast for Cocoon. They had narrowed it down to two—Rodeo Drive in Beverly Hills, right next to Bijan, where a vacancy was coming up, and Union Square in San Francisco. Both were everything Astrid could have hoped for, prestigious, high-visibility locations that screamed luxury. Carol would review everything with Astrid as soon as she returned from Palm Springs.

Julie, however, had no time to think about real estate. The cab ride home from the airport was a blur. She showered quickly, desperate to wash off the stale scent of the plane, then stood in front of her closet, staring blankly. What in the world could she wear to this family gathering? She had asked for this to happen— backing out was not an option now.

When Davie stepped into the bedroom to check on her, she didn't recognize him at first. She had never seen the preppy side of Davie Rose, and it took her a moment to take it all in.

"Where's your polo horse?" she teased.

"Well, we're going to need a horse if you don't hurry it up, Jules," he shot back with a grin.

She finally reached for the Diane von Furstenberg wrap dress she had scored on sale. It flattered her figure and, more importantly, always made her feel confident, like she belonged in any room.

At exactly 7:00 p.m., the car pulled up to whisk them off to Turnberry Country Club. Sliding into the seat beside Davie, Julie felt an uneasiness she had not felt in years. She folded her hands tightly in her lap, whispered under her breath, Please God… let this go well.

They were all there waiting as Davie and Julie were escorted to the Rosere family's reserved table for nine.

"Davie! Davie, so great to see you," Alan said, slapping his brother across the back. "Julie, good to see you again. Please meet my wife, Francis."

Lisa was next to stand, throwing her arms around Julie. "Welcome, Julie, so great to meet you." Then she grabbed the top of Davie's head, giving him a playful noogiee. "Missed you, little creep," she teased. "Welcome home."

That left Justin, whom Julie knew well from her days parading around his office in Phillipe Leon dresses. "Good to see you again, Julie. And I don't think you've ever met…"

"Me," Karen chimed in, stepping forward with a smile. "Wonderful to meet you, Julie. We need to have lunch soon."

"I look forward to that," Julie said.

Davie pulled out Julie's chair, and drinks were quickly served to ease the tension. David rose from his chair, and with a gracious smile, he lifted his glass.

"Tonight, we celebrate something long overdue—our son, Davie, home again. You've been missed, my boy, more than you could ever imagine."

He turned slightly to face Julie. "And to Julie," he said, lifting his glass. "Barbara and I welcome you to this crazy family. We are passionate, opinionated, and occasionally impossible, but I have a feeling you will hold your own just fine. L'chaim, Cheers."

Glasses clinked, and the conversation flowed with surprising ease. But across the dining room, Alan thought he caught sight of someone familiar. The view was obscured by a waiter, but when she sensed his stare, their eyes locked— there was no avoiding it. Slowly, unsteadily, Casey rose from her chair as if she were rising from the ashes and stumbled toward the Rosere table. David and Barbara's backs were turned, but Alan was in full view of his drunken ex-mistress staggering toward his table.

Casey was in rare form, intent on making her presence known. "Well... HELLOOOO Alan! How are you?" "Helooooo Roserereressss family" she slurred.

David and Barbara both looked up, stunned, trying to make sense of what was happening. She looked vaguely familiar to David, though he couldn't place her, at least not at first.

With a theatrical flair, Casey plopped herself onto Alan's lap. "How's my luver boy? You must be the little wifey, Francis, right? Have you missed me, baby?" She flashed a sloppy smile at the others. "Oh, hello, everyone. I'm Casey, Alan's mistwress. Nice to meet you alls."

Francis, seated next to Barbara, reached under the table to grip her mother-in-law's leg, shooting her a look that said plainly, I told you so.

Lisa sat perfectly still, as if waiting for a cue. For once, she had no smart remark, no protest sign to hold up to capture the absurdity of the moment. She simply stared, wide-eyed, caught between shock and disbelief.

Justin and Karen kept darting glances at each other, each silently waiting for the other to speak. Davie and Julie sat still, in disbelief.

It was Barbara who finally broke the silence. "Casey, dear, I think you might have had a little too much to drink. Heaven knows, we've all been there. You must be mistaken, dear. Let's get you some coffee."

The country club manager rushed over to investigate the commotion, but Barbara kept her composure, her voice calm and practiced.

Casey twirled a lock of Alan's hair between her fingers, smirking. "Oh really? No, I'm not mistwaken. If I was mistwaken, how would I know that little Al, Al here has a birthmark shaped like a wittle star… on the side of his left cheek?" She giggled; her voice pitched like a schoolgirl ready to set off fireworks. "It's the weft cheek, baby, right? And I don't mean this little bitty cheek," she pinched Alan's face playfully. "I mean this little bitty cheek."

With that, she slid her hand onto the bottom of Alan's lap. "Do you want to show everybody, Al, Al?" Her giggle spilled into a sing-song tease. "Tinkle, tinkle, little star… that's how we used to sing it, baby, right?"

The table went silent. Forks clattered against plates; glasses paused halfway to lips. Lisa's mouth hung open. Justin stared hard at his napkin as if it could swallow him whole. Barbara blinked once, twice, her left eye twitching again, while David's hand tightened around the stem of his wine glass until it looked like it might snap in two. The only sound left was Casey's laughter, echoing too loudly through the stunned hush of the country club dining room.

Only two people knew her statement to be true— Alan's wife, Francis, and his mother. Francis, embarrassed and humiliated, shot to her feet, her face red with fury, and stormed away from the table, leaving Alan struggling to pry Casey off his lap.

In that instant, the lightbulb went off in David's mind, the real reason this model had been chosen to represent Gordon Gabriel. Rage surged through him so dark, so consuming, he had to grip the edge of the table just to stop himself from acting on it. Barbara, sensing the room closing in on them, straightened in her chair and slipped on her most gracious smile, the one she used when disaster struck in public. Her voice was calm, almost musical, as if nothing at all were wrong.

     — — — B A R B A R A A. D A V I S

"Casey, darling," she said smoothly, "thank you for stopping by. But I think you have said quite enough for tonight."

She rose halfway, gesturing to the hovering manager. "Would you be a dear and help our guest find her companion and her way home?"

The manager nodded quickly, stepping forward, but Casey clung stubbornly to Alan's arm. "Oh, don't mind me, I'm just getting comfortable," she slurred, her laugh high and sharp.

Barbara didn't flinch. "Comfort," she replied evenly, "is best found at home. This is a family dinner, sweetheart. It's time you let Alan rejoin his family."

Her tone left no room for argument. The manager and a waiter gently lifted Casey to her feet and ushered her toward the exit, her protests echoing through the dining room.

Barbara sat down slowly and smoothed her napkin on her lap as though nothing had happened, her right eye twitching despite her steady smile. "Well then," she said, turning back to the table. "Where were we? Ah yes, dessert."

The staff hurried to refill glasses and reset the mood, but the air around them remained tight, heavy with unspoken words.

David hadn't moved, his knuckles white against the tablecloth. He caught Barbara's eye across the table, and for a moment, husband and wife shared the same unspoken thought—this was not good.

Davie held Julie's hand tightly, trying to comfort her. She looked back at him with a soft expression that said, It's okay, it's not your fault. But then, out of nowhere, she lost control. Whether it was the jet lag, the exhaustion of traveling through California with Carol, or simply her nerves giving way, Julie burst into laughter. Not just a chuckle, an uncontrollable wave of laughter that spilled out and refused to stop.

Lisa, always ready to cut through life's chaos, quickly joined in, her own laughter bubbling up until she was nearly doubled over. Within moments, the table, minus Alan, who had run off after Francis, was caught up in the uproar, hysterical with laughter. What had begun as disaster twisted itself into something else entirely—a release, a reminder that sometimes all you can do is laugh.

"I'm so sorry," she said once she finally caught her breath. "I'm just a little tired from—"

"Don't you dare say another word, Julie," Barbara cut in with a laugh. "What else can you possibly do at a time like this but laugh?"

She kept smiling, but inside she knew exactly how the rest of the night would go. As soon as she got home, she would have to sit through her husband raging on about what a mess Alan had made, then listen to

Francis talk about leaving her son, though both of them knew that was never going to happen.

Barbara straightened in her chair, determined to keep the mood light. "Now," she said brightly, "can I interest anyone in an after-dinner drink?"

Every hand at the table went up.

— 47 —

Alan smoothed things out with Francis by spinning a ridiculous lie about a photo shoot with Casey, claiming she had walked in on him in the bathroom and seen his birthmark by accident. It was a flimsy story, but far easier than facing the truth or the years of misery that would come with a divorce.

"You of all people know how those shoots go, Fran," he said quickly. "One bathroom for everyone, no lock on the door. She was upset about being fired after only being featured in just one Gordon Gabriel ad and threatened to get back at me. This was her way of doing it. Please believe me. She's hardly my type."

Francis pretended she did. But when she left for work that Monday, she carried the weight of knowing that the trust was gone in her marriage. She had too many things to do that day to think about her husband's affair, yet the sharp turn of the wheel as she left betrayed the fury she carried inside.

Alan watched her go, relief washing over him for only a moment, before the heavier truth returned. His real problem was still waiting for him. His father. The home phone rang just as he was heading out the door. He picked it up, his voice on edge.

"Alan, come to the house. Please."

"I'll be there in thirty minutes," Alan replied, and hung up. He muttered under his breath, Shit. Not the house. At least at the office, there were people around to diffuse the heated conversation.

– – – – –

The drive felt endless. His mind rehearsing excuses that sounded weaker with every mile. When he pulled into the driveway, his father's Rolls was parked waiting to take his father to work. Alan stepped inside, dropped his keys on the table, and barely had time to breathe before he heard the heavy footsteps pacing in the study.

"Alan." His father's voice was sharp, cold. "Get in here."

Alan obeyed, each step heavier than the last. David stood by the fireplace, a cup of hot coffee in his hand, the other gripping the mantel so tightly his veins stood out.

"You have embarrassed this family," David said flatly, not even looking at him at first. "At the club. In front of everyone. Do you have any idea what that woman," he spat the word out like poison, "has done to our name?" Alan opened his mouth, ready to tell the bathroom story again, but David turned on him, eyes blazing.

"Don't. Don't insult me with your lies."

Alan's throat went dry. He swallowed hard, but nothing came.

"You think this is about you and your… indiscretions?" David continued, his voice rising. "It isn't. This is about our business. Our reputation. Everything I built, everything your grandfather built, is in the balance now because you couldn't keep your hands off a fucking model hired to represent our label." His voice dropped to a deadly growl. "Do you know what will happen if Gordon Gabriel hears about this? He'll cancel our contract. We'll be finished." He slammed the cup down on the desk, coffee splashing across the papers.

Alan flinched. He'd seen his father angry before, but never like this. "What do you want me to do?" he whispered.

David straightened, his voice low and cutting. "Fix it. Clean it up. Make sure it stays far away from Gordon Gabriel. Do you understand me?" Alan nodded slowly, his chest aching.

"Good," David said, turning back to the fire, dismissing him with a flick of his hand. "Now get out of my sight."

Alan left the study, the weight of his father's ultimatum pressing down on him. He knew he couldn't fix it, not this time. He had no control over Casey and had no idea if she was planning another attack on him.

Alan drove to work with a pit in his stomach. He had always been the bright star of the family, the golden boy. Praise had been his lifeblood, especially from his father. Criticism was foreign to him. And now it lingered in his ears, stinging worse than he ever imagined. He needed to fix this. He needed to get her out of his life. His thoughts spun wildly as his Porsche hugged the highway, speeding toward New York City.

– – – – –

What Alan did not know was that Francis was already working on her own plan to deal with the Casey Jordan problem. The moment she sat down at her desk, she pressed the intercom button.

"Get me Wilhelmina Models," she told her secretary.

Wilhelmina specialized in runway, editorial, and commercial work, and Francis had connections at the very top. She had sent them Beth Taylor the year before, who had gone on to become one of their fastest-rising stars. Someone there owed her.

"Hi, Bethany. Francis Rosere, darling. How are you?" The niceties were exchanged before Francis cut to the chase.

"I seem to be in need of a favor," she began smoothly. "We have a very disgruntled model who was let go after one ad campaign at my husband's company. She hasn't taken it well, and she's becoming… an annoyance. Any chance there's an opening for your European tour scheduled next month?"

Bethany's voice was apologetic. "I just filled the last spot, Francis. But we always need a backup, someone to step in if a girl falls ill. Let me reach out to her for her portfolio. Are you talking about Casey Jordan? She's the model who did the latest Gordon Gabriel shoot, right?"

Francis exhaled, long and tired. "Yes. That's the one."

"Okay. I'll be sure to reach out to her. The tour lasts a year, so at least it would keep her occupied. Hopefully that helps you out."

"Yes," Francis said, her voice cool. "It certainly will. And Bethany, please, just between the two of us. Don't mention my name."

"Of course, Francis, not a problem at all" Bethany replied without hesitation.

Francis hung up the phone and allowed herself the faintest smile. With a single call, Casey Jordan's fate was decided. If all went according to plan, by this time next month, she would be out of the country and out of their lives.

— — — — —

Casey had just stepped out of the shower when the phone rang. At first, she almost didn't answer, but something made her grab the receiver. "Hello, is this Casey Jordan?"

"Yes… yes, it is.

"This is Bethany Rodgers from Wilhelmina. We would like to invite you to join us as a backup model for the upcoming European runway shows. I can't guarantee you'll walk in every show, but you would be in at least half. We saw your Gérard Jeans ad and thought you would be a perfect fit," she lied.

Casey thought this must be a dream as she put her hand over the receiver and squealed so loudly she nearly dropped the towel wrapped around her. It fell to the floor as she started bouncing up and down, her voice tumbling out faster than she could control. "Why yes, yes, it would be my pleasure!"

"Wonderful. Please come down to the office this afternoon at three o'clock to fill out the paperwork. We're located at 300 Park Avenue South, 22nd Street, in the Flatiron District."

Casey nodded furiously at every word, like one of those little toy dogs with the bobbing heads. Of course, she knew exactly where Wilhelmina was—she had dropped her headshots there more times than she could count, never hearing a word back.

When she finally hung up the phone, she stood naked in front of her full-length mirror, her heart racing. A slow smile spread across her face. "Well," she whispered, "Gordon Gabriel Jeans did help me with something after all."

Then her voice hardened, sharp as broken glass. "Fuck you, Alan."

Casey paced the length of her apartment, from the kitchen to the hallway and back again, over and over, her bare feet echoing on the worn wooden floor. She argued with herself, shaking her head one moment, nodding the next, unable to settle. But in the end, she knew she had to do it. She grabbed her coat and stepped outside. She knew exactly where Alan kept his Porsche, tucked into a small lot on 37th Street, and she knew his schedule well enough to time it perfectly.

Just as he rounded the corner, she stepped out of the phone booth and came face-to-face with her birthmarked boyfriend. For a split second, she saw fear in his eyes. He hesitated, ready to turn and walk away, when she caught his arm and whispered, "Please, Alan, give me two minutes."

He was furious at himself for stopping, but there it was, this woman still had a hold on him. He hated to admit it, but he genuinely had feelings for her. And that perfume, the one he knew so well, the one he had bought for her, pulled him back to their Chelsea love nest and the nights that had felt so intoxicating.

"What is it, Casey?" Alan asked, his voice edged with annoyance, but curiosity slipped through.

She drew in a breath, her tone soft but steady. "I just wanted to tell you how sorry I am. Truly sorry. I was out of my mind, drunk, and seeing you with your family… it brought out the worst in me. I'm leaving soon, but before I go, I need you to know that I'm thankful that we met. I really did care about you."

She meant every word, yet beneath the apology was another message entirely. She wanted him to know that Wilhelmina wanted her, Casey Jordan, for their European tour, even if he didn't. That was the point she needed to drive home.

"I really hope we can put this little episode behind us," she said quietly. "I don't want to burn any bridges. If it hadn't been for the Gordon Gabriel ad, I wouldn't have been invited on the Wilhelmina European Tour. So… thank you for that." She hesitated, then added softly, "Take care of yourself, Alan. Goodbye."

And with that, she turned, gliding down the sidewalk as if it were her runway. Alan stood for a moment, a wave of relief crashing over him. As he watched her disappear into the crowd, he began plotting how he would spin this to his wife and father, how he would tell them he had handled it. The golden boy was back.

Alan had made reservations at Francis's favorite restaurant in Westchester. La Crémaillère, was a French culinary delight tucked inside a white farmhouse. She always ordered the rack of lamb and loved their chocolate soufflés, while Alan prided himself on knowing his way through the restaurant's extensive wine cellar. To him, it felt like the perfect place to make his announcement— that he had taken care of the Casey situation.

When Francis walked through the door that evening, work had al-

ready drained every ounce of her. All she wanted was a quiet night to herself, something simple to eat, maybe cottage cheese and fruit, a few pages
of her favorite book, and bed before nine. That's what she kept telling
herself on the drive home. But the moment she stepped into the kitchen,
she stopped short. On the counter sat a vase of fresh flowers, a handwritten
note propped against the glass— I love you… dinner at 7:00 at La Crémaillère?

Alan appeared in the doorway just then; a smile stretched across his
face. She was too tired to play along, so tempted to say no. But then she
thought, He's trying, at least. With a small sigh she managed, "Give me
twenty minutes to freshen up, and I'll meet you in the car."

It was a very quiet ride to the restaurant. Alan turned the volume
knob on the radio up and started singing along, as if his voice could smooth
over the awkward silence. Francis stared out the window, counting the
passing lights, too drained to humor him.

At La Crémaillère, the valet slipped Alan a ticket, and moments later, they were seated at a table for two by the window. The setting was
perfect for what he was so eager to share. For a while, they sat not saying
anything, until Francis finally spoke. "It's so nice here," she said, breaking
the silence.

"Yes, I know it's your favorite," Alan replied with a practiced smile.

The first course arrived. Francis's lamb was perfectly tender; Alan's
sole baked to perfection. Wine flowed, and slowly, so did the conversation.
By her second glass, Francis felt her shoulders unclench, easing back into
their natural place.

"I have some good news, Fran," Alan said, leaning forward.

"Really?" Her face lit up, hungry for something, anything, to soften
the edges of her day.

"I have taken care of the Casey Jordan problem."

Francis grabbed her napkin on her lap, treating it as if it were a life
preserver. "The Casey Jordan problem? Did I hear that right?"

"Yes," Alan said, grinning with self-satisfaction, his chest slightly puffed.

Francis watched him, her expression unreadable. At that moment, he reminded her of a baboon at the zoo. She hated baboons.

"What do you mean, taken care of?" she asked carefully.

"She's leaving the country," Alan said smoothly. "She won't be around to make false accusations about me, or our family."

Two things struck Francis at once—how would Alan know she was leaving the country unless he had spoken to her directly, and why was he now taking credit for something she had orchestrated herself, something she had never intended to share? Her first fleeting thought was Bethany from Wilhelmina, but no, the more obvious explanation was staring her in the face. Her husband had been in contact with Casey Jordan.

She sank her head into her hands, elbows pressing into the table, unsure what to do next. Alan watched her, waiting for any sign, any word, from her.

Inside, everything screamed, take the plate and smash it over his cheating head, scream, "You liar," punch him, walk out, and never look back. The visual of it was so satisfying, and for a second, it comforted her. But she didn't move. She drew a slow breath, smoothed her crumpled napkin over her knees, and let the anger cool into an insincere calm.

"Well, well," she said finally, voice even, the words measured on purpose, "I'm glad to hear that, Alan. Let's wish her well."

The ride home from the restaurant was anything but pleasant. Alan hummed along to the radio, convinced the evening had gone well, while Francis sat in silence, her eyes fixed on the blur of white lines racing past the car. In her mind, the golden boy she once admired was tarnished beyond repair, and no amount of polish would ever restore the shine.

By the time they pulled into the driveway, she felt only emptiness. No pain, no rage, no love, just nothing. At the door, she kissed his cheek lightly and told him she was going straight to bed. Then, without another

    - - - B A R B A R A A. D A V I S

word, she ascended the long, winding staircase to her bedroom.

All she wanted was her bed, the one place left that felt safe. She opened the nightstand drawer, shook two sleeping pills into her hand, and swallowed them dry. With their help, she could wash away the day and what little respect she once had for her husband. "Sweet dreams," she muttered to herself, curling beneath the covers as the waves of unconsciousness began to pull her under.

Alan made a beeline to the library, as if the night were his alone to claim. He poured himself a generous glass of Rémy Martin, lifted it high, and toasted his own reflection in the darkened window. In his mind, life was good, and the night ended in victory.

– – – – –

Alan had a pep in his step as he walked into Gordon Gabriel the following morning and headed straight for his father's office. "Has my father arrived yet, Debbie?" he asked the receptionist.

"Yes, Alan, about thirty minutes ago." What am I, a fucking time clock, she whispered under her breath.

"Great." He straightened his jacket and pushed through the door. "Good morning, Dad."

David glanced up from his desk, his expression hardening at the unusual cheer in his son's voice. His brows came together as he studied him. How in the world could Alan be this upbeat? Their last conversation about Casey Jordan had been a disaster, yet here he was, grinning like he had just won the lottery. David leaned back in his chair, baffled.

"How in God's name are you smiling, Alan?" David finally said, his tone sharp. "Did I miss something? Or are you living in a different universe? Because the last I checked, you left the house a man with his tail between his two unfaithful balls."

"I have great news, Dad," Alan announced, ignoring his father's last comment. "Casey Jordan is joining Wilhelmina's European tour. She will be gone for a year, and I'm sure that will be the end of her."

Two immediate thoughts flashed through David's mind—first, how in the hell had that little waif of a girl landed such a prestigious assignment? And second, how did Alan know about it?

"Really?" David asked, his eyes narrowing as he studied his son. "And how exactly would you know that Casey, whatever the fuck her last name is, is going on this tour?"

Alan stumbled over his words, scrambling, before deciding it was safer to blurt out the truth.

David grunted, brushing the matter aside with a flick of his hand. "Fine. Good riddance to that disaster."

Alan left the office feeling like a champ, chest puffed, strutting down the hall punching the air like Muhammad Ali. In his mind, he had floated like a butterfly and stung like a bee. He hadn't just won; he had claimed the title.

— 48 —

Samantha Akiko Tanaka, Akiko after** Kenji's beloved grandmother, was born on April 17, 1980, at 2:15 in the morning, weighing in at 6 pounds, 11 ounces. The delivery room was quiet for a moment, just the steady beeping of monitors and the low murmur of nurses moving quickly around Carol. Then came the sound that changed everything, a sharp, loud cry that filled the air. Carol's head fell back against the pillow, tears streaming down her cheeks. Her body ached with exhaustion, but her heart swelled in a way she had never known before.

When the nurse placed the tiny bundle in her arms, Carol could hardly breathe. "Hello, my precious little baby," she whispered, her voice trembling with awe. "Welcome to the world, Samantha. Mommy and Daddy are so happy you're finally here." She pressed her lips gently against the newborn's tender head, inhaling that unmistakable baby scent, warm, soft, and perfectly new.

Kenji stood beside her, his own tears spilling freely. He had held it together through the hours of labor, but now, seeing his daughter in Carol's arms, he was undone. Overwhelmed, he rushed to the nurses' station, practically shouting into the phone as he called his parents. "It's a girl! She's here!" His voice cracked with joy.

On the other end of the line, his mother and father hugged each other, their own tears of happiness flowing. Their first grandchild. "Good job, son," his mother said, her voice full of emotion, overjoyed that the baby carried her own mother's name. "We'll come as soon as we can. We have to meet our granddaughter."

Back in the room, Carol studied every detail of Samantha's face, the tiny bow of her mouth, the flutter of her eyelids as she settled, the delicate fingers curling instinctively around her own. She traced the baby's cheek with her fingertip and looked up at Kenji, who had returned to her side. "She's perfect," Carol whispered.

Kenji leaned down, brushing a kiss across Carol's damp forehead before resting his hand gently on Samantha's back. "We're a family of three now," he said softly, almost in disbelief. And in that quiet, tender moment, under the fluorescent lights of the hospital room, Carol and Kenji knew their lives would be forever blessed.

– – – – –

It was Ruby who knocked gently on Astrid's bedroom door, balancing a breakfast tray with two poached eggs on white toast, a bowl of fresh fruit, a neatly folded linen napkin, and a glass of fresh-squeezed orange juice. A single pink rose stood in a crystal vase, as it always did.

"Miss Astrid," Ruby said softly as she set the tray down, "Mr. Tanaka phoned this morning. They've had the baby."

Astrid shot upright, her silk robe slipping from her shoulders as her face lit up. "How wonderful, Ruby! What wonderful news. Did he say how Carol is? And… was it a little boy or girl?"

Ruby's smile widened. "He said to tell you that Carol is beaming. And they've had a little girl; her name is Samantha."

   – – – B A R B A R A A. D A V I S

"Samantha…" Astrid repeated the word curling on her tongue like a treasure. She pressed her hand to her chest, eyes shining. "How precious. How very, very precious."

She dressed quickly and had the car take her straight to The Factory, Andy Warhol's legendary New York art studio. No appointment was ever needed; Astrid didn't make appointments. She was Astrid. She swept into the East 33rd Street loft in all her glory.

"Andy, Andy, Darling, I need you."

Andy lit up the moment he saw her. He adored her. Moving toward her at once, he air-kissed her cheeks in his usual deliberate way—one side, then the other. "My Astrid," he said, his voice soft but brimming with delight. "To what do I owe this glorious pleasure?"

She always loved being around Andy. His life amazed her, the contradictions of him. Painfully shy, yet always the center of attention. Quiet, but with eyes that absorbed everything, sketching the world in silence. He was the "Pope of Pop," the man who transformed everyday objects into icons of art. To the world, he was a genius. To Astrid, he was simply Andy.

"I have a commission for you," she announced, her tone playful but resolute. "A very special one."

His pale eyes flicked toward her, curious. "Do you have anything in mind?"

"Of course, my darling, when don't I?" she laughed. "I want you to paint a baby block. On it, the name Samantha, her birthdate, and the exact time she entered the world this morning. Make it girlish, yes, but not too sweet. I will leave the rest to you."

Andy nodded, already turning the idea over in his mind, as if he could see it forming on a canvas that only he could see.

"And one more thing," Astrid added, her voice softening but losing none of its command. "I need it finished in two weeks. I'm throwing a party for my little angel, and this will be the centerpiece."

The Factory buzzed around them, models, musicians, and dreamers drifting in and out, living their lives in colors much louder than hers. Yet Astrid always felt at home here, among the so-called misfits who chose to live differently and wildly, and who, in their own way, made the world a little more open-minded and open-hearted.

— 49 —

That hot pretzel smell got her every time, but Davie laughed and warned, "It will ruin your appetite, Jules." He had surprised her with two tickets to *Evita* by Andrew Lloyd Webber and Tim Rice. It was playing at the Broadway Theatre, and the thought of seeing Patti LuPone in person made Julie scream the second Davie handed her the envelope.

"CRAZY!" she shouted, clutching the tickets like they were made of gold. Julie was a huge fan of Webber's, and she couldn't wait to get there. They had missed out on *Jesus Christ Superstar*, but this time Davie had come through big time, orchestra seats, dead center, right in the middle of the row.

She couldn't stop squeezing his hand, so grateful to be there, so swept up in the moment. The Broadway Theatre was enormous, its ceilings soaring high above them, and Julie could hardly believe she was actually there, waiting for the curtain to rise.

As soon as the curtain came down, Julie leapt out of her seat and wrapped her arms around Davie. "Oh my God, that was amazing!" she cried, almost laughing with the words. "I didn't even breathe half the time.

They gave it everything up there, you could feel it. It wasn't just a play, Davie, it was like… a whole journey. I loved every minute of it!"

Davie loved seeing her this excited. He smiled, still humming "Don't Cry for Me Argentina" under his breath.

"I loved it too, Jules. Ok, let's grab something to eat before I pass out."

As they left the theater, Julie felt the music still singing inside her, Patti LuPone's voice echoing in her ears. *Evita* had amazed her, but it also left her unsettled. Walking beside Davie through the crowded streets, she kept replaying the story in her mind, the rise to power, the adoration, the illusion of control. All that glory, all that ambition, and yet Eva Perón had died so young.

Julie found herself asking a question she wasn't sure she wanted the answer to—was the sacrifice, the suffering, the endless striving for power really worth it? And in that moment, she couldn't help but wonder if the same was true for her own dreams.

By the time they slid into a corner booth at Joe Allen's, a quiet Midtown restaurant in the heart of the theatre district, Julie finally let the thoughts spill out, like water from a dam that had just given way.

"Davie," she began softly, her hands wrapped around a glass of water, "watching Evita tonight made me wonder… am I chasing the wrong kind of dream? Am I fooling myself into thinking I can just step into that powerful world of Seventh Ave, what if it isn't who I am at all?"

Davie sat back in the booth. It was going to be a long night, he thought to himself, and waved for the waiter to bring the bread to the table.

Julie leaned back, her head resting against the cool leather of the booth. And then, for the first time, it struck her; it was as if a light bulb had gone off in her head. Maybe the proverbial brass ring, the dream she had been chasing since she was a little girl, wasn't what she thought it was. The idea of becoming someone big, like the next Barbara Walters or a star of Seventh Avenue, had once felt like the ultimate prize. But now, after *Evita*, she wasn't so sure. She had seen enough of that world in her everyday life to question if she ever even wanted to be part of it. Was all the sacrifice worth it?

Davie listened to every word, not interrupting once, his eyes never leaving her face. When she finished, he reached across the table and took her hand. "Julie," he said softly, "I can only promise you this—we can live in a cabin in the woods in Maine or an Upper East Side penthouse—you know who my family is, and what that world is. I'll leave the choice to you. Just know that whatever you decide, I'll be happy. Because, Jules, I love you. The only thing that matters to me is you, just you."

Julie listened to his words, and she knew in that exact moment that God and all the mothers she had prayed to that day in church had guided her to the right man.

Across the table, Davie felt it too. For the first time, it was clear to him: *God is good*. He had brought him Julie, and for that, he would always be thankful.

$$- 50 -$$

S ami had called Jérôme over and over, begging to come home. Four weeks in the Betty Ford Clinic already felt like a lifetime. Each time he swore the same promise—he would never touch cocaine again, never even look at it. But Jérôme ignored his cries. Kelly had already broken things off, not wanting to be dragged down with him, and that rejection had gutted him. He begged, he pleaded, but Jérôme stayed firm.

"Four more weeks, Sami. I'll be there to pick you up. Hang in there, brother. Your counselor says you're not quite there yet. One more month, and I promise, you'll be home."

Sami slammed the receiver down, knowing Jérôme was right, but the truth only made it worse. The thought of one more month trapped in this place made him want to crawl out of his own skin. Rehab was its own world, a strange mix of punishment and salvation. Intake had been a blur. The nurses were kind and had the daily task of checking his vitals, weighing him, and handing him a plain plastic cup for a drug test. The air smelled like hospital soap and burned coffee.

The days ran on a military clock. A knock on the door at 6:30 a.m.

Meditation circles where some prayed, some wept, and some just stared blankly at the floor. Breakfast was eggs and toast, coffee strong enough to jolt even the weakest of them awake. Group sessions filled the mornings. At first, he sat silent, listening to others spill their sad stories, overdoses, broken families, and relapses that nearly killed them. Eventually, he opened his mouth, his voice low as he admitted how cocaine had ruined him, how every morning he swore he would quit only to find himself snorting lines by noon.

Chores kept them grounded. Sami scrubbed trays in the kitchen alongside actors, bankers, housewives, all stripped down to the same thing—addicts. Afternoons were for one-on-one counseling, questions hard enough to break even the strongest among them. "What are you running from? What's the story you don't want to tell?" Evenings brought AA and CA meetings. At first, the 12 Steps felt like empty words, but by week two, they felt like his lifeline.

Cravings came in waves. He would smoke his cigarettes outside under the desert sky, staring out at the palo verde trees and date palms, pretending the stars could hold him steady. Family Day destroyed him, even though deep down he understood his brothers were too far away to come. Seeing everyone else surrounded by their loved ones, held up by some kind of support, split him in two. He realized that the damage he caused wasn't his alone; it had rippled through everyone he loved. By the final week, they were forced to plan for the outside world. Relapse-prevention plans. Trigger lists. Role-playing what to say when temptation came calling. He hated it, but he also knew he needed it.

On his last night, sitting in the circle, he surprised himself. "I came here empty," he said, his voice rough. "I'm not leaving cured, but I'm leaving with a chance. I hope that's enough."

When the meeting ended, Catherine Rigby, the head counselor and director of the clinic, crossed the room and pulled Sami in for the biggest hug. "I'm very proud of you, Sam the Man," she said, using the nickname

                                    — — — B A R B A R A A. D A V I S

he had grown fond of during his stay. Then she pulled back, her eyes sharp but kind. "But I never want to see you here again. You hear me?"

"Yes, Catherine," Sami said with a sheepish grin. "But if you're ever in New York, come see me. I owe you a few pairs of jeans," he added with a laugh, before his eyes grew serious. "And so, so much more."

Catherine held his gaze for a moment, her expression caught between pride and worry, before finally nodding.

— — — — —

The next morning, Sami packed his suitcase. No champagne sendoff, no applause, just a firm handshake from his counselors and the reminder — one day at a time. When he stepped outside, Jérôme was waiting, exactly as promised. They embraced for what seemed like forever before finally breaking apart. Jérôme looked lovingly at his baby brother. "I missed you, Sami. Let's get you home."

As the car pulled away, Sami looked back at the low desert buildings. Those two months had felt like boot camp for the soul, and maybe the only thing standing between him and a coffin.

Daniel and Bernard had already agreed with him — Sami should stay with Jérôme for a few months before returning to his own apartment. It was a tough couple of weeks. The brothers moved carefully around Sami, each one gingerly dancing on eggshells, doing their best to keep life steady and calm for him, even though nothing about this business was ever steady or calm. At first, he came in later in the mornings, easing himself into the daily routine, but by the end of the month, he was back full-time, finding his way again. Toni and Barry were thrilled to hand back the responsibilities they had carried while he was gone.

Sami clung close to Jérôme outside the office, trailing him home after work like a lost puppy waiting for his next command. Jérôme didn't complain. He was happy to put his life on hold for him, cancelling dinner dates with women his friends tried to set him up with. It never felt like much of a sacrifice anyway. Julie still lived in his heart. But she had made up her mind.

Through Bernard, he had heard that the wedding was set for some time in the spring. The thought of her as a bride flashed through his mind more often than he cared to admit, and he could almost see her, beautiful Julie, radiant, breathtaking, everything he had once imagined she might be for him.

When she first left, he dreamed of her often. Dreams so vivid he would wake with his heart soaring, certain she had come running back to him, only to be crushed by the truth that she was gone. Each morning, he reminded himself to forget Julie Glass, to let her go. But he was happy that at least he had told her he loved her before she left. That was something he would never be sorry for. He had lost her, and now it was time to try again.

— — — — —

"Who's Kell, Sam? Who are you talking to, brother?"

Sami panicked, the phone still pressed to his ear. His heart dropped as he turned and saw Bernard standing in his office doorway. He had not even heard him come in.

Bernard's face darkened. "Please, Sam. Tell me you're not back with that piece of shit wannabe actress. Tell me my brother is smarter than that. Who is Kell?"

Sami's throat went dry. Before he could answer, Daniel pushed through the door, closing it behind him. "What now, you two?" His eyes darted between them, then landed on Sami. The look of surprise spread across his face. "What's going on here?"

"Tell him, Sam," Bernard snapped. "Tell Daniel who you were just talking to."

Sami couldn't lie, not to them. Not after everything they had done for him. They deserved the truth, no matter how ugly it was. He opened his mouth, fumbling for words when Jérôme happened to walk by. Seeing his three brothers huddled together, he stepped in, hopeful it might be good news.

Instead, Sami slumped into his chair, the weight of his guilt crashing down. "I've been talking to Kelly again. She wants to get back together. Says she misses me."

Daniel's hand shot up, ready to smack the back of Sami's head, but Jérôme caught his arm midair. His voice was calm but firm, the tone that always cut straight through the noise.

"And what did you tell her, Sam? What do you think the right thing is? What would Catherine Rigby tell you to do?"

Sami said nothing. Defeat was written all over his face. For a moment, he couldn't meet their eyes. His fingers drummed restlessly against the arm of the chair, torn between shame and longing. He knew exactly what Catherine Rigby would tell him to do—cut ties, walk away, save himself. But in his chest, the ache for Kelly and the lifestyle he left behind still burned, pulling him back toward everything he was supposed to leave behind. Sami swallowed hard. His eyes lowered. The truth he couldn't yet admit out loud was simple—he wanted to see Kelly Laurent again, and he wanted to get high.

It took all of five seconds for Jérôme to make up his mind. He picked up the phone and dialed.

"Aunt Fanny, it's Jérôme."

"Jérôme! Oh, Jérôme, my beautiful boy, how are you, sweet boy?"

Her voice was like a blanket, soft and familiar, and for a moment, the weight on his shoulders felt a little lighter. Aunt Fanny had been his rock ever since their parents died, the one steady presence who helped guide him and his brothers as they struggled to keep the family textile mill alive. Jérôme spoke quietly, choosing each word with care. He didn't want to upset her; at her age, bad news seemed to cut deeper, the armor thinner with every passing year.

"I was hoping Sami could stay with you and Uncle François for a while," he said gently. "He needs to get out of New York. The temptation here… it's just too much for him."

"Of course," she replied without hesitation, her voice warm. "Anything for my boys. Tell him Uncle Francois will be there to pick him up. Just tell us when, and he'll be there."

The plan was set. Jérôme called Catherine Rigby to arrange for an escort, someone who would travel with Sami and keep a close eye on him once he arrived at his aunt's home in Roubaix.

To the brothers' surprise, Sami didn't push back. Not a scream, not an argument, he didn't say a single word. He just sat there, silent, as Jérôme held his hand, steady and strong, giving him all the love and reassurance he had been starving for.

"This is my fault, Sam," Jérôme said tenderly. "This dream of making a mark in fashion—it was mine. I wanted it for me, and for all of us. But I never once stopped to ask if it was something you even wanted. Go home, brother. Rest. Let Aunt Fanny spoil you. Build your own life back there. And know this Sami, if New York ever calls your name to come back to this office, the door will always be open. You will forever be part of Gérard Jeans. You helped build this company, and nothing will ever change that."

He squeezed his brother's hand, his voice filled with emotion. "Think of how you can live like a king there, Sam. I just want you to be happy. I love you, brother, we all do. We'll all come visit right before the holidays. Just picture it, all four of us back together again, back home in Roubaix."

For the first time in weeks, Sami's eyes softened. A single tear slid down his cheek, but his lips curved into the faintest of smiles. He gave Jérôme a small nod, a silent promise that he understood. And in that moment, Jérôme knew his brother was finally ready to let go and begin the long road back home to heal, surrounded by Aunt Fanny's cooking, Uncle François's steadiness, and the familiar comfort of Roubaix.

It felt strange, sitting in the conference room with just the three of them. When Sami had been away in rehab, it had also been three, but that absence had always felt temporary. They knew he would be back eventually, so they treated it like a seat being held open at the table. This was different. This felt permanent.

Jérôme studied his brother's faces and knew he had to say out loud what he had confessed to Sami. "Look," he began, his voice low, steady. "This isn't easy. It's always been the four of us. We have to keep moving forward, carrying Sami with us in spirit, but we also need to accept there's a chance he won't come back. And I want to be honest, I never asked any of you if this was your dream, too. I wanted it so badly, I just assumed. But if anyone doesn't want this, now's the time to say it. I need to know you're really in."

Daniel and Bernard exchanged a glance, a silent language only brothers share. Then Daniel coughed, dragging on his cigarette. "Are you insane, Jérôme? I pinch myself every day."

"Me too," Bernard added quickly. "We're right up there with Gordon Gabriel. Did you see last quarter's report? Twenty-five percent market share increase over the number one competitor."

He shook his head in disbelief, almost grinning. "Why would I ever want to leave this?"

Jérôme felt the heaviness lift slightly. Daniel leaned forward, his voice softening. "We're all together, and together we'll always be." It was something their mother used to say, and the words wrapped around them like a blessing. For a moment, all three sat in silence, letting it sink in. "Alright then," Jérôme said, his tone snapping back to business. "Let's get to work."

Toni had been waiting for them to finish their meeting. She knew the brothers could talk for hours; there had been plenty of times when she had thrown her arms up, muttered under her breath, and marched back to her office. But not this time. This time, she had something too important to keep to herself, design sketches she had been obsessing over, three sleepless nights in a row. And she was ready.

"Nobody goes anywhere!" Toni shouted as she burst into the conference room, waving her oversized sketch pad. "Take a seat. I am so excited to show you what I have been working on these last two weeks."

The brothers exchanged amused glances and sat back in their chairs behind the conference table. Toni planted herself at the head of the table, her eyes gleaming. "We all know Gordon Gabriel set the market on fire with their white button-down shirts…" She paused, smirking. "Good for them."

With a dramatic gesture, she flipped back the cardboard cover of her sketch pad. "Now, meet Sophia, the first of five sexy silk blouses designed to pair with your favorite dark-wash denim jeans. Gordon dresses his customer for the day. We," she leaned forward, her voice sharp and playful, "we take over the nights. Our customers dress for Studio 54, not the carpool. How's this for a new slogan—Gérard Jeans…where denim gets sexy."

Page after page turned, revealing five different silhouettes, each one bolder than the last. Five silk styles. Five jewel-toned colors. A complete look, they had not even realized they were missing. Just then, Barry appeared in the doorway, grinning from ear to ear. "Pretty fucking great, right?"

The brothers burst into applause, the sound filling the room. Jérôme leaned forward, eyes still on the sketches. "Brilliant," he said simply, his tone carrying the weight of final approval. "Green light. Start sourcing fabric. We want this ready to ship by the end of September, early enough for the holiday selling period."

Toni straightened, gave them a theatrical royal bow, and high-fived Barry on her way out. "Told you," she tossed over her shoulder with a grin, before heading back toward the design studio to get to work.

— 51 —

Astrid realized that in the 1980s, the corporate world was still very much a man's game, which made her bold move irresistible to gossip columnists like Liza Jones. The moment Liza caught wind of Astrid's latest idea, she wasted no time. She stormed into Cocoon's offices, zeroing in on Julie, the closest target in her path.

"Honestly, Miss Jones," Julie said carefully, keeping her composure, "they haven't even started the room yet. I think it's best if you speak directly with Astrid. Would you like me to see if she's available?"

"Definitely," Liza snapped back, her eyes already darting past Julie. Spotting Astrid within earshot, she raised her voice dramatically. "This is the best idea I have heard in years!"

"Darlin' Liza!" Astrid purred, gliding over with outstretched arms. "Come, sit, have a cup of tea with me."

Julie stepped aside as Astrid launched into her pitch with her trademark flair. "I'm calling it the Caterpillar Nursery. I plan to put one not only here in this office, but in all my freestanding stores. Imagine it, Liza, mothers shopping while their babies are cared for, safe and happy. A win-

win, don't you think, dear Liza?"

Liza leaned forward, practically vibrating with excitement. She scribbled furiously, her red nails tapping the page between notes. "Adorable name, Astrid. Clever. When does it open? I want to be the first, photos, feature, the whole spread. My readers will eat this alive. When will you be up and running? I love everything about it. I want to send in my photographer and run a full-page spread, featuring you standing in front of the nursery. Do we have a deal?"

"Done!" Astrid declared, rising smoothly to her feet, the unspoken signal that the meeting was finished.

Liza snapped her notebook shut with a grin. "Fabulous. I'll hold you to it." With that, she swept out the door, already rehearsing the lead line for her future column—"Astrid's Cocoon Hatches Caterpillar." Or maybe even better, "High Fashion Meets Highchairs." Either way, she knew she had her front-page sensation.

"Julie, could you be a love and call for my car, darling? Did Carol leave you my home number in East Hampton?"

"Yes, Astrid," Julie answered. "I have a copy of her phone book on my desk."

"Splendid. Ring me if anything comes up, but I doubt I will be hearing from you. You seem to have everything well under control. Just a few more weeks and Carol will be back with us. Isn't that exciting, dear?"

You have no idea, Julie thought. What a nightmare these past months had been while Carol was on maternity leave. Construction noise, endless boutique promotions, back-to-back product launches, people calling in sick, and all the stress of running this business falling on her shoulders. She could barely sit down to lunch without her eyes closing shut. Having Astrid out of the office for June was a small blessing. The woman's drawn-out way of speaking, stretching every syllable as if speech itself were an ordeal, was grating on her last nerve. Even the way she called her name made Julie want to scream. "Juuuuuulieeeeee..." Davie always laughed when she imitated it for him, but to Julie it was anything but funny.

As soon as Astrid left the office, Julie dove into work. She called each of the three boutique managers to check stock. They weren't allowed to place supplier orders themselves; everything had to funnel through the New York office. Julie liked seeing the sales trends firsthand—which products flew off the shelves and which ones just gathered dust. "If it needs dusting," Carol always said, "it's a loser. Mark it down and move it out."

The candles were different, though; they were selling fast. Astrid had discovered the idea one summer afternoon in East Hampton. She had wandered into a tiny boutique when a fragrance stopped her in her tracks. The scent was so wonderful and so unforgettable. "What in the world smells so divine?" she asked the girl behind the counter.

She handed Astrid a plain glass jar. Astrid studied it like a gem. "These have been very popular," the girl said. Astrid bought five on the spot, each in a different fragrance, and shipped them to her New York team with a note, "I want candles, but not just for dining tables. I want a signature, something people buy because it feels like a piece of a dream, a luxury lifestyle brand."

– – – – –

Astrid always claimed her best ideas came from her visits to her Hampton compound. The Atlantic breeze carried her back to her childhood summers, a time when her parents were still alive and happy. Lauren Minkoff had redecorated all of Astrid's other homes, some of them twice, but not this one. It remained untouched, her private time capsule, sacred and unchanging.

She had Ruby unpack the few things she had brought from the city, though, as in all of Astrid's homes, the closets were already filled with everything she could ever need for the season. "Please make sure you arrange the shoes to match the coordinating outfits, dear Ruby." Ruby had been with her for more than twenty years. She knew the drill by heart, but Astrid still felt compelled to issue instructions aloud, as if speaking them into the air reinforced her sense of order.

Without lingering, Astrid swept toward the car, pausing only to take in the hydrangeas that flanked the entrance beside the door. Their blossoms framed the house like a painting, the salty sea air drifting in from the Atlantic, waves crashing faintly in the distance. She closed her eyes for a moment. *Home*, she whispered. *Welcome home to me.*

Her driver took her to Hedges & Company, where she wandered the store, browsing the stylish home accessories. She selected a leather-bound antique book on etiquette, turning it over thoughtfully. *Something like this would be perfect for my stores… I'll have to run it by Carol*, she thought.

Oh, dear, she muttered under her breath, spinning quickly on her heel to avoid the figure walking through the door. Too late. Barbara Rosere had already spotted her. Astrid liked Barbara well enough and was so grateful she had sent Carol her way, but small talk was the last thing she wanted right now. She glanced down at the etiquette book in her hand and couldn't help but wonder what it would say about avoiding someone in public. She would have to look that one up as soon as she returned home.

"Hello, Astrid," Barbara called cheerfully. "Are you here for the summer?"

Astrid smoothed her expression into a polite smile. "No, just the month. Then I will be off to St. Tropez for a month or two." She tilted her head graciously. "And you, dear, how about you?"

"Just a short visit this time," Barbara said. "I'm looking for a new home with a better ocean view than our current home, but it's been nothing less than challenging. I'm working with Alan M. Schneider Real Estate, and, so far, I'm not liking a thing. Honestly, it's exhausting."

"I'm sure that's true," Astrid replied kindly.

Barbara's expression softened. "I hear Carol had a little girl. I'm so happy for her. Is she planning to come back to work, or has motherhood become her new role?"

"Yes, that's right, little Samantha," Astrid said, her voice warm as if savoring the name. "I think both," she added with a gentle smile. Still, she wasn't about to mention Caterpillar; that secret was reserved for Liza Jones alone.

They wrapped up their conversation with two very insincere air kisses before parting ways. Barbara, off to torment some poor real estate agent who would never quite live up to her impossible standards, and Astrid already spinning her next idea—a best-selling etiquette book for her boutiques. She had a dinner planned later at Nick & Toni's with Wesley Lord, but first it was back home for her standing appointment with Gérard Bollei, the hairdresser to the Hamptons' elite who made house calls for his most important clients. Astrid adored that about him; thank heavens she didn't have to trudge to one of the high-end salons on Newton Lane like everyone else.

– – – – –

Julie was just finishing up, getting ready to meet Davie at the SoHo gallery, when her father and sister, Malerie, arrived, right on time, as always. The moment she saw them, she started jumping up and down like a little girl. To have them here, seeing where she worked, meant everything. She couldn't wait to show them around.

"Is that a Wa—" her father started.

"Yup," Julie grinned. "It's Andy Warhol. An original."

"Wow," he said softly, shaking his head. He had never been that close to one before.

"Who's Warhol?" Malerie piped up, wide-eyed, trying to take it all in. She had never seen anything like this office in her life.

Julie laughed, tugging her sister closer. Her father beamed, pride written all over his face. "Look at my girl," he said, smiling ear to ear. "I'm so proud of you, honey."

After the little tour, they climbed into the car service Julie had arranged and headed downtown. Malerie pressed her face to the window. "This is so cool!"

"Just wait until you see SoHo," Julie said, laughing. "You're going to love it. The buildings aren't so tall, and there are cobblestone streets, so if you're walking in heels, be prepared to fall." She kissed the top of Malerie's head, her heart full.

Julie wanted to show them some of Davie's paintings before heading over to Raoul's, the cozy French bistro where Barbara and David would be waiting. Dinner there would be all about the wedding plans.

As they stepped into the gallery, Davie was already waiting near the entrance, his smile breaking wide the moment he spotted them.

"Davie, my son, so good to see you."

"You too, Ed," Davie said warmly before turning to Malerie. "And Malerie Ann Glass, is that really you?"

"Yes, it is, Hi Davie!" Malerie laughed, her whole face lighting up. She adored Davie and was so excited when Julie asked her to be in their wedding party. The thought of calling Davie her brother-in-law made her even happier.

Davie slipped an arm around Julie's waist and began leading them through the gallery, pointing out a few of his favorite pieces and telling little stories about the artists along the way.

"And here's me," Davie said, stopping in front of one of his own canvases. He looked straight at Ed, waiting for his reaction. Ed took his time, leaning in a little, as if he were studying it like an expert. Finally, he nodded with a slow smile. "Well, let me tell you something, I think I like this better than the Warhol I just saw in Julie's office." He winked at his two daughters. "Really, beautiful work, son."

Davie's shoulders eased, his grin widening. "Thanks. That really means the world to me."

Ed's eyes couldn't resist darting to the small card beside the painting. When he caught sight of the price, he chuckled to himself. Well, he thought, my daughter will never starve.

Davie pushed open the narrow door at 180 Prince Street and let Julie, Mal, and Ed step in ahead of him. He had always loved Raoul's, famous for their delicious steaks smothered in garlic butter, its tiny, crowded dining room alive with energy. To him, the casual charm made it the perfect place to share the casual news—there would be no country club wedding this time around.

He had already told Julie he didn't think his mother would be upset, after all, Alan and Karen had gone that route, complete with a full orchestra and flowers designed to overwhelm the senses. Their wedding had checked every box of extravagance. Theirs, however, was going to be different—simpler, and more them.

Julie wasn't so sure Davie was right, and as she slid into her seat, her heart thudded hard against her chest. Barbara and David had met her family several times before and always seemed to enjoy their company.

"Where's your brother, Julie?" Barbara asked as the menus were passed around.

"He's at a sports camp this week, but he says hello," Julie answered with a smile.

They settled in quickly, everyone ordering Raoul's famous sizzling steaks, while David selected a beautiful Château Margaux to pair with the meal. Conversation flowed easily. David asked Ed how he was enjoying retirement, teased Mal about junior high, and Julie leaned in to ask about the business. Barbara, meanwhile, beamed when she noticed Julie wearing a pair of Gordon Gabriel jeans, a thoughtful gesture that felt both kind and deliberate.

Talk eventually turned to the wedding. Julie had already joked about the "lack of a wedding budget," but Ed had insisted on contributing something. Barbara had waved it off immediately, only to feel David's hand clamp gently on her leg under the table, his look warning her not to argue. "So, any ideas about dates for the big day?" Barbara asked, her smile bright and eager.

"We're thinking about next April," Julie said with a small smile.

"A spring wedding, how perfect." Barbara straightened in her chair, the way she always did when she was gearing up to organize something as important as a wedding.

Davie caught it instantly, the spark in his mother's eyes. She was revving up. Before she could go further, he glanced across the table at Julie, then began the speech they had carefully worked out the day before.

"Mom, Dad," he started, his tone warm but deliberate. "You have always been so generous, and I want you to know how much Julie and I appreciate all you have done and continue to do for us. Mom, I know how much you love the grandeur of it all, and no one throws a party like you. Every detail is perfect."

Barbara's eyes glistened, her chin lifting with pride. "Yes, dear…" she leaned forward, ready to hear more, while David's hand found her leg under the table, a silent brace for what he anticipated was coming.

"But," Davie said, drawing a breath, "Julie and I want something very different from a wedding at the Country Club."

"Oh?" Barbara tilted her head, trying to keep her smile steady. "Well… what did you have in mind? A destination wedding abroad? Paris, England, Italy?" She leaned in, her voice picking up speed. "I hear it's the newest thing, Margaret's daughter Penny was just married in Cannes." The suspense was killing her.

Julie gulped down a large sip of wine, giving Davie the floor.

"We did some research," he said carefully, "and we have fallen in love with a beautiful little inn in upstate New York."

David's grip on Barbara's leg tightened beneath the table.

"Oh. Well… that's um—" Barbara stumbled, her usual fluency failing her. "That's… um… different." She couldn't manage more; her carefully rehearsed visions of grandeur dissolved before her eyes.

"Davie, Julie," David cut in smoothly, his tone warm and controlled, "that sounds wonderful."

"Yes," Ed chimed in, eager to follow his lead. "That sounds just like you two. Please tell us more."

David kept the conversation moving. He knew Barbara had no words left, and he wasn't about to let the silence stretch into something no amount of wine could fix.

Julie jumped in quickly, determined to fill the air. She began talking about the Beekman Arms Inn in Rhinebeck, the place where she and Davie had spent their very first weekend away together. They had both fallen in love with it then, and now it felt only right to begin their married life in a place that already held a piece of their story. Her eyes lit up as she described the inn's charm, the gardens, and the intimate dining room where they imagined celebrating with family and friends.

Barbara's smile froze midair. "Isn't that the place we used to take the kids when they were little?" she asked, turning sharply toward David as if to say, please tell me that's not the place.

Julie went on, oblivious to the chill in the air. "They said we can rent a tent, and we've already spoken to the wedding planner. We will be meeting with her soon, so we'll have more to share once we have all the details."

Barbara, listening in her perfectly poised way, was already doing what only Barbara could—calculating how to turn this disaster of a plan into something her social circle would envy, not pity.

The dinner ended with hugs, kisses, and very full bellies. Julie had arranged a car service to take her father and sister back to the parking lot near her office, while David and Barbara headed home to Scarsdale in their Rolls.

As soon as they stepped outside, Davie leaned close, grinning. "We did it, Jules. No one was harmed in the delivery of our wedding news."

Julie laughed, the tension finally breaking. They hailed a cab, still giggling like kids all the way home.

— 52 —

"**Gérard Jeans does it again.**" That was the headline Bernice Greyson chose for *WWD*, simple but sharp, splashed above a full-page photo of the new silk blouse on the August issue's cover. Toni nearly burst with pride when she saw her name in print as head designer. Julie had called her from her office the minute she read it, her voice bubbling with excitement.

"Congratulations, my dear friend!" Julie cheered.

"I know," Toni laughed breathlessly. "I still can't believe what's happening with this blouse. We honestly can't keep up with the orders, Jules."

"That's wonderful! I'm sure the brothers are ecstatic. Let's have dinner soon, Toni. I miss you."

"Definitely. We'll make that happen. But I've got to run, it's crazy here!"

Meanwhile, Jérôme, Daniel, and Bernard were on the phone with Sami, practically screaming through the receiver about the headline. He put Aunt Fanny on the line so she could share in the celebration.

"Look at my amazing nephews," she said, her voice warm with pride. "Your mother and father are looking down at you, smiling from heaven. I couldn't be happier for you."

When the call ended, Sami set the phone down gently and stepped outside. The narrow streets of Roubaix stretched around him, cobblestones still damp from the morning rain. He breathed in the crisp air and made his way to the cafe on the corner. He had made the right decision to come home. This was where he belonged, where his story had started, and where it would begin again.

Within minutes after hanging up the phone with Sami, Paula Jennings waltzed into the showroom looking like the cat who had just swallowed the mouse, a copy of the morning's *WWD* tucked neatly under her arm. "I hear Gérard Jeans has done it again," she laughed, her eyes sparkling as she waved the paper above her head. Bernard hurried over to wrap her in a hug.

"To what do we owe this great honor?" he teased.

"The buyer from Bloomingdale's is making a surprise visit," Jérôme added with a grin.

"I come bearing good news," Paula said, lowering her voice just enough to build suspense. "My general merchandise manager, Andrew Fishman, wants to know if you boys would be interested in having your very own department, front and center, right in the middle of Contemporary."

She paused, studying their stunned expressions, then chuckled. "I was going to call, but honestly? The look on your faces just made the walk over here worth every step." Paula leaned back, eyes dancing as she delivered the punch. "So… I should tell him no, right?" She burst out laughing, the sound so infectious that Daniel rushed over to see what was happening.

"No shot, really?" he blurted, his grin as wide as Bernard's. And with that, it was settled—construction would begin on their very first in-store shop at Bloomingdale's. A landmark day for Gérard Jeans.

"Hey, older brother," Paula said, glancing at Jérôme with a teasing smile. "Got a spot where we can talk in private?"

Daniel threw up his hands. "Alright, alright, we'll get lost," he said, already backing toward the door. Bernard chuckled. "Yeah, message received."

Jérôme grabbed a chair at one of the showroom tables, spinning it around to face her. "Okay," he said, leaning in a little. "What's on your mind?"

"I want you to meet someone," Paula said, her eyes sparkling. "Someone very special. She's absolutely beautiful, kind, sweet, and she loves this business. She's my assistant's cousin, she just moved here from L.A., and I really think you two would be perfect together."

Jérôme smirked. "And if I say no, do we lose the Bloomingdale's shop?"

"Absolutely," Paula shot back with a laugh.

Jérôme shook his head, chuckling. "You don't fight fair."

"Never have," she said, scribbling a name and number on a piece of paper. She slid it across the table with a grin before strutting out of the showroom like a peacock, clearly pleased with herself.

Jérôme let the slip of paper sit on his dresser for three days, staring at the name and number, avoiding the moment when he would have to decide what to do with it. Each morning, he thought about tossing it; each night, he found himself picking it up again, running his thumb across the neat handwriting. By the third evening, he sighed, gave in, and finally picked up the phone.

Her voice caught him off guard; it was warm and friendly. He liked her right away. The conversation flowed without effort, and before long, they had settled on dinner at Mortimer's, the cozy spot on Lexington and 75th Street. Friday night, they agreed.

"Would you like me to pick you up, Jackie?" he asked.

"No, that's okay," she said lightly. "I can walk, it's very close to my apartment."

When the call ended, Jérôme sat still for a long moment, the quiet of the room closing around him. Goodbye, Julie, he thought, the words final but oddly freeing. It's time.

To say Jérôme was pleasantly surprised would have been an understatement. The moment she walked in, he noticed her instantly. She was striking, so striking that every head in the room seemed to turn as she was escorted to their table. Jérôme rose to greet her, unable to take his eyes off her. Her thick black hair tumbled in waves all the way down to her waist and there was something about her hazel eyes that was impossible to ignore.

"It's so nice to meet you, Jérôme," she said warmly, brushing a friendly kiss against his cheek. "Paula told me so much about you. I've been so excited to finally meet you tonight."

And she was French! Jackie Duval was French. He had suspected it when they first spoke to arrange the date, but he hadn't been sure. The accent was unmistakable, making even the simplest words sound elegant. They talked for hours, the conversation flowing so easily that Jérôme could barely remember eating his meal. Before he knew it, the waiter had returned, sliding the dessert menu between them.

"You know what I'm thinking, Jérôme?" Jackie leaned in with a mischievous smile. "How about we skip this and have dessert across the street at the new Ben & Jerry's? Have you tried it yet? It's amazing."

Jérôme nearly laughed out loud, relieved she meant ice cream and not her apartment. He wanted to take things slow with Jackie. This girl was different, special, very special.

The night air was warm as they stepped out of Mortimer's, the yellow taxis rushed by, and the noise of the Upper East Side wrapped around them. Jackie slipped her arm through Jérôme's as if it were the most natural thing in the world.

Across the street, Ben & Jerry's was crazy busy, its big windows spilling a bright light onto the sidewalk. Inside, families, students, and couples leaned over tubs of Maple Walnut and Peanut Butter Brickle like it was the greatest treasure in New York. Jackie pressed her finger to the glass, studying the flavors like she was making the most important decision of her life.

"Strawberry," she announced with a grin. "What about you?"

Jérôme smirked. "Classic. Coffee. Never disappoints."

They carried their cones outside and found a spot on the stoop of a brownstone a few doors down. Jackie licked her ice cream with a happy sigh, her hazel eyes catching the moonlight.

"See? Better than soufflé, no?" she teased.

Jérôme couldn't help but laugh, watching her. He realized he had not thought about work, about his brothers, or even about Julie all night. For the first time in a long while, he felt happy.

And as Jackie leaned her head against his shoulder, Jérôme thought to himself, *This is exactly where I want to be.* Life was starting to feel good again.

— 53 —

Finally, **it was ready, more** spectacular than Astrid could have ever envisioned. Liza Jones was there as promised, flanked by her entire media team, as the first of many Caterpillar Nurseries was unveiled. Carol and Kenji, with baby Samantha in her arms, could hardly believe what Astrid had created. Kenji drifted toward the striking painting of the baby block hanging on the back wall, and as he leaned in, his suspicion was confirmed—it was signed by Andy Warhol himself.

"Incredible," he whispered, almost speechless.

Astrid, radiant and composed, played the role of gracious host to perfection. This was her element, and no one did it better than Astrid Peyton. Wesley Lord lingered nearby at first, in case she needed anything, but quickly realized no assistance was required, she was entirely in her glory.

The room was alive with photographers, every major magazine and newspaper represented. And then, as if on cue, C.Z. Guest appeared on the arm of Truman Capote, making a grand entrance in support of their dear friend. "Darling, you have outdone yourself," Truman said warmly, kissing Astrid's hand before taking his leave. The moment shimmered with the sort of society glamour only Astrid could command.

"This is all because of you, darling Samantha. You are my inspiration, my precious girl," Astrid whispered into her ear as she carried her gently across the nursery. The guests, the press, the big players, all had gone. Now it was just the two of them walking together in the nursery. Carol, Kenji, and Julie stood quietly nearby, watching as Astrid moved slowly through the room, showing Samantha the space that would be her second home for many, many years to come.

"Oh my God, Carol, it's so good to have you back," Julie whispered warmly. "You'll be here on Monday?"

"Yes, I can't wait," Carol replied with a tired but happy smile. "It's going to be so nice to have both my worlds under one roof. Honestly, my brain is turning into mush. I can't wait to be back."

Thank God, Julie thought to herself as she hurried off to grab the ringing phone.

"What book is Susan from the Upper West Side store talking about, Julie? Did we do a book?" Carol asked, still trying to catch up after months away. There was so much she had missed while on maternity leave.

"Yes," Julie explained quickly. "Astrid found an antique etiquette book while she was summering in the Hamptons, had it copied, and it's flying off the shelves. Literally flying."

"Great," Carol said with a wink. "Show me the projection sheets; we're obviously going to need to order a lot more."

As a small favor, Carol had given Julie a week off in August, and she was counting the days. She and Davie planned to head up to Rhinebeck to meet with their wedding planner and finally nail down all the details.

The rest of the week was a blur. Astrid swept in and out of the office daily, always with a new "brilliant" idea for Carol to write down, sometimes a new fragrance, sometimes a limited-edition packaging design, sometimes a whole new product line that made Julie's head spin. Lauren Minkoff stopped by with new fabric swatches for the nursery pillows As-

   - - - B A R B A R A A. D A V I S

trid wanted to add to the room, insisting that Astrid approve every shade of pastel. And Susan from the Upper West Side kept calling, begging for more candles and etiquette books because her shelves were already bare.

Julie ran interference where she could, juggling vendor calls, organizing boutique promotions, and quietly keeping Carol up to speed without overwhelming her. By Friday, her desk was stacked with folders and her notepad crammed with reminders, but she felt good about it, like she had survived a tornado and kept the place standing.

The weekend finally rolled around, and Julie was ready for a little life outside Cocoon. She and Davie spent Saturday walking through Central Park, the heavy August air with cicadas buzzing in the trees as they wandered the shaded paths. For Julie, it was bittersweet. She had not set foot in the park since Pepper died. Walking past the wide lawns she could almost see her little baby trotting beside her, tail wagging, filling that quiet ache in her heart.

That dog had carried her through some of the loneliest days of her life, the memory hit so hard she had to sit down on a park bench to get herself together. She blinked quickly, willing the sadness away, but the heaviness stayed with her. I'm so sorry, Davie, but we need to leave, I'm about ready to lose it."

To lift the mood, Davie steered them downtown. They browsed old vinyl at Bleeker Bob's in Greenwich Village, grabbed late-night pizza at John's of Bleecker Street, and listened to jazz at Davie's favorite place, the Village Vanguard. They slept in on Sunday and finally made it out of bed to catch a matinee at the Paris Theater before ducking into a café for cappuccinos.

The weekend flew by, and before Julie could blink, Monday morning had arrived. She was back at Cocoon, sliding into the booth across from Carol for their breakfast meeting, a ritual Carol insisted on. "It's a wonderful way to start the workday," she always said. And Julie, still carrying the glow of her city weekend, couldn't argue with her.

It was waiting for her when she got home from work on Tuesday— a big box sitting in the middle of the apartment with a hand-painted sign that read: Open Me.

"What is this all about?" she asked, eyeing Davie.

"Read the sign, Jules. Jeez, even the simplest directions throw you off," he teased.

Julie bent down and jumped back when something inside moved. Then she heard it—the unmistakable sound of a puppy's cries. "Davie… what have you done?"

He couldn't hold it in any longer. Grinning ear to ear, he whisked off the top of the box. Out tumbled the most adorable little puppy with a shiny black nose and curly red hair, yipping and wriggling right into Julie's arms.

As Julie looked into her tiny face, she caught something familiar in those eyes. Her father always told her that when you lose a dog, the special one, not just any dog, but the one who stays with you even after they're gone, that dog will come again and find you. Staring at this little pup, Julie knew it was true. Beneath the red curls, it was her Pepper.

She kissed the puppy's head again, and again, and again, her voice breaking into a whisper. "Welcome home, baby… welcome home."

After much back-and-forth, Davie pushed for Ginger, but Julie stood firm on Poppy, the "P" in honor of Pepper. And so, Poppy it was. Every morning, Davie tucked her under his arm and took her on the subway to his art studio, where she quickly became the underground's little superstar. Commuters stopped to pet her, coo over her curls, and she soaked up every second of the attention. By evening, Julie would take over, doting on her new adorable four-legged best friend.

There was, however, one rule Davie insisted on, the only thing he had ever put his foot down about since the day they met. "No sleeping in bed with us, Jules. I'm serious. I'm really firm about this." Julie had every intention of following through, but the first time Poppy whimpered in the middle of the night, her resolve melted. By morning, the puppy was curled between them, snoring softly.

"Well, so glad I have a say in things around here, Poppy," Davie sighed, shaking his head. Still, he had to admit, her sweet puppy smell was impossible to resist.

Her vacation week finally rolled around. They dropped Poppy at Toni and Barry's apartment before catching the train to Rhinebeck. Julie's checklist looked more like a scroll, packed with hundreds of details to review with the wedding planner, Colette. They spent as much time as they could lingering over coffee, wandering the town, and just being together without the usual rush of their day-to-day life in the city.

It was Davie who suggested it. "Since we're here… why not look at some real estate?" They had been talking about buying a home in the Hudson Valley, and this felt like the perfect chance to casually explore. There was something about the light up there, the way it bathed everything in a golden amber glow, that they both loved. Davie wanted to be close enough to Market Street to walk to dinner or the bookstore, but still have space to breathe, space that felt like theirs.

The first house stopped them cold. A nineteenth-century Victorian, painted sage green with pink and yellow gingerbread trim, it looked like something plucked from a storybook. Julie grabbed Davie's arm; her knees suddenly felt like jelly. A wide wraparound lemonade porch hugged the house, and inside, pocket doors slid effortlessly across the original wide-plank floors. The kitchen needed updating, but it had charm, and the high ceilings in the bedrooms were cooled by antique ceiling fans that seemed to whisper of summers past.

But it was the stained-glass window on the landing that Julie couldn't take her eyes off. Its jewel tones lit by the afternoon sun seemed to cast the whole staircase in warmth. Standing there, she felt strangely at home.

Julie crossed the kitchen and stepped into the backyard, taking in the quiet. She thought about all the people who had called this place home, the laughter that once filled the air during parties and cookouts, and the quieter moments, too. The ones that people tucked in their hearts for a rainy day.

The garden was so still she could hear the bees buzzing. Julie sat down by the rose bushes; they smelled almost too good to be true. It was at that moment that something inside her finally unlocked. Life, she thought, was meant to be lived one day at a time, one messy, beautiful, ordinary day at a time. You take what it gives you, and then you let it go.

"That's life, isn't it?" she whispered to the bee hovering near a rose petal. It's a mix of happy and hard, all tangled together. You want the people you love to be there with you forever, but when they are gone, it's just you. And somehow, that was the plan all along. You keep going, figuring it out as you do. It is not perfect, but maybe it was never supposed to be.

She felt the weight that had tightened around her heart since her mother's passing began to lift. For the first time, she could feel herself breathing, really breathing. She tilted her face towards the sky and whispered to her mother that she wished they had had more time together, but this sadness she was holding on to was not what her mother would want for her. "I have decided I want to be happy now, Mom, because if I'm not, then all the love you poured into me will mean nothing."

She hugged herself as if her mother's arms were around her. "I will think of you and love you always." Julie closed her eyes. "Mom, this is where I am going to live. I will light a candle so you can find me."

The Realtor was in Davie's ear, reminding him what a rare find this was. He nodded, then crossed the lawn to where Julie was sitting. "What do you think, Jules?" Davie asked, watching her.

Julie looked up at him, her eyes steady and clear, her decision already made. "This is our home, Davie," she said quietly. I want us to live here like the Rose family, not the Rosere family."

Davie pulled her close and, with the biggest smile, told her, "That is exactly what I want too. From now on, it will only be Mr. & Mrs. Rose."

By the end of the week, they had accomplished two things. The

  — — — B A R B A R A A. D A V I S

wedding checklist was complete, and the Roses had bought themselves a home. Not just a place with walls and a garden, but a beginning. A home where laughter would return, where ordinary days would matter, and where love, imperfect as it is, would have a safe place to land. For the first time in a long time, Julie felt certain she was standing exactly where she was meant to be.

— 54 —

"**L**ook at us!" **Bernard shouted** from his office to Jérôme's. They had just received their table seating assignment for the Black Tie Christmas Ball. We are seated right next to the VIPs. "Not bad, considering we were eating with the kitchen staff last year!"

Daniel pounded the top of his desk in hysterics, the sound carrying across the room. Jérôme sat back in wonder. Had it really been a whole year since the last Christmas Ball? Everything was so different now. Gérard Jeans had secured its place as a powerhouse on Seventh Avenue. Sami was thriving back in Roubaix, where the brothers had flown with Jackie to visit him before the Jewish holidays.

Aunt Fanny was overjoyed, her kitchen brimming with noise and laughter as all her boys were finally under one roof again. Jérôme was especially proud to have Jackie by his side, introducing her not just to Sami but to the two people who had carried them through so much. Uncle François wasted no time giving his verdict, clapping Jérôme on the back with a grin. "She's a ten, my boy."

This year, the brothers arrived at the Waldorf Astoria in custom Brioni tuxedos, no longer the scrappy newcomers in Santa suits handing out Gérard jeans to receptionists. They belonged. Jackie, dazzling in Oscar de la Renta, was easily the most beautiful woman in the room.

They were still settling into conversation when Astrid Peyton and her entourage swept into the ballroom. Jérôme caught Carol's eye, and she returned his smile with her signature brow lift and a wink. Julie followed with Davie, which raised its own tension because Barbara had wanted them at her table. David, once again, came to Davie's rescue "He's not ours anymore, Barbara. Please, let him be. His place is supporting Julie, not sitting with us." He was right. At least the tables were close enough for Barbara to reach over and hug them both. Jérôme glanced across the room. For him, it would always be there, that soft tug whenever he saw Julie, but she wasn't his to have.

Julie, meanwhile, soaked it all in. The chandeliers, the gowns, the music playing through the ballroom, it was dazzling, but she knew now, it wasn't for her. This glittering life of the rich and famous, the one she had once thought she wanted more than anything, no longer fit. This was not her brass ring to grab.

"What's so funny, Julie?" Davie called over the music.

"Just the difference a year can make, that's all," she answered, still smiling.

"Come, come, all you beautiful people! I need all my denim mavens together for a photo," Liza Jones called out, her voice carrying across the ballroom. "My next story involves every one of you. Just wait until I tell you all about it, you're gonna love it."

They stood tall, knowing they had done it, each in their own way, in their own style, and on their own terms. They had carved out their place, and tonight was theirs.

"Smile, say Denim!" Liza shouted.

The three powerhouse companies stepped forward, shoulder to

shoulder. Julie slipped into place among them. A quiet pride settled over her. To stand here, in the middle of it all, part of the so-called denim wars, she had never felt prouder. They had taken women out of dowdy daytime dresses and slipped them into denim that spoke of independence and power. For the first time, jeans were a declaration of identity. Together, the very names that had redefined denim, changed the way women dressed, and set trends the world would follow, lifted their voices in unison.

"Denim!"

ACKNOWLEDGEMENTS

To my most sacred and loving men, Bob & Ian—you are my everything.

To Mom and Dad—there really are no words except forever grateful you were mine.

To my family and friends—you have left footprints on my heart, bunions and all. Life is better because of you!

To Maddy—thank you for opening the door I had stopped knocking on.

To my Seventh Avenue peeps—you have no idea how you shaped my life, and I will forever be thankful to every one of you.

To God—thank you for never leaving my side, even though there were times I'm sure you wanted to.

XOXO,
Barbara

ABOUT THE AUTHOR

Barbara Davis launched her career on Seventh Avenue at the height of the denim revolution, immersed in the creativity and camaraderie that inspired her debut novel, *Denim Wars*.

A natural storyteller grounded in lived experience, she gravitates toward the resilience beneath the surface, the unexpected turns that shape us, and the courage it takes to move forward.

Her writing reflects a quiet truth: we are rarely prepared for the moments that define us—we become ready by stepping into them. *Denim Wars* is her tribute to the dreamers who dared to do just that.

www.ingramcontent.com/pod-product-compliance
Lightning Source LLC
Chambersburg PA
CBHW051507150726
47997CB00001B/143